PRAISE FOR SIGRÍÐUR HAGALÍN BJÖRNSDÓTTIR

"Sigríður, probably best known to Icelanders for reporting the news, has written her third book, *The Fires*, and if things continue this way, she may disappear from our TV screens. This book is so good, excellent even, that more writing must be seen from her and consequently less screen time. Sigríður succeeds extremely well in weaving together the thrilling volcanology and [Anna's] love life . . . Disasters at work and in private intertwine in a particularly interesting way, resulting in an explosion in both places. Anna tries her best to fight against love, but her reasoning is no match against the fire that has been ignited . . . The author's characters and philosophical reflections are extremely strong. All the puzzle pieces seem to fall into place in Sigríður's writing, but the story itself is such that it is impossible to put the book down, yet at the same time you sometimes don't want to read on as it becomes clear that things will not end well. *The Fires* is a thriller, a love story, and a tragedy. It is absolutely fantastic, though one cannot help but hope that Reykjanes will not start to shake and tremble with as much force as in the book . . . *The Fires* is a must read. Except maybe for those who are very terrified of earthquakes."

—★ ★ ★ ★ ★ *Morgunblaðið*

"The novel is a dystopian thriller about what could happen when and if an active volcano wakes from its slumber when it least should. The storyline—set near the capital area of Reykjavík shortly after the pandemic—is convincing, especially the clashes between the scientists and the business community during civil defense meetings, where one group sees eruptions as an amazing, dangerous subject while the other sees them as an ideal marketing opportunity. Sigríður Hagalín Björnsdóttir choreographs a fascinating dance between volcanic eruptions and emotions as smoldering magma looms under the surface of both earth and woman, erupting without warning. Violent earthquakes and doomsday disasters intertwine with personal calamity when nature, desire, and passion clash with common sense, comfort, and affection. *The Fires* is an exceptionally well-written and addictive story. The love described in the novel is not the beautiful and nourishing kind but a veritable force of nature, destructive and cataclysmic, creative and devastating. The geological part is, in this critic's opinion, extremely well done, the references are impressive, strong, and poetic, and the danger that lies both within the heroine and in the seething magma chambers under the surface is, like the story itself, haunting and powerful."

—★★★★★ *Fréttablaðið*

" *The Fires* by Sigríður Hagalín Björnsdóttir is, in more ways than one, a shocking love story as well as an existential speculation about the role of the mother, but first and foremost it is an extremely accomplished thriller . . . It is a testament to Sigríður's narrative force that the reader follows the author without hesitation through conversations and speculations about fissures and vicissitudes without ever once losing the thread."

—*Viðsjá*

"'The various strands are woven together well, not only the earth sciences and the related specialist knowledge but also the inner turmoil of the volcanologist's life. The book is incredibly exciting, and the last chapter is a nail-biter,' says Sunna Dís Másdóttir, while Þorgeir Tryggvason admires the author's ruthlessness: 'It's a terrible catastrophe,' he says, 'and she just lets it happen. If Reykjavík must collapse, then Reykjavík will collapse. This is the Sigríður we know from [her first novel,] *Eyland*, where everything was laid to waste and people had to start digging for potatoes. But then there is also Sigríður from *The Holy Word*, which is the philosophical Sigríður, who here weaves together the hearts of men and the hearts of the earth and the magma of the earth and does it so wonderfully. *The Fires* is a huge success. Such a profound, well-thought-out, romantic thriller.'"

—*Kiljan*, Iceland's foremost literary TV program

"Science and literature may not always seem the best bedfellows, but this novel unites them with an unexpected force. On the surface it appears to be a classic love triangle . . . But this thread of the novel is merely a part of a more complex and exciting web, where her profession plays the main role. On the Reykjanes Peninsula, a string of earthquakes has been measured, and fears of an eruption start growing . . . What evolves is an enormously exciting story that reads like a thriller of the best sort, and yet at the same time we can contemplate both moral and practical questions of how to survive, as people in relationships and as humans facing the forces of nature, forces which have no moral message in their destructive power. The pace of the short novel is perfectly timed, and this reader became completely absorbed, as there is never a lull in the narrative. A gem of a book."

—Prof. Gauti Kristmannsson

THE
FIRES

THE FIRES

A NOVEL

SIGRÍÐUR HAGALÍN BJÖRNSDÓTTIR

TRANSLATED BY LARISSA KYZER

AMAZON **CROSSING**

Previously published as *Eldarnir. Ástin og aðrar hamfarir* by Benedikt Bókaútgáfa in Iceland in 2020. Translated from Icelandic by Larissa Kyzer. First published in English by Amazon Crossing in 2023.

Published by Amazon Crossing, Seattle

www.apub.com

ISBN-13: 9781662500145 (hardcover)
ISBN-13: 9781662500152 (paperback)
ISBN-13: 9781662500169 (digital)

Cover design by Sarah Congdon

Cover images: ©klyaksun/ Shutterstock; ©d1sk / Shutterstock; Paradoxe on Offset / Shutterstock; Kseniya Ivashkevich / Shutterstock; Arctic-Images / Getty

Printed in the United States of America

First edition

One could say that the melting zone, where magma forms, is the "burning heart" of Iceland.

—Freysteinn Sigmundsson, Magnús Tumi Guðmundsson, and Sigurður Steinþórsson, "The Internal Structure of Volcanoes," in *Natural Hazards in Iceland*

Explosives have nothing compared to these sparks
So let's fall apart
And then lie with me, breathing in the den of the dark
It's firesmoke

—Kae Tempest, "Firesmoke"

CAST OF CHARACTERS

ANNA ARNARDÓTTIR—Professor of volcanology and director of the Institute of Earth Sciences

KRISTINN FJALAR ÖRVARSSON—Her husband, a tax lawyer

ÖRN ÖGMUNDUR KRISTINSSON (ÖDDI)—Their son, age twenty-three, who works at an aluminum smelter

SALKA SNÆFRÍÐUR KRISTINSDÓTTIR—Their daughter, age eight

TÓMAS ADLER—Photographer

ÖRN ÖGMUNDSSON—Anna's father, a geoscientist, deceased

GUÐRÚN OLGA JAFETSDÓTTIR—Anna's mother, a translator and poet

ÁSTRÍÐUR LIND—Interior designer

ELÍSABET KAABER (EBBA)—Geophysicist and chair of the board, Institute of Earth Sciences

JÓHANNES RÚRIKSSON (JÓI)—Volcanologist at the Institute of Earth Sciences

EIRÍKUR STEINARSSON—Geologist at the Institute of Earth Sciences

JÚLÍUS ÓSKARSSON—Director, Earthquake Hazard Monitoring Department at the Icelandic Meteorological Office (the Met)

HALLDÓRA RÖGNVALDSDÓTTIR—Meteorologist at the Met

MILAN PETROVIC—Chief superintendent, Department of Civil Protection and Emergency Management

RAGNAR SNÆBJÖRNSSON—National commissioner of the Icelandic Police

SIGRÍÐUR MARÍA VIÐARSDÓTTIR—Executive director, SAF, the Icelandic Travel Industry Association

STEFÁN RÚNAR JÓHANNSSON—Middle manager at the Ministry of Justice

ÚLFAR ÁSBJARNARSON—Technologist, Iceland GeoSurvey (ÍSOR)

ÓFEIGUR KÚLD—Director, Icelandic Coast Guard

ÓLÖF INGIMARSDÓTTIR—Chief security officer, Isavia (the national airport and air service provider of Iceland)

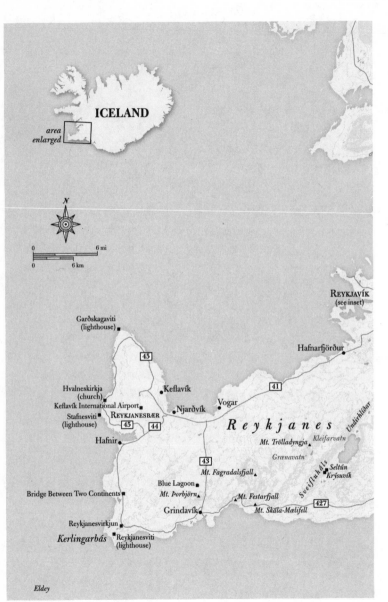

ICELAND

area
enlarged

N

0   6 mi
0   6 km

REYKJAVÍK
(see inset)

Garðskagaviti
(lighthouse)

Hafnarfjörður

45

Hvalneskirkja
(church)
Keflavík International Airport
Stafnesviti
(lighthouse)   REYKJANESBÆR

Keflavík

Njarðvík   Vogar

41

Reykjanes

45   44

Hafnir

Mt. Trölladyngja   *Kleifarvatn*

Undirhlíðar

Grænavatn

43

Mt. Fagradalsfjall

Sveifluháls   Seltún
                Krýsuvík

Bridge Between Two Continents

Blue Lagoon
Mt. Þorbjörn

Mt. Festarfjall

Grindavík   *Mt. Skála-Mælifell*

427

Reykjanesvirkjun

Kerlingarbás   Reykjanesviti
                (lighthouse)

Eldey

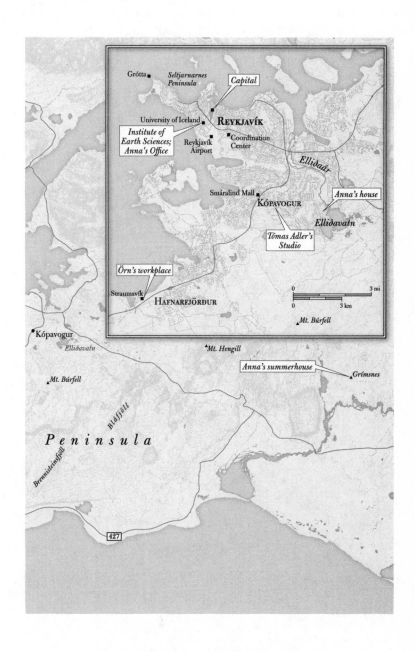

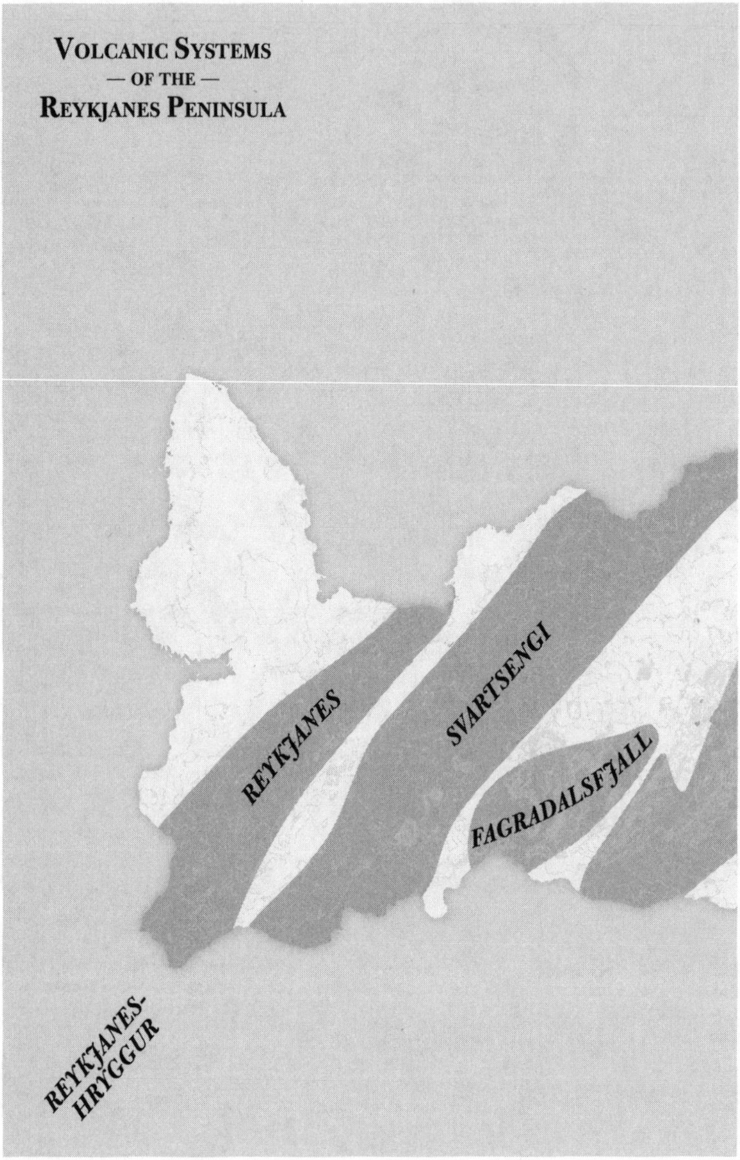

VOLCANIC SYSTEMS
— OF THE —
REYKJANES PENINSULA

REYKJANES

SVARTSENGI

FAGRADALSFJALL

REYKJANES-
HRYGGUR

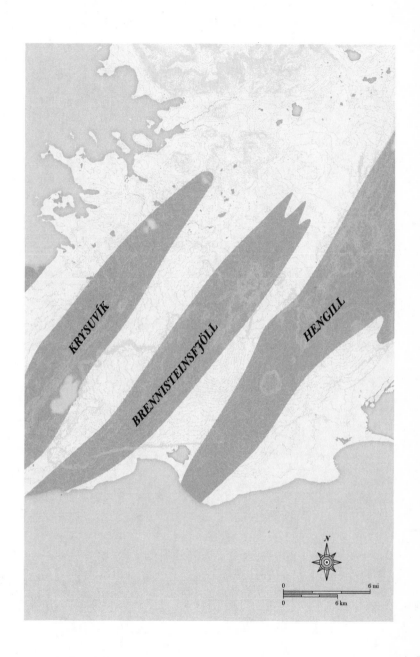

KRYSUVÍK

BRENNISTEINSFJÖLL

HENGILL

N

0 ——————————— 6 mi
0 ——————————— 6 km

AUTHOR'S NOTE

Books often know more than the people who write them.

This was one of the most surprising facts I discovered when I began writing, and this book is a prime example. It came out in Iceland in November 2020, four months before a volcanic eruption began for real on the Reykjanes Peninsula, just a few kilometers and a mere handful of days apart from the fictional eruption described in these pages.

I'm not psychic; I was just as surprised about this as everyone else. This book is, however, based on scientific articles and my extensive conversations with geoscientists who not only shared with me anecdotes from their profession and conjectures about coming volcanic events but also granted me ready access to new information and research in the lead-up to the real eruption.

Thus did science blend with fiction and this story become a part of reality.

The world is, after all, made of more than stone.

This is how it ends.

The earth envelops me, with all her eons, all her 4.5 billion years. Her weight presses down upon me, steadily and without pity, like the beating of her blazing heart. Laws that spare no one, the dawn of life and its dusk. I am in her power, an insect in her dark, velvety palm.

I try to move my head, but it doesn't budge. I open my eyes and close them, full of darkness, once again. Best to keep them closed, to concentrate on just doing that.

Don't think.

Don't let my mind wander to the thought that I'm dead, that this is what it's like to be dead.

It's not an unreasonable conclusion to draw. And it would solve a lot. Spare me the decisions, be a perfect excuse not to face the things I've done. No more sleepless nights, no more tears, no more regret.

Nothing, never, not ever again.

Dust I am, and to dust I shall return, but my mind refuses to let go. It continues its obsessive maundering about the end of the world, projecting images of houses crumbling into black fissures, hovering for a moment on the brink before sinking slowly sideways, settling into the fire with a heavy sigh. Furniture, paintings, photo albums, pianos, microwaves—everything vanishes under the black tongue that protrudes from this red jaw, slithers across the land and destroys everything in its path. All the memories and caresses, the children's drawings and dutifully vacuumed carpets—everything submits to its insatiable hunger and vanishes into the darkness.

It's beautiful, don't you think?

Your voice echoes in my head as though you're right here beside me, your face glows with childlike enthusiasm. You smile at me, and your eyes are full of laughter; my mind knows it's an illusion, knows you're not here, but my heart sings with joy anyway, then breaks in that selfsame moment. But at least I got to love.

Stop this, I say to myself. Stop reminiscing and remembering and missing. Stop hyperventilating and wasting what little oxygen you have left—be rational, woman. Put that brilliant mind of yours to use, *Homo sapiens*—you, the so-called crown of creation. What good is logic to you now? Here you lie, curled like a worm in the womb of the earth, a mouse beneath the moss. An overgrown brain swollen with memories and facts and regrets, formulas and decimals and information and dreams, your worst presumption being that you could differentiate them, that you, in your great wisdom, would be able to fathom the universe. You, who couldn't even understand your own heart, its simple, universal laws.

This is where it ends, but it's not where it began.

It all started last winter. Remember?

THE REYKJANES RIDGE

N 63°48′56″ W 22°42′15″

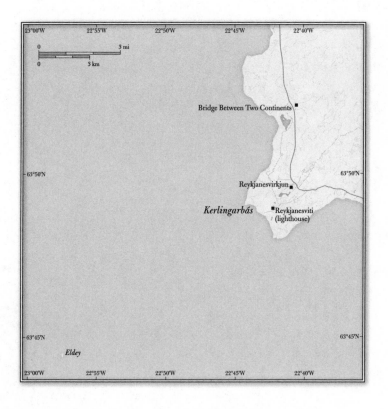

The Reykjanes Ridge is in many ways unique on Earth. One of the longest obliquely divergent plate boundaries along the Mid-Atlantic Ridge, it is the longest such plate boundary that doesn't lie at a right angle to its spreading center. The Ridge stretches 559 miles south from Reykjanes to the Bight transform fault, near 56.5°N.

Submarine volcanoes are more common along the Reykjanes Ridge than anywhere else on the Mid-Atlantic Ridge.

Ármann Höskuldsson, Einar Kjartansson, Árni Þór Vésteinsson, Sigurður Steinþórsson, and Oddur Sigurðsson. 2013. "Submarine Volcanoes." In *Natural Hazards in Iceland: Volcanoes and Earthquakes*, ed. Júlíus Sólnes. Reykjavík: University of Iceland Press.

PAVANE FOR A DEAD PRINCESS

(SIX MONTHS EARLIER)

The north magnetic pole is an extremely volatile place. Unlike its steadfast sibling in the south, it's changeable and constantly in motion, hovering beneath the earth's crust on a ceaseless search for sanctuary, unable to help its itinerant nature. It pulls compass needles along behind it, leading them from Nunavut, Canada, to just east of the North Pole—the geographic North Pole, that is. The geographic North Pole is stationary; meanwhile, the north magnetic pole seems to be drifting toward Siberia. But no one knows why, what business it has there.

The mysterious ramblings of the north magnetic pole plague me as I lie half-awake, pretending to be asleep while I think about rolling groundswells in the bowels of the earth, her mantle tossing and turning like a sleeping dragon, like my husband who murmurs beside me and turns onto his side, reaching out to touch my shoulder in his sleep. Our alarms will go off soon, I can feel it even though my eyes are closed, can almost count down to the moment his phone will play its harp melody and then three minutes later when the sirens blare from mine loud enough to wake the dead on Doomsday and me on a Monday morning. I'm usually a deep sleeper—I make the most of my nights—but today I wake early from restless dreams about the north magnetic pole and the molten iron at the earth's core that hounds it, driving it ever eastward. The earth's mysterious, subterranean movements sometimes haunt me in my sleep: mantle convection, the plume that rises up under this island, stoked by the planet's white-hot core. It drifts through my subconscious, having ensconced itself there long ago.

Dad never told me bedtime stories; Poppycock, he'd say, and then read instead from tomes on geology, astronomy, and magnetics. He'd lie beside me in my narrow bed and read and explain, drawing diagrams of strata and orbits, PET scans of the earth, expound on the internal logic of the universe, how it came into being. My dad smelled of pipe smoke, his big glasses were always smudged, and he was older and grayer than other dads, but he was the center of my universe. When Hekla erupted in 1980, I was so scared for him I thought my five-year-old heart would stop beating. But home again he came, rapturous and tired with sand in his hair.

Take a look at this, Stubby: our earth, fresh from the oven, he said, handing me a chunk of lava as if it were fragile, priceless. I was almost afraid to touch it—it seemed like it was still glowing, but it was probably just warm from Dad's big hands, reddish purple, about the size of a bread roll, rough all over and strangely weightless. It shed sharp grains of sand that I rubbed into my palm, licked from my fingertips when he wasn't looking. They tasted of blood.

The first alarm goes off, and my husband rolls over, flings out his arm and silences the burbling harp. I lie there, eyes closed, trying to stretch out these last three minutes under the duvet before the sirens go off on my phone.

We lie side by side with our eyes closed, pretending we're asleep. I know he's awake, and he knows I'm awake—it's the kind of thing you just feel after decades of marriage. But there are worse things than lying side by side with someone, pretending to be asleep.

He sits up, stretches, yawns, gets out of bed, opens the door, and walks down the hall, his heels reverberating on the white-stained oak floors—how can footsteps be so familiar?

I don't open my eyes until I hear the toilet flush, then let them adjust to the darkness for a moment, reach for my phone on the nightstand and shut off the alarm right before it sounds; it's March 4, 7:02 a.m. The Meteorological Office is forecasting a northeasterly breeze of nine to fourteen yards per second and intermittent sunshine that will turn overcast along the south coast later in the day, looks like snow, temperature's hovering right around freezing. We'll need to be in the air before noon if we're going to see anything. According to the Met's readings, there's an ongoing earthquake swarm off the coast of the Reykjanes Peninsula; they measured several quakes over 5.0 last night, all about four miles east-northeast of Eldey Island.

In all other respects, it's an entirely ordinary Monday morning: I take a shower, open Salka's door, Wake up, Stubby. Up and at 'em, Örn, I shout and pound vigorously on his door, try the knob, but my son's locked himself in. I knock again, he's supposed to be in the potroom by 8:00 a.m. Still no sign of life, but he's a grown man—well over twenty—and he's got to learn to be responsible for himself.

My husband and I do circuits around the house without crossing paths, like planets on different orbits; we divvy up the morning's tasks without a word. He's turned on the coffee machine by the time I come down to juice the oranges and set out muesli and yogurt, he hangs up the laundry, I make the lunches, we take turns calling the kids, rustling them out of bed.

An entirely ordinary Monday morning, the radio purrs in the kitchen and I stop to listen to the headlines at seven thirty, but there's no mention of the earthquakes. People have gotten used to them, they're not news anymore. They'll read the headlines again at eight, but they're done for now, and there's a brief silence before piano music starts, a bittersweet chord progression: Ravel's *Pavane pour une infante défunte*,

Pavane for a Dead Princess. Tender and sorrowful and infinitely beautiful, an elegy for a dead child, I close my eyes and let it wash over me, this incomprehensible beauty that stops me short in the midst of the morning chores.

My husband comes into the kitchen, pops a pod into the coffee machine and presses the button, the delicate music drowned out by the din.

What? he asks when he sees my face. What'd I do? Is something wrong?

No, nothing, I say, turning away.

Hey, now, he says with a laugh. Are you crying? Weeping at the radio? What's going on?

I just shake my head. He puts his arms around me, and I know he loves me. We've been married for over twenty years.

He kisses me and shouts goodbye to the kids, tax day's approaching and he needs to be at work early to advise clients on protecting their assets and earnings. Accounting is a narrative art, he sometimes says, and it's a good line—always gets a laugh at parties. These days he's writing fairy tales for the state treasury from morning till night.

I pound on Örn's door again, there's nothing, not a peep. Salka is sitting at the kitchen table when I come back down, sleepy and bedheaded in a yellow sundress and tights.

Morning, Stubby, I say, pouring some cod liver oil into a spoon for her. You need to put on something warmer—it's freezing outside.

I'm not cold, I weared a dress last week and was fine, she says, swallowing the fish oil and quickly washing it down with orange juice.

Wore, I say. Not weared. And it was unusually warm last week, remember? It doesn't make sense not to dress for the weather. And what do we call people who don't use common sense?

Dum-dums, she mumbles.

And are we dum-dums?

No, Mommy. But I still want to wore a dress, she says, dolloping yogurt and muesli into a bowl before counting out nine blueberries, like she always does, and popping them one by one into her mouth with a determined frown between her eyebrows. She's eight and young for her age, she really leans into her role as the baby of the family—it's like she's trying to hold off getting older for as long as she can.

Heavy footsteps shuffle down the hallway, and my eldest lumbers in, squints at the kitchen clock, and swears. He's got his uniform on, royal blue and orange coveralls with reflective stripes crisscrossing the chest, his dark locks are uncombed, and there's stubble on his upper lip.

Greetings, my good sir, nice of you to finally join us. You want some breakfast? A shave, maybe?

I hear it come out of my mouth, hear the officious, meddling tone before I can stop myself. He shakes his head, no time, he's already running late as it is. He towers over me, my beautiful boy, gives me a dutiful kiss on the cheek, pilfers my coffee cup, takes a deep swig, burns his tongue and swears again, drops a paw on his sister's head, ruffles her dark curls, mumbles, Bye, Stubbs, and then he's gone.

Be careful, I call as the door closes behind him. His old Ford coughs and sputters to life, the engine rumble heads toward the street, becomes muffled, fades away.

Get a move on, please, I tell Salka. Don't you need to feed your rats?

They're not rats. They're degus.

Degus, tassel-tail rats, whatever. You need to feed them before we go.

Mommy, Máni getted a cat. I want a cat.

Got. Máni got a cat. And what do you think your rats would have to say about that?

They wouldn't mind.

You're allergic to cats, sweetheart. And you need to learn to be responsible for your degus and take care of them. Now hurry up. Do you have your phone, your key, your inhaler?

I rinse the dishes and glasses, put them in the dishwasher, run a cloth over the kitchen table, and push the chairs in. I do Salka's hair while she brushes her teeth, pin her bangs back with a barrette so they don't get in her face, our eyes meet in the mirror, and we exchange a smile. She nuzzles her head in the crook of my neck and yawns sleepily. I'm tearing up again, I've no idea what's the matter with me today.

Okay, Stubby, I say, patting her on the shoulder. Hurry up now. No nonsense, no dillydallying.

Ten minutes later we're in the Benz and backing out of the now warm garage. Dropping Salka off now means I'll be stuck in traffic on my way into the city. Our house isn't particularly well situated for public transportation, it's one of the trade-offs of living out here by Elliðavatn Lake with a wood in our backyard and limitless views of the mountains out on Reykjanes. Delicate flora stretches into our garden: moss, crowberry and wild thyme, violets, the occasional wildflower. Right now—as the headlights cast a cold light across the crusted snow—they're all asleep underground, but they're there all the same, waiting for the spring, their roots curled around stones.

He was so happy when he found the house. For you, he said.

C'mon, I said. Forget it, it's way too big, too much.

But his mind was made up, it was the only house that would do, he said, perfect for the best geoscientist in the country.

Nonsense, I said, but I caved in the end. I liked the idea of living out here by the lake, surrounded by these blue mountains, these monuments to ancient eruptions, long since gone cold. I could be content here, could do my work and relax; the landscape would be my constant inspiration.

The house makes me happy, he was right—our home always brings me pleasure, even if I never imagined I'd live like this. So extravagantly. It's smartly laid out: bright rooms on the top floor with 360-degree views; on the ground floor, a quiet wing for bedrooms sheltered by trees and vegetation. We lived in Dad's apartment in Vesturbær on the west side of the city when we came back from our studies abroad, and I thought maybe we'd get a place with a bit more room after Salka was born, enough space, perhaps, for a small home office, but nothing like this—I'd never dreamed of this palace or this neighborhood, a secluded corner of the world on the outskirts of my consciousness, it couldn't have surprised me more if he'd found a house for us in Australia.

My dear husband.

And so here we are in the suburbs with all the associated pros and cons. At school, my daughter clambers out of the car and joins the other suburban kids streaming through the doors, all of them raised in relative wealth and security: vacations abroad, iPhones and a new coat every fall, three cars in the driveways of their spacious homes. Parents who skim the cream off the clangoring centrifuge of the free market economy, who maybe drink a little too much red wine, who sometimes raise their voices, slurred, but not at our house. Everything's smooth sailing at our house.

Bye, Mommy, she says without looking over her shoulder, and I drive away, toasty in the Benz, tune the dial to the classical station, and try to focus on the day's business—seismic activity on the ocean floor—but my mind wanders. Red taillights form a continuous chain into the city, and the traffic's unusually slow, but there's no point getting worked up about the delay, stupid to waste energy on that. And I actually like these long mornings in the car, enjoy the friendly hum of the engine and the powerful speaker system. The tank's full, the tire pressure is as it should be—all the gauges and meters on the sleek dashboard show that everything is working just the way it should, the scent of the coffee in my travel mug fills the car.

My attention drifts to the surrounding cars, the one next to me is full of smoke, the driver sucking greedily on a vape. The woman in the car in front of him is hunched over her phone and not paying attention to traffic, whenever she notices that it's moved forward, she stomps on the gas pedal and her car lurches three, four yards ahead—you can feel the irritation in the line behind her, it's like the vaper's car is the head of a furious dragon, preparing to spew fire and death. Maybe these people have terrible secrets, maybe their lives are in shambles. Maybe the vaper isn't allowed to see his kids, maybe the woman on her phone is sending an email to her divorce lawyer. Maybe he's about to serve a prison sentence for some horrible crime, maybe she's been diagnosed with terminal cancer. People struggle with the most unbelievable things without anyone being the wiser, they keep going to meetings, doing the shopping and brushing their teeth, even though no one would blame them if they spent their days curled up in bed, crying in agony.

I shake my head, surprised at myself, flip from Brahms to the news. They're just bad drivers, there's nothing more to it. It's not like me to start imagining things—facts are good enough for me. What's all this sentimentality? Poppycock.

UNDER OUR FEET BEATS A BURNING HEART

Mantle plumes are postulated mechanisms that push anomalously hot material from the depths of the earth's mantle and up toward the surface. Many theories claim that one of the most powerful plumes is located under Iceland and the tectonic plate boundaries that cross through it, thereby weakening the earth's crust and stimulating tectonic shift. According to these theories, Iceland owes its existence to the Iceland Plume.

Örn Ögmundsson. 1987. "The Mantle Plume Theory."
In *A Textbook in Geoscience for Icelandic Gymnasia.*
Reykjavík: Íþaka.

The Reykjanes Ridge has been shaking for three weeks. It's always been in motion, of course, ever since the earth's crust started pulling apart sixty-six million years ago and Norway and Greenland began their slow sail, each in their own direction. This is not news in and of itself, but in the past few days the seismic waves around Eldey Island have become more powerful and moved closer to land. It's nothing to get worked up about and my colleagues carry on as usual, shuffling papers around their desks and peering at computer screens, standing in the break room and discussing the situation over cups of coffee, rolling their weight from their heels to their toes and back again, hmming and mmming, the suspense is palpable. They all go silent when they see me—everyone wants to be in the helicopter, but there are only two seats this time.

Jóhannes Rúriksson leans against the shabby kitchen cabinets, narrowing his eyes under gray-streaked brows.

So, I hear you're taking the helicopter out for a spin, eh, Miss Anna? What the hell for? The Ridge is shaking, like it's always done. Just like it did last year and the year before that. It's a whole lot of nothing.

No one says a word. The old coot lifts his chin and squares his shoulders in his holey sweater, looms over me with arms crossed, chomps his nicotine gum and eyes me defiantly. I meet his gaze and lift my brows: No harm in checking it out.

Hysterics, plain and simple, just like when you all went to pieces over Þorbjörn. You'd be better served taking the helicopter over Bárðarbunga and checking out the calderas in Vatnajökull. That's my opinion.

He knows as well as I do there's nothing happening at Bárðarbunga right now, but he's as obstinate as a teenage boy, never mind that he's well over sixty. Sometime ago I had to have a serious talk with him about run-ins with female colleagues and the unnecessary risks he was taking in the field, but he's done surprisingly well since and I've only had to remind him once, after he made the front page of a foreign newspaper during the Holuhraun eruption by jumping onto a stone slab floating down a river of lava and grinning for the cameras like a surfer from hell.

Call it hysterics if you like, I say, but last I checked, geoscience doesn't revolve around your opinions, but measurements and scientific observations.

All we need to do is to lift the Uncertainty Phase—there's not a damn thing going on out there. No more than there is at Grindavík.

I walk up to him and cross my arms, look him dead in the eyes, Oh, of course, I forgot: Jói knows all. Maybe the Met should unplug its instruments and just plug you in instead.

We stand there, staring each other down, our coworkers watching and waiting to see what will happen next. Then he looks away with a smirk, rubs his gray head: Clearly a morning person, aren't we, Your Highness?

You know as well as I do how imprecise data can be with quakes at sea, I say, we could have a submarine eruption happening right now along the coastline and not even know it. There's no harm in flying over and taking a look. But maybe you think you're better qualified to go?

The chair of Institute of Earth Sciences' board sticks her head out of her office and puts an end to our duel by asking me for a quick word. Elísabet Kaaber's mousy hair is a bit ruffled, and there's a coffee stain on her pale pink sweater.

Don't provoke the boys, Anna, dear, you know they're scared of you, she says, peering myopically at the Met Office website on her computer screen, fidgeting in her chair. Every horizontal surface in her office is covered: with books, with maps, with files, coffee cups, flower vases, and chunks of rock—the chaos is a direct extension of the disarray and genius of her person.

Be honest: do you really think there's something happening out there? You don't think the flyover is a waste of time? There *is* a lot of activity—I can't remember anything like it. Not there, at least.

It's probably nothing, but it doesn't hurt to take a closer look. This is atypical behavior, and we know the Ridge is capable of anything, I say, glancing around with a grimace. And while we're being honest, Ebba, isn't it time to clean up a bit? How do you find anything in here?

Hush now, don't start. I've got a very precise system, I know where everything is. The Ridge could start moving at any moment and Reykjanes, too, for that matter.

Hold your horses, let's not get ahead of ourselves. We'll start with the flyover and go from there.

She nods. Eiríkur will go with you, and some media people will tag along for the ride too. The usual suspects—RÚV needs aerial shots, Channel 2, *Morgunblaðið*, and there's some photographer too. I don't know him—he's got a foreign name.

Oh, for the love of God. Ebba, we're conducting scientific observations. I shake my head. We don't have time for this. That lot'll just plonk themselves down in the window seats, and we won't be able to see anything. We might as well not go.

Anna, dear. We have to be accommodating, she sighs, looking at me imploringly. You've got to understand that. It's important for us to be on good terms with the media, to keep them on our side.

I open my mouth to complain, but she holds up a hand to cut me off.

Stop. It isn't just about funding and PR. It's important for us to maintain the nation's confidence—that people see what we're doing and trust information from us when it matters the most. You're our public face; you've got to talk to the media.

Okay, fine, I relent. But I'm not a babysitter, I don't have time to explain every little thing for them. I just want to do my job in peace.

She flashes me one of her rare shy smiles, follows me out and claps me on the shoulder in parting. Have a good trip and good luck, she says. And be nice to them, okay? Hopefully, you won't see a damn thing out there.

Walking to the airport would probably have been faster than driving, but it's cold out, so I offer Eiríkur a ride. He's an awkward, highly intelligent young man with a thick shock of hair atop his large, squarish head; his obsession with the medieval formation of Reykjanes has cast new light on the volcanic eruptions of the thirteenth century. He stops at a vending machine and buys himself a carton of chocolate milk and a shrimp sandwich that he proceeds to unwrap as soon as he gets in my sparkling-clean SUV. I shoot him a sharp look, and he hesitates before wrapping it back up with a sullen expression.

The media people arrived ahead of us; I recognize the two camera operators and the photographer from the newspaper, all men, and then a pale, nervous girl who introduces herself as a reporter from the national radio station. We're all buckled in the helicopter when a fifth man runs up with a camera bag on his shoulder, out of breath and smiling from ear to ear, he hoists himself into his seat, puts the headphones on his tousled head, and doesn't seem to be even slightly embarrassed that he almost missed the flight.

I've never met him before, he looks at me and smiles, his lips moving and his eyes laughing, his teeth are white and uniform, and he's unshaven. I can't hear what he's saying—the din from the rotor drowns out his words, and he irritates me, unpunctual and self-satisfied, his whole presence obtrusive and distracting, filling the helicopter with an unruly sort of energy. I don't return the smile, look away and focus on the work at hand.

The helicopter heaves itself into the air and heads west-southwest over the Reykjanes Peninsula toward Eldey Island. The sun is up, and the land below is deserted, the vast, empty landscape around the capital unfurls below us like a geological history chart. I shake off my irritation, flip on my microphone, and turn to the passengers, flashing them my most ingratiating smile.

Shall I bore you with a crash course in geoscience?

They nod eagerly, and I start reeling off facts, descriptions of how the Reykjanes Peninsula has come to be, built up over time along the plate boundary of the Mid-Atlantic Ridge, how tuff mountains were thrust upward under the pressure of the ice age glacier, how the largest lava field was formed after the glaciers started retreating and the land started rising.

This peninsula is the youngest part of Iceland, I say. People were around to see the formation of many of these lava fields. That big one there between the Bláfjöll Mountains and Heiðmörk Nature Preserve is called Húsfellsbruni and was formed around the year 1000. And though it's not far, a large portion of the lava fields around Hafnarfjörður are even younger, Kapelluhraun, Chapel Lava Field, for instance—the tongue that runs alongside the Straumsvík aluminum smelter—that was formed in 1151. It probably buried a church, which is how it got its name.

The man who deigned to grace us with his presence says something, but none of it is audible until he fumbles with his headphones and he manages to turn on his mic.

Did the lava all come from the same volcano?

No, I reply. There's no central volcano here on the peninsula. No real volcano like Hekla or Katla or Öræfajökull. The eruptions occur in a fracture zone that extends from Reykjanes, around the Svartsengi and Krýsuvík geothermal areas, and all the way to the Brennisteinsfjöll Mountains. People sometimes count Hengill Volcano as part of the Reykjanes Peninsula, but it's a central volcano and doesn't have much connection to the other systems. Eruption episodes out here can occur over the course of many decades and move between systems. The last time there was an eruption on Reykjanes, in the thirteenth century, the fires continued for over thirty years. Intermittently, I should say.

A thirty-year eruption? That must've been crazy.

There aren't any precise descriptions of it, but there don't seem to have been any fatalities. They were medium-sized eruptions that came and went, always cropping up somewhere new. Eruptions like that are called "fires." The sources we have from that time describe considerable ashfall, how the fissures diverged and the land cracked and transformed. Vegetation had a hard time taking root in the area for decades after the Reykjanes Fires ended. My colleague Eiríkur can tell you more about this, it's visible in all the strata.

I fetch a well-thumbed page from a plastic folder in my backpack and hand it back. The pale girl from the national radio examines it attentively before taking pictures of it with her phone and passing it to the photographer.

This was quite a happening place in the thirteenth century, I say. Ten eruptions in thirty years. The place names tell us that people witnessed these events. Bruni means "fire," of course, so it's a common appellation for lava fields around the country. Here, right below us, is Háibruni, High Fire, and just plain Bruni is there to the right. That's where you find Óbrennishólmi, or "unburnt islet," where the lava flowed around hills and knolls in the landscape. And it's easy to spot the boundary where new lava flowed over old, again and again, which is how the peninsula was formed.

The reporter turns on her mic. Why was the capital built here if people knew about all these volcanoes?

I smile at her.

Historical Volcanic Eruptions on the Reykjanes Peninsula		
Year	Location	Type
1926	Eldey	Submarine
1884	Eldey	Submarine
1879	Geirfuglasker	Submarine
1783	Eldeyjarboði	Submarine
1583	Reykjanes Ridge	Submarine
1422	Reykjanes Ridge	Submarine
1340	Reykjanes Ridge	Submarine
1325	Trölladyngja	Fissure
1210–40	Reykjanes Fires 10 eruptions	Submarine, Phreatic, Fissure
1200	Brennisteinsfjöll	Fissure
1151–88	Krýsuvík Fires 5 eruptions	Fissure
950–1000	Brennisteinsfjöll Fires 6 eruptions	Fissure

They forgot. The city was built a long time after the last eruption, which was hundreds of years before the old village became a city and we started building on the lava. Human history goes much faster than geological history, we have such short memories. For people, a thousand years is thirty generations, but in geological terms, that's just the blink of an eye. It's like a single day.

She looks at me, her eyes wide. Isn't that dangerous?

Dangerous? Everything's dangerous. You've got a greater chance of dying in a car accident or breaking your neck getting out of the bath than being in a volcanic eruption. And the volcanic activity here on the peninsula hasn't been particularly dangerous—not really. Sure, it can cause some logistical headaches, generally due to the movement of the earth's crust. Roads pull apart, water supplies get destroyed, power lines snap, and so on. But we've just got to live with it if we're going to live on this island. We're right on top of a hot spot, over a melt zone in the mantle where magma forms. Without it, we wouldn't be here, this country simply wouldn't exist. Under our feet beats a burning heart—it's just a part of life.

That's awesome, says Mister Come Lately, his eyes shining. All this feral, fertile energy bubbling up again and again, forming the land. Creation and destruction at the same time. Wild job you've got.

I give him a thin smile.

Scientists have to stick to facts and scientific conclusions. There's nothing "wild" about it.

He chuckles, and the light glints off his teeth.

Mother Nature, baby. She doesn't care about your scientific conclusions. She's pure chaos.

I shake my head and turn my attention to the landscape below. What an ass.

We fly over the ocean, over Eldey and Geirfuglasker, the helicopter almost touching the surface of the sea, waves receding under the beating rotor. We can't make out any strange movement—no air bubbles or color changes, no sign of anything unusual happening beneath the surface—turn and fly back over the lava fields, watching in silence as we near the city with dizzying speed.

Three days later the earth's crust tears apart just south of the southernmost tip of the Reykjanes Peninsula, fissures open along the ocean floor just beyond Kerlingarbás Cove with an earsplitting crack, plumes of lava shoot miles into the air, and thousands of square yards of lapilli and ash rain down over Keflavík.

Thirteen minutes before it happens the sirens on my phone wake me up. It takes me a few seconds to realize that the alert from the Met Office is for an event that's just about to happen.

Pure chaos, baby.

EXPLANATORY NOTE I

HEKLA 1947

Experience has taught us that our favorite volcanoes can turn on a dime and we need to be on our guard against them.

Páll Einarsson. "Volcanoes in Iceland: Monitoring, Warnings, Achievements, and Prospects." Christmas Lecture, University of Iceland, Reykjavík, December 19, 2019.

Hekla is the central volcano in the mountain ridge to which it lends its name, a ridge that's cleft longways by the Heklugjá volcanic fissure, the westernmost volcano in Iceland's Eastern Volcanic Zone. She's the stately queen of Icelandic volcanoes, the virgin princess, the dragon that hovers over the fertile lands in the south of the country, the gateway to hell. Hekla is all of this, but she's also just a heap of lava that, over the course of 7,000 years of eruptions, has grown into a 4,921-foot peak.

Hekla is also a geological riddle. We've spent many human lifetimes working to solve it, searching for her mysterious magma chamber, which we know hides deep within the bowels of the earth, perhaps as much as twelve miles below the surface. And why hasn't she erupted this century, after having done so at ten-year intervals up until now, as regular as the clapper of a bell? What's she waiting for?

I'd spent years researching Hekla before I realized what a complicated relationship Icelanders have with her. And not just with Hekla, but with all the other volcanoes in this country as well. I always took it as a given, that blend of cheerful and anxious expectation Icelanders get anytime an eruption begins, but when I started traveling to other volcanic regions, I discovered that our fondness for volcanic events is virtually unmatched. Elsewhere in the world, active volcanoes are viewed as threatening monsters. Filipinos and Indonesians fear and hate their volcanoes, whereas Icelanders baptize their children in honor of their most dangerous ones, as though they were beloved, if capricious, aunts. No one's ever named a child Tambora or Krakatoa, but in Iceland, we're knee deep in little Heklas and Katlas.

My father had an explanation for this. It was our lot in life, he said, to settle this difficult and beautiful land, but we had to see ourselves as worthy of it. It couldn't be just anyone who endured such adversity, and as a result, the nation had an obligation to educate a rugged bunch of scientists and see to it that the country continued to be inhabited. But there weren't any geoscientists in Iceland when Katla erupted in 1918.

To our everlasting shame, he said with a shake of his head. We'd trained poets and pastors instead of scientists. Foreign scientists oversaw the majority of the research that took place during that great eruption, but they lacked a connection with the land and its history. They didn't have fire in their blood, he said, his eyes darkening as he tapped out his pipe as though it were full of foreigners.

The Society of Icelandic Scientists was founded that very same year, 1918, in part to address this shortage, and so after the 1938 glacial outburst flood on the Skeiðará River, only Icelandic scientists participated in the first observation flight over Vatnajökull to examine the caldera north of the Grímsvötn volcano. Okay, so the pilot was half-Danish and educated by Nazis, but we can't look a gift horse in the mouth, said Dad with a wink. But then he went quiet and solemn because dear, departed Steinþór had been on that flight. Steinþór perished in the Hekla eruption nine years later, the only Icelandic geologist to lose their life in the field, to die a hero's death in the service of Icelandic earth science. Dad was studying abroad when it happened, but he remembered it well, saved a newspaper clipping like some kind of holy relic that he'd let me read sometimes.

> TRAGEDY STRUCK on the Hekluhraun lava field last Sunday, a sudden accident in which geologist Steinþór Sigurðsson, MSci, was killed by a fist-size chunk of lava stone after it rolled off the edge of a lava fall. He died instantly. Steinþór was researching and filming one of the main lava falls, a torrent of red-hot lava flowing down a hillside. He was standing close to the 32-foot-high flow edge. He either didn't see the fiery lava stone—which slid over the edge at an unusually high speed—or didn't have time to escape its path. Steinþór was felled, his body lifeless before it hit the ground. The stone struck him on the chest, right over his heart.
>
> *Morgunblaðið*, November 3, 1947.

I thought about his death a lot when I was a child: to be struck in the heart by a red-hot lava stone. Pictured Steinþór's heart in flames, his amazement when it went up in smoke.

When I started traveling around the world and lecturing on volcanic activity in Iceland, I explained our love for volcanoes like this:

Our nation didn't witness an eruption in the vicinity of a populated area from the time of the Katla eruption in 1918 until Hekla erupted in 1947. In the intervening years, Icelanders conveniently misplaced their memories of the horrors these events had rained down upon them. We'd freed ourselves from the yoke of the Danish crown and somewhere on the way to independence the country's volcanic activity became part of our self-image. Iceland's volcanoes became its crown jewels, the symbolic essence of the relationship between the land and us, its people, which is why it's always like a national holiday when the earth opens and spews fire and blazing ash over the country. People hop in their cars and drive as far as they have to in order to see the spectacle in person, sneak across the Department of Civil Protection's safety cordons, endanger their lives and those of their families to see an eruption with their own eyes. Overwrought reporters interview grave-looking scientists who've been transformed overnight from dusty scholars into soothsayers and national heroes; the most imaginative restaurateurs fly tycoons up to the lava's edge, serve them flambéed duck breasts and vintage champagne on white-clothed tables, ash crunching between their guests' teeth.

It's a cause for celebration when our country gets bigger, I'd say with a shrug, and this generally yielded a laugh from the auditorium. That's why we don't need an army in Iceland, why we don't have to invade other countries. Our land expands all on its own.

Needless to say, my opinion on this has since changed.

Nearly a quarter of the nation perished as a result of the Skaftá Fires. Since then, eight generations have been born and died. We are the progeny of those who survived, with fire, ash, and hunger in our DNA. We've no control over it, we're drawn to the fire like moths to a flame.

WE LIVE ON AN ACTIVE VOLCANO

Phreatic eruptions are eruptions that occur when magma in volcanic conduits or vents comes into contact with water; these are called *tætigos* in Icelandic. The Surtseyan eruption, a type of phreatic eruption, was named for the island of Surtsey off the southern coast of Iceland, and the eruption that formed it in the mid-1960s. In phreatic eruptions a high proportion of small particles increase heat transfer to the ash plume, which causes the plume to reach higher altitudes than in other kinds of eruptions. Indeed, alkaline magma that comes into contact with water can easily create a massive ash plume that may rise as high as six to twelve miles into the air, but would have otherwise turned to lava.

Ármann Höskuldsson, Magnús Tumi Guðmundsson, Guðrún Larsen, and Þorvaldur Þórðarson. 2013. "Eruptions." In *Natural Hazards in Iceland: Volcanoes and Earthquakes*, ed. Júlíus Sólnes. Reykjavík: University of Iceland Press.

How could this happen? How the hell could Keflavík Airport just erupt without warning?

The national police commissioner is reading the riot act to the Met Office employees who have been trying for weeks to convince him that the unusual seismic activity off the tip of the Reykjanes Peninsula was worthy of his attention, with no success. He stands in the middle of the Department of Civil Protection's coordination center, turning in circles and shouting into his phone, which he's holding in front of his face; people stream into the room and watch him, wide-eyed.

Advance warning? What the hell do you think the words "Uncertainty Phase" mean?

I can make out the husky, ill-tempered voice of Júlíus, the director of the Met's Earthquake Hazard Monitoring Department, on the other end of the line, and he's not amused. It's a terrible shock that the Met's instruments didn't pick up the microquakes leading up to the eruption, but that's one of the difficulties of measuring volcanic activity on the ocean floor. That and there's the ominous ash plume that formed when red-hot magma burst from the depths, shot to the surface, ripped through the stratosphere, rained truckloads of tephra over Keflavík, and shut down air traffic in this part of the North Atlantic indefinitely. Flights that were unable to turn around have been redirected to airports in Akureyri and Egilsstaðir, Nuuk in Greenland, and Tórshavn in the Faroe Islands, throwing into chaos the travel plans of thousands of passengers and airlines, the commissioner's shirt has big blotches under the arms, this whole thing is so god-awful—so overwhelming and unlucky—and it's all landed squarely on his desk.

Good morning, I say, trying to sound encouraging, he's the highest-ranking superior in Civil Protection and needs to be fit to make levelheaded decisions. At the moment he looks anything but, his face is red and his brow shiny with sweat, his eyes wander uncertainly over the screens on the wall. Someone needs to give him a hug and calm him down: there there, we're here, the members of the Scientific Council are gathering, leaders from ICE-SAR, Icelandic Search and Rescue, are trickling in, and here comes Milan, chief superintendent of the Department of Civil Protection, calm and crewcutted, his shoulders broad enough to hold up the heavens. It'll be okay.

We settle around the stained conference table, everyone disheveled and jumpy, Isavia's chief security officer apparently didn't give herself time to change out of her pajamas, but she's already done her part—they redirected all flights away from the Keflavík airport, activated the diversion airports, notified the Volcanic Ash Advisory Center in London, and paused air traffic around the North Atlantic. She's looking rather dazed from the effort.

Thank you all for coming on such short notice at this time of day, says Milan, looking out over the motley, sleepy gathering. We thought it was important to convene the Scientific Council to discuss the volcanic eruption out beyond Reykjanes. We're still missing a few people; the representatives from the Environment Agency and the Met Office are on the way. We've got coffee brewing, but I think we should get started. Anna Arnardóttir is here from the Institute of Earth Sciences at the University of Iceland, and Anna, while we wait on the Met, I think it would be best for you to start us off. What do we know so far?

I don't know much more than you, I say. Based on the limited information we have, it seems like a volcanic fissure has opened on the ocean floor not far from Kerlingarbás Cove, in the southwest of the peninsula. It looks to be a classic Surtseyan phreatic eruption, and the ash plume is currently just under six miles high. We can monitor it in real time using Keflavík Airport's meteorological radar.

How bad is it?

Hard to say. It all depends on how it develops. The eruption is happening underwater—for now, at least—and the volcanic debris is breaking through the surface as tephra. The tephra fall could be considerable in Grindavík and Hafnir, cause damage to the power plants, and create some real inconveniences around Keflavík and at the airport. The ash could make for slippery roadways across a wide area, but the greatest danger will probably be for flights, from the ash plume.

Is it too early to say how it will develop?

Yes. Submarine eruptions like this come and go, and how long they last on the surface varies. This burst could continue for a few hours or maybe several days.

This burst?

Milan glances up from his computer screen and sends me an inquiring look. He enunciates his words just a tad too precisely, but otherwise, there's not much to remind you that somewhere in the distant past, he was part of the Yugoslav military police. His voice is deep and calm, as if we were just talking about the weather, he's dealt with far more complicated matters than this eruption.

It's much too early to say. Submarine eruptions that reach the surface often occur in bursts and surface again and again. For instance, the Surtsey eruption went on intermittently for three and a half years from 1963 until 1967. We don't know much about volcanic activity on the ocean floor beyond Reykjanes, there've been occasional, small-scale eruptions around there since the fourteenth century. The last was northeast of Eldey in 1926, it was a short eruption—only lasted a few hours. So far as we know, there hasn't been a real eruption in this part of the country since the thirteenth century. In that case the bursts started on land and then moved out to the ocean.

How long did those go on?

In total, thirty years. But again, only intermittently.

Thirty years?

Milan's forehead wrinkles, the first sign of concern he's shown since he arrived.

Yes, the Reykjanes Fires lasted thirty years. They were the conclusion to a nearly three-hundred-year period of volcanic activity on the peninsula. First there was the eruption at the Brennisteinsfjöll Mountains around the year 1000, then the Krýsuvík Fires started up in the twelfth century, and then there were the Reykjanes Fires from 1210 to 1240. Eruptions popped up here and there, traveling east to west along the peninsula's fracture zone.

Sorry, is this what's happening now? Ólöf, Isavia's chief security officer, looks at me disbelievingly, as if it's the first she's heard of it.

It's difficult to say, I reply. The eruption only began a few minutes ago, and we don't have any scientific sources to refer to from medieval times, of course, all we can do is try to puzzle together hints from strata in the area and draw comparisons with recent eruptions elsewhere in the country. But it's been more than eight hundred years since the last eruption. We can't rule anything out.

Why haven't we heard anything about this before? she asks. We've invested millions in an international airport, marketed it as the North Atlantic's premier airline hub, we're just getting back on our feet after the pandemic—what happens if there's a thirty-year eruption now?

This is all clearly explained in the risk assessment report, I say, starting to get angry. The latest version has been available for three years. None of this should come as a surprise. We live on an active volcanic island that erupts, on average, every four years. Where exactly do you think all the lava that your airport's built on came from?

We can discuss this later, Milan interjects. We need to respond to the situation as it stands now and implement the contingency plan. We've sounded the alarms, we've started evacuating Hafnir and Grindavík. ICE-SAR is setting up shelters in schools in Keflavík and Vogar. Passengers and tourists can sit tight in the airport for the time being, at least for a few hours.

The meeting is supposed to be short and strategic, but the Scientific Council abides by its own unwritten rules; people have to stand up and hold forth about what their field or institution has to say about the situation. The geophysicists are concerned about the movement of the earth's crust, and the petrologists muse about isotopes from the old lava in the area, Maurice from Iceland GeoSurvey reviews the latest satellite images of Reykjanes, and Bárður from the Environment Agency predicts that roofs will start to cave in when the ash layer reaches a thickness of almost three feet—every square foot of dry ash weighs 123 pounds, he states darkly, a whole ton if the ash is wet.

The door screeches open, a group of journalists shove past the coffee corner and into the middle of the coordination center. TV cameras are shouldered, tripods splayed, and phones aimed, flashes go off in rapid succession. Milan remains expressionless, stands up to meet the fourth estate.

Good morning and welcome, he says. Unfortunately, we do not have a great deal of information right now, we're still in the middle of the Scientific Council meeting and have just begun to acquaint ourselves with the situation. What we know is this: An eruption has begun in the ocean beneath Reykjanes, just beyond Kerlingarbás. The eruption is thought to be small or medium in size, but a substantial ash cloud has developed as a result, and that could have serious consequences for airline passengers. There's considerable ashfall across the Reykjanes Peninsula, and we cannot rule out the risk of carbon monoxide poisoning. We've enacted the Civil Protection contingency plan and announced a state of emergency in Grindavík, Reykjanesbær, and Vogar. Grindavík and Hafnir are being evacuated as we speak, and residents directed to the Red Cross's disaster shelters for assistance. The police and ICE-SAR teams are assisting with evacuations. All flights to and from Keflavík Airport have been canceled for the time being.

Milan reels off the information as though he's reading it from a paper, he's a mountain of calm, he's taken all the tumult of the room and boiled it down into this concise summary. The journalists listen attentively, hold out their microphones, and take notes as if their lives depended on it. He invites them to ask questions, and a solemn-faced reporter, a veteran Knight of the Natural Disaster, steps forward and asks loudly: Are people's lives in danger?

I roll my eyes, it's everything I can't stand about the media in times of crisis: their insatiable hunger for catastrophe and tragedy, their need to appeal to the public's basest impulses—fear and sentimentality. Milan remains impassive.

We declared a state of emergency in order to save lives, he says. We need to evacuate the area while we investigate local conditions, but nothing thus far indicates that people are currently in any serious danger.

There's an outburst of questions, the reporters all talking at once, but Milord Doomsday raises his voice above the din. It's long been said that the Reykjanes Ridge is due for an eruption. Shouldn't you have been better prepared?

I stand up and take my place beside Milan. You're mistaken, I say, frowning at the reporter. Volcanoes are never "due" for an eruption. They don't have a schedule. They erupt when the conditions beneath the earth's crust demand it. Sometimes this happens at fairly regular intervals, but no one can predict the next eruption. If we could, our jobs would be easy.

Sir Catastrophe doesn't proffer another question, but the pale girl from the national radio station is here, and she raises a slender hand. Milan nods at her.

Can we expect more eruptions in the area? As I understand it, the last eruption went on for several decades and occurred all over the peninsula. She looks down at her notebook and then up again. Can we expect another Reykjanes Fires?

It's too soon to say, I reply. Our job now is to respond to this submarine volcano. The Met Office operates an extensive network of seismographs in the area, and we'll be warned of volcanic activity.

But you weren't this time, she says. You only got thirteen minutes' notice.

It would be best for the Met Office to respond to that. But it's always difficult to predict eruptions at sea.

Milan calls an end to the press conference.

ICE-SAR's PR officer will be your contact. You can put in requests for interviews and images with her. But whatever happens, we need to ensure that from here on out, we only publish accurate and verified information. It's important that we maintain calm and don't encourage unnecessary unrest. This depends on all of us.

We sit back down and, grumbling, the journalists settle around the press table. Júlíus from the Met Office has finally arrived, long-bearded and scowling like a thundercloud, which means I can head over to the Reykjavík airport and prepare for the observation flight that will be taking off before sunrise. I wave a wary greeting at Júlíus; he nods and slings his backpack onto his desk.

Money, he spits out. It always comes down to money. We've been begging to increase the instrumentation on the Reykjanes Ridge since this burst began, and they batted the request back and forth between ministries until this happened. And now it's all blown up in our faces.

If you'd had more equipment out there, would we have had more warning?

What do you think? We need triple what we have now, especially out on Reykjanes. But no one thought it was unusual or important enough . . .

He falls silent, then looks me dead in the eye, his beard quivering. Think if this had happened just a bit later, around now, six, with the flight from the US getting ready to land. Huh? That would've been a fun thing to be responsible for—seeing them plummet from the sky like a shot goose.

Now, c'mon, that wouldn't have happened, I say reassuringly. Surely you'd have had enough time to redirect them.

Maybe, he says, sinking into his chair. Whatever makes you feel better.

THERE'S NO SUCH THING
AS EDEN

TF-Sif, the Coast Guard's Bombardier Dash, isn't as agile as its helicopters, but it's equipped with the radar equipment and thermographs we need to analyze the eruption and its ash plume. It's also a much more comfortable aircraft. While the crew readies for takeoff, Eiríkur, two scientists from the Met, and I buckle in. The sun is coming up, but it's a strange dawn—it looks like an old photograph, the eastern light is diffuse, only piercing through the haze here and there. The darkness to the west is endless, the silence broken only by the occasional crack of distant thunder.

I sip my coffee, clench my teeth, and try to hide the fact that I'm chattering; the cold, my lack of sleep, the excitement of the past few hours, it all seems to be conspiring against me—I'm keyed up, my body is vibrating like a taut string even as my mind remains sharp and clear, we've got to get going, I have to see this eruption for myself.

The door of the plane opens, and in bustles the director of the Icelandic Coast Guard, Ófeigur Kúld, short, energetic, and always with this toothy grin plastered on his face—a real spark plug, my dad would say.

Well, here we are, he greets us. It's all happening now, isn't it?

He looks at his watch. You should be able to take off in about twenty minutes. We just have to wait for the others.

Others? I ask. What others?

Government folks, he says. And the media.

I don't believe what I'm hearing.

Government folks? What the hell are you talking about?

We got a call from the ministry offices. The National Security Council wants to take a peek at this thing, and the PM, and the minister for foreign affairs, and the minister for justice. They're en route, the media's just arrived.

I'm sorry—you're delaying our observation flight so you can fill the plane with politicians? Have you lost your mind?

This is a matter for Civil Protection, Halldóra from the Met Office agrees. A research trip. Can't you take them on their own flight later?

Ófeigur leans back, his face hardening. Let's not forget, shall we, that this aircraft belongs to the Coast Guard, as do the helicopters you take for your flyovers. I oversee the Coast Guard, and the minister of justice oversees me. So you two just sit back and relax and accept that we will take off when and with whom I say or you won't go at all. Is that understood?

He storms out, and we exchange a wordless glance.

Awful little man, mutters Halldóra after a long pause.

I take out my phone and call Milan. He answers after one ring, his voice level.

It's up to him, he says after I've explained the situation. I don't agree, but I can't tell the director how to do his job. And I don't have time for this now—Keflavík is being buried in ash as we speak.

He hangs up, and we sit there dejectedly until people start filing into the plane. The ministers and their assistants say hello, and everyone's excited and bundled up in practical parkas except for the minister for foreign affairs, who reminds me of a sleepy, double-chinned bear in her thick fur coat and hat. She's done her makeup, even put on lipstick. The ministers greet one another and settle into the window seats; the media will have to make do with the aisle.

What a joke, Halldóra grumbles, and we hunch over our laptops, try to ignore the lot of them.

Finally, we're ready for takeoff, the plane coasts down the runway and hefts itself into the air. We scientists sit in the observation seats facing the windows, while the Coasties pore over the screens on the instrument panel. The day is starting to dawn, and a coal-gray plume of smoke rises from Reykjanes, like a curled fist punching into the dawn. Lightning plays around it, and thunder shakes the plane, as if two mountains are crashing against one another; we cower with every roll.

It's dark, I say, gesturing at the plume, and Halldóra nods. Surprisingly dark for a submarine eruption, the color indicates there's a considerable amount of magma streaming from the fissure, turning into tephra, and shooting into the atmosphere in a cloud of white steam. It might be bigger than we thought.

The passengers ooh and ahh and ohmygod until the TV guys shush them—they're drowning out the background sound. The plane flies toward the plume, which has already reached a height of seven miles. The crest is drifting northward, drawing a shadowy veil across Keflavík and the upper half of Reykjanes, which itself has been cast into total darkness amid a blizzard of ash. South of the plume, the gunmetal sea churns and roils like a hot spring around the eruption site, which appears to be extraordinarily close to land.

Maybe Reykjanes will get bigger, stretch farther into the sea, says Halldóra. Unless the eruption moves ashore.

I nod, craning my neck for a better view before unbuckling and stepping over to the Coasties, who are huddled over the infrared cameras and radar. I study the images, trying to figure out if the eruption originates from a single spot or several places along the seabed.

Can we get any closer? I ask the man overseeing the radar.

Sure, we should be able to, he replies. There's a no-fly zone in effect for a ten-mile radius at twenty thousand feet, so we should have a few miles to work with. But it's up to him, he says, nodding in the direction of the cockpit. He might not dare go any closer with half the government on board.

The closer we get to the eruption, the more the plane shakes, I totter back to my seat and fasten my seat belt. I stare as though hypnotized by the gray plume curling out of the ocean against the blue sky, its billows steadily puffing and blooming like ghastly flowers, tumorous outgrowths of steam, gas, and tephra. It's as if the gates of hell have opened, as if evil is streaming into Eden unchecked, and I suddenly feel a primal, gut-level fear wash over me. It surprises me, I've got to get a hold of myself, remind myself that there's no such thing as creation or hell, that this eruption isn't evil, just a product of the earth, like me and everything else, no better or worse, it's simply adhering to the laws of nature, doing what it does. I don't understand this apprehension; there's only concentration on the faces of my fellow scientists. I bite my cheek and try to drive these illogical feelings from my mind. Glance to one side and see all the passengers gazing raptly at the eruption, or all but one. The photographer, Mister Tardy, has let his camera fall to his lap and is looking straight at me.

I inhale sharply and hurriedly look back out the window. He's seen how I feel, he's read me. His eyes aren't laughing now, rather, they're searching, thoughtful. I swear under my breath and stare into the plume, as though that seething cumulus could tell me something.

The plane turns around and flies back south of the plume, only lower and closer this time. The passengers shift uneasily, the ministers clearly think we've gotten close enough, but the ends justify the means: this way, we'll get usable pictures of the eruption. Turns out, it isn't as close to land as we thought.

By the time the plane lands, the plume has shifted and a black cloud envelops the capital. The ash falls like fat demonic snowflakes, everything's gone gray—the houses, the cars, the trees. I'm careful not to look at the photographer. We pull up collars and cloths to cover our faces before running into the hangar, the minister of foreign affairs' assistant holds up an umbrella to protect her fancy fur coat, and Halldóra and I exchange a grin.

Ófeigur is waiting for us with a subdued expression on his face, distributes face masks, and tells us to be careful out there. The public has been told to stay indoors and keep children at home, but there are always people who miss such advisories or just disregard them, insist on running some vital errand that can't wait. Cars inch along the shrouded streets, streetlights punching dimly through the smoky darkness.

The kids. Where are they? Where's my husband? In all the commotion, I haven't thought about them, haven't called. I fish my phone out of my pocket, the networks are under a lot of stress; I don't get through until the third try.

Nice to hear your voice, says Kristinn. Everything's fine. Salka is watching a movie, and Öddi's asleep. They asked him to come in at noon to help keep the smelter running. I'll work from home today, look after hearth and home. You're being careful, right?

Yes, of course, I say. This is the job, we know how to take care of ourselves. Have you sealed the windows?

He has—with tape, even, no particles will get in. I talk to Salka next, tell her there's no danger but that she has to stay indoors while the ash is falling.

It's really creepy, she says. Like that TV show, *Stranger Things*.

Ash is basically like sand, I tell her. Brand-new and powdery and freshly baked in the earth. It'll be over before we know it.

Her voice starts to wobble.

When are you coming home, Mommy? What are you doing?

We have to research this eruption. So that we'll know more about our earth and also so the police and ICE-SAR will know what they need to do.

I'm scared for you.

Don't be silly, Stubby. There's no reason to be scared, I say, trying to brush away my guilt, remembering how scared I used to be for Dad.

I'll be careful. Can you keep an eye on everything at home? Look after Öddi and Daddy and your rats?

They aren't rats, Mommy. They're degus.

But you're going to take good care of them, right?

Yes. I love you, Mommy.

I love you, too, my big girl. Be brave and use your sense. There's nothing to be afraid of.

There's nothing to be afraid of, back at the coordination center things are moving along at a rapid but orderly clip; in the face of chaos, stability rules the day. Milan sits at the end of the conference table in a worn office chair, sipping coffee from a paper cup and issuing instructions to the police and ICE-SAR with steady focus. His superior, the commissioner, seems to have regained his footing, comes in wearing a jacket with brass buttons, weaves between the desks asking how things are going, tries to encourage people and give the impression that he serves some purpose here. He lights up when he sees Halldóra, Eiríkur, and me: You're finally back! We need to talk.

We close ourselves in the conference room to review the images and the situation. Ash is accumulating on Reykjanes, ICE-SAR members from all over the southwest have been called in to dig out roofs and important buildings, but they don't think there's any reason to evacuate more residences. People from Grindavík are upset they had to leave; with the current wind conditions, the town has gotten far less ashfall than those on the northern end of the peninsula.

The good news is that no gas pollution has been detected, says Milan. People have been told to stay inside and seal their doors and windows while we're waiting for the full assessment. But we need to evacuate the Keflavík airport this afternoon, transport tourists to the city, and find them lodgings. People are frightened and hungry, a lot of them don't speak much English, and Isavia is only now getting information translated into other languages.

The other thing we should mention is that the minister of justice has made some small changes to Civil Protection's reporting structure, says the commissioner. It's for the best, just making the channels of communication more efficient.

What changes? I ask suspiciously.

The Scientific Council has been given a new name, he says. From now on, it will be known as the Natural Disasters Advisory Board.

For what possible reason? The Scientific Council is a perfectly good name.

The Scientific Council will be the name of Civil Protection's new administrative authority, he continues. During disasters like this, it will assess conditions in light of current scientific knowledge and public safety concerns and make decisions about what measures should be taken.

But that's Milan's job, in collaboration with us, the Scientific Council.

The old Scientific Council—now the Advisory Board—is remarkable, the commissioner continues. Truly. It comprises the most brilliant scientific minds in the nation. But it's too large and disorganized, people ramble, argue amongst themselves, it takes forever to reach any conclusions. No one agrees on anything. We need an intermediate point of contact between the scientists and Civil Protection. People who can think fast and make decisions on their feet.

The Scientific Council has always been an informal, academic forum where the Society of Icelandic Scientists and the heads of Civil Protection can come together, I say. We get the best and most accurate advice when specialists approach the same problem from different angles, when they have the freedom to talk things over, put forth theories, and reach a mutual conclusion. That's the scientific method.

We don't always have time for the scientific method, he says. Like this morning—why should we waste time talking about isotopes when we should be evacuating Grindavík?

It can have an impact, offers Eiríkur timidly. And it's not a good idea to alienate the petrologists. You don't want to get on their bad side.

The commissioner shakes his head: We need something more direct. Anna, you've been designated the university's representative on the new Scientific Council, along with Júlíus from the Met Office, Milan, and myself. We'll start there.

What you're actually doing is disbanding the Scientific Council, says Halldóra. It won't have any power.

The Advisory Board will advise the new Scientific Council, says the commissioner.

Milan, what do you think about all this? I ask.

He shrugs. I follow orders. Do what I'm asked and try to be of some use. And we don't really have time to debate this right now.

He's right, of course. So I report on the images that were taken during the observation flight, and Halldóra goes over the measurements we've gotten from the meteorological radar at the airport. We take a stab at calculating how much volcanic debris there will be, try to estimate how powerful the eruption is, its depth and whether it's originating in one spot or several. Our best guess is that the eruption began in a fissure on the bottom of the ocean about a mile and a half off the coast of Kerlingarbás Cove and that it's bigger than we first thought. The Met is sending data about the ash to the Volcanic Ash Advisory Center in London, and for now, the plume has only impacted the airports in Keflavík and Reykjavík, but airlines and aviation authorities on both sides of the Atlantic have already started bickering about how safe it is to transport passengers under these conditions, weighing human safety against financial losses.

I try to pay attention to the discussion, but I feel my mind wandering, I think about my family at home under the darkened sky, and the bright, attentive eyes of the photographer, how he looked straight through me, saw my irrational fear. The thought of having shown him that side of myself makes me feel sick, like he's seen me naked.

BULGAKOV IN THE OVEN

Þú munt heyra þrumur og minnast mín
og hugsa: Hún þráði storma.
Brún himinsins harðnar og roðnar
og hjarta þitt brennur á ný.

Anna Akhmatova „Þú munt heyra þrumur"
Translated by Guðrún Olga Jafetsdóttir

You will hear thunder and remember me,
And think: she wanted storms. The rim
Of the sky will be the color of hard crimson,
And your heart, as it was then, will be on fire.

Anna Akhmatova, "You Will Hear Thunder"
Translated by D. M. Thomas

I make a snap decision to stop by her apartment on the way home
from the coordination center. I don't call ahead—she wouldn't answer
anyway. I doubt she's even noticed there's an eruption going on. It's far
too worldly and mundane to merit her attention.

The ashfall is letting up, and the wipers are turning the dust into a gray paste that scratches the windshield. I try not to think about the SUV's champagne paint job, my husband won't be happy, but it's not like it's my fault.

I park in front of the apartment building and take the stairs to the top floor, following the stench of smoke that gets stronger the closer I get. Her poor neighbors. I knock on the door—softly at first, then harder—before digging the key from my bag and opening it, sticking my head into the sweltering apartment.

Anyone home?

She's sitting in front of an ancient desktop computer in her cramped office and turns around when she hears my voice, narrows her eyes over the top of her glasses, seems surprised, and not entirely pleased, to see me.

Anna? What are you doing here? Shouldn't you be dealing with that eruption?

Yes, I've been at it since early this morning, just going home to have dinner and take a nap. I thought I'd check on you, see if you needed anything.

Me? No. What could I possibly need?

Food? Company? Something to read?

This last bit is an attempt at humor, her apartment is wall-to-wall bookshelves—there are books stacked on tables, on the piano, in the windows, and I suspect she keeps them in the oven too.

She doesn't crack a smile, just pats a book on top of a pile on her desk: Have no fear, I have my dear Akhmatova, and there's always plenty to work on. I have so much unfinished business, and my time's almost up, my days are numbered.

I hate hearing her talk about her imminent death, so I go into her tiny kitchen, open the empty refrigerator, sigh at the unwashed ashtrays and old sardine tins in the sink, the overflowing, foul-smelling trash.

You haven't sealed the windows, I gripe and go into the bathroom to fetch a few threadbare towels, wet them, and stuff them into the sills of her drafty windows. This, she finds funny.

You think that volcano is going to manage what old Winston couldn't in sixty years? Snuff me out? she asks. Her laughter becomes a racking cough, a rattle deep within her chest, she fumbles for a pack of cigarettes, lights one, inhales greedily, and I look away. She's gotten so gaunt and unkempt that I find it hard to look at her, curled like a shrimp after a lifetime spent smoking and stooped over a keyboard. When I was a child, I thought she was so beautiful; now she's just a specter, a gray ghost.

You want to come have dinner at ours? I ask, even though I already know the answer. I could drive you home on my way back to work tonight.

She doesn't dignify this with an answer, sitting there in a chair that looks like it may well have once belonged to Trotsky, just turns to the gramophone on the bookshelf next to her desk and sets the needle on the record, Shostakovich, before turning back to her computer, squinting over the top of her glasses, and making a show of thumbing through a book to indicate that my presence is no longer desired.

I sigh and turn to leave.

Call if you need anything.

No answer.

I'll tell Kristinn and the kids you said hi.

Hi! she shouts, her voice cross and raspy.

I close the door behind me and walk down the stairs with a catch in my throat. It was a bad idea to come here, exhausted after a long day. Childish to think that she might show any interest in me, praise me for the interview today, tell me she sees how hard I work, how smart I am. The only thing ever awaiting me at my mother's house is disappointment.

WHO NEEDS AN INTERIOR DESIGNER IN THE MIDDLE OF AN ERUPTION?

Salka comes running when I open the front door, throws her arms around my neck like she's just wrested me from the jaws of hell—or maybe she's just happy for the diversion after having been stuck inside all day.

Easy, Stubby, I give her a hug before extricating myself from her fierce embrace, wash my hands, and take a seat at the kitchen table. My husband has dinner waiting for me, a quiche and a salad, he's opened a bottle of white wine, but I wave off the glass he offers me—I have to be back at work at midnight. He's happy to see me, eager for my company after a long day, but I'm really too tired to talk. I tell him about the flight with the government ministers and the confounding decision to sideline the Scientific Council in favor of a new one with a more rapid response to disasters.

And before we know it, the new council will be crowded with dusty middle managers from the Energy Authority who're more interested in regulations than geoscience, I say. The whole thing's so poorly thought out. The ministers don't understand that the old Scientific Council has been our greatest strength—a free, open forum for debate between scientists and Civil Protection.

My husband shakes his head and cuts me a slice of quiche.

Politicians and scientists don't speak the same language, he says. Information is a weapon for politicians and officials, their power lies in valuable secrets. They're always trying to hold information close to the vest, to use it to their advantage. Meanwhile, you all live to synthesize knowledge and keep the public informed. You don't live on the same planet.

I'm not sure I want to be party to this. What I really want is to resign from the council.

You can't do that, and you know it, he says. You're the best there is at this, the quickest thinker, the most rational. No one can do this as well as you.

I smile at him. He's so good to me. Then I smother a yawn—I've no appetite at all, I'm overcome with exhaustion. He understands, takes up the conversation, tells me what he worked on today, launches into an intense discussion of specific points of law, initial capital investments and bank rates, sips his white wine and chews with relish. I poke at my food with my fork and pretend I'm listening, think about the incident with the photographer on the plane, think about my mother. I miss my dad with a sudden fierceness, wish with all my heart that he was lying on the sofa with a thick book atop his big belly, talking about geophysics, that his quiet, warm voice was echoing around the living room.

Could you check?

Huh? I mumble, distractedly. Sorry, I zoned out.

Could you check your calendar and find a time for the interior designer to come? Her earliest available appointment is three weeks from now.

Interior designer? I look at him blankly.

Yes, remember? Ástríður Lind—we were going to have her take a look at the living room with you. The curtains and sofa and all that.

Oh, right—sure, I'll check when things slow down a little. I've no idea what the situation is going to be in three weeks.

I stand up, and fatigue washes over me.

Thanks for dinner, I say. I'm going to lie down for a bit. When is Örn supposed to come home?

He was supposed to be home by eight but decided to work over-time—they get crisis pay if they stay and shovel the roof of the smelter. Quite an adventure our man's having.

He's got to be careful. I hope they're wearing masks.

He's a big boy, he can look after himself.

I take a shower, swallow an aspirin, and get into bed. I don't fall asleep right away—Salka is practicing the piano, and her dad is washing up in the kitchen, clanging pots and pans, the TV is murmuring in the living room. All sound carries in this big, beautiful house, maybe that's something I can discuss with Ástríður Whatsherface.

Still, I think, just before I manage to settle into a jittery, restless sleep: an interior designer at a time like this, in the middle of a volcanic eruption?

EXPLANATORY NOTE II

THE CORONA OF THE SUN

In the firmament are black holes
where time vanishes in impressionless deep
taking all its happenings and souls
in a frenzy as it fades from the earth.
And on the thicketed mountains are deep ravines
where the gateway to hell can be found. Verðandi, norn
of fate,
forges there her manifold shafts of fire—and hurls these,
her flaming signals, to the heavens!
Our history is written in cinders . . .

"Fire Signals," Hannes Sigfússon

My father wasn't a geoscientist by training, not originally. First, he went
to university in Göttingen, Germany, where he studied astronomy, this
was right after the big astrophysics institute was rebuilt, following the
Second World War. He was entranced by the sun—blinded, you might
say—and wrote his thesis about the solar corona, the outermost layer of
the sun's atmosphere, which extends five million miles out into space,

the white light that streams from its photosphere, hotter than the sun itself.

It was only after Dad graduated that he realized he had no employment prospects, there was no demand for young Icelandic astronomers who specialized in the corona of the sun. He sought the advice of a benevolent professor at his alma mater, who told him he was wasting his energy. Anyone, anywhere on the globe, could pursue solar science, except perhaps a young man in Iceland, where the sun is a seldom-seen wonder. My father was, on the other hand, in a unique position to focus his attentions lower, to redirect his academic interest away from the sun in all her glory to the mysterious forces stirring below the earth's crust.

Hekla erwartet Sie, said the professor, his eyes sparkling. Hekla awaits you. My father was young and optimistic, but more than anything else he was a rational man; he swallowed his disappointment, sailed home on the MV Gullfoss, and turned his talents to the inner workings of the earth, dull echoes of the sun's might. He started by researching atmospheric refractions, then got interested in magnetic measurements, and he was the first to map the gravity field of Iceland. The volcanoes came later, his deep understanding of physics and mechanics made it possible for him to posit theories about how the acidity and viscosity of lava affect its flow—ideas that marked a real turning point in the history of geological research in Iceland.

He wasn't perfect, my dad, not by any means. I've no intention of making any such claim. He was, for instance, never fond of maps and diagrams. Presented most of his theories alongside cryptic physics equations that were difficult for the layman to understand, distrusted stratigraphic work and other geological research methods, and never stopped loving the sun. Sat in it at every opportunity—hatless, with his pipe and coffee in a chipped mug, eyes closed or reading. He always got a sunburn on the top of his head in the summer, no matter how much I nagged him or how many layers of sunscreen I slathered on his pate.

But Dad was a storyteller, like all good geoscientists. Long-cooled volcanic eruptions gushed into our living room, flowed over the dinner table, the foot of my bed. Askja, Surtsey, Hekla, and Krafla—he'd faced them all and spoke of them with respect and affection, like old flames.

The greatest story of them all, however, was the one about the eruption on Heimaey, the largest and only inhabited isle in the Westman Island archipelago, just off the south coast of Iceland. I'd whine and beg, and he'd sigh: You just heard that one! But then he'd settle at the foot of my bed with a smile, furrow his brow, and begin the story, always the same, like all good fairy tales:

No one suspected a thing. No one knew that Heimaey, Home Island, was actually an active volcano rising from the sea, and when, on January 21, 1973, the first earthquakes were detected from the mainland, most people thought it was Hekla that was preparing to erupt. The quakes were happening so deep in the ocean under Heimaey that the people who lived there didn't even feel them.

His voice was deep and resonant, and he took long pauses, always in the same places: when the earth ripped open and an unbroken wall of fire formed along the full length of the fissure; when the people were shaken from their sleep and had to flee by boat in their pajamas; when the houses in town collapsed under the weight of the ash, scorched by incandescent tephra. Bright-eyed university students flocked to the island to shovel ash from rooftops but forgot their shovels on the mainland; a daring expedition rescued all the cows at Kirkjubær Farm before the lava engulfed it, only for the cows to be taken to slaughter at the local fish factory. But all the fish at the local aquarium were saved, he added, which was a great consolation to me.

My favorite part, of course, was the part where Dad entered the story, like a superhero. He and a dashing group of geoscientists arrived together with one crazy idea: they wanted to try and slow the lava's progress by spraying it down with ice-cold seawater.

It was Þorbjörn Sigurgeirsson, my father's friend and mentor, who first had the idea, he'd experimented with it on Surtsey, another isle in the Westman archipelago that had formed in its own submarine volcanic eruption just a few years before. Dad helped him carry out his plan but quickly saw from his calculations that fire hoses would be of little use, they'd need pumps at least ten times as powerful if they were going to save Heimaey Harbor and what remained of the town. First, they called for a dredger ship, and then the US Air Force, which was still stationed at the base in Keflavík at the time, sent cargo planes loaded with enormous pumps that were used for transporting oil from battleships to land. They pumped 265 gallons of seawater a second onto the lava flow, which was threatening to block the harbor, the lifeblood of the island; the scheme worked, and the harbor was saved—as was civilization as the islanders knew it.

If a "civilization" you can call it, Dad smirked good-naturedly, he was a leftie and held a deep-seated, politically motivated antipathy toward the more conservative islanders, though not so deep that he'd allow the eruption to strip them of their harbor.

And there I'd lie, snuggled in bed with my blanket pulled up to my chin, eyes closed as I pictured him on the pier in Heimaey, his big glasses on and his pipe in his mouth, hunched over his notes, doing his equations in black pencil—viscosity, heat, and acceleration—his thoughts stream from his mind and through his pencil onto the crumpled, wet page. Ash falls all around him, houses turn to soft black masses with only the white-painted eaves and electric poles protruding from the darkness to remind you that here, a home once stood, here, people once lived; the volcano roars and spews fire and embers, but my father stands his ground. He carries on with his calculations undaunted, calculates how to save the world, *Homo sapiens*, wise man, armed with rationality and the scientific method, challenging a volcano to a duel and emerging victorious with the laws of physics.

HEMINGWAY IN THE LIGHTHOUSE

Everyone is relieved when the sun finally reemerges. The wind has changed direction and is carrying most of the ashfall southward; people in the southwest can finally see the sun again. They revel in the light, go out with ladders and shovels to dig out their roofs in the pale sunshine. Everything is possible now that the eruption has lifted its black paw from the city and the sooty murk has dissipated—what do we care if ash is falling in the Faroe Islands, in Scotland and Ireland, if it's been carried all the way to Siberia, creating innumerable flight delays?

I yawn in the back of an orange ICE-SAR jeep. The night shift was uneventful. The volcano is maintaining a low boil out at sea, but the situation appears to have stabilized—no casualties, no major accidents, our country has put us to the test, and we've passed, yet again. I want to go out to the eruption site. My rationale for doing so is logistical, we need to sync up our measurements and ascertain that the instruments are all where they should be, although, of course, other people are responsible for that. It's more that I've simply got to see this phenomenon with my own eyes.

The farther west we go, the thicker the ash in the air becomes. It sprays out from under the tires, shrouds the landscape like heavy, dark snow. Everything looks dead and gray, there's no sign of life except for the steady stream of traffic in both directions: Reykjavíkers headed south to the edge of the restricted area to watch the eruption; evacuees from the south headed toward the city to shelter with family and friends, their cars packed to the gills with children, pets, and luggage. All of the nation's conflicting feelings toward the volcano colliding right there on Rte. 41: angst, anxiety, gleeful anticipation.

The restricted area is a twelve-mile radius around the volcano, but people hike nearby Mt. Þorbjörn or drive even closer to the lighthouses at Stafnes or Garðskagi to get a better view of it. Traffic crawls along, the Road Administration has brought out snowplows to clear ash from the roads. We drive with our flashers on, passing one car after another; one is decorated with white ribbons, and a bride sits in the passenger seat, clutching a glass of champagne and staring out the window wide-eyed, thrilled to be getting married in her white gown with the black plume of ash in the background—the pictures are going to be incredible.

This country is insane, I say to the ICE-SAR guy beside me. At least when it comes to volcanoes.

He takes a bite of his doughnut, shrugs. Course. It beats low-pressure systems. Nothing else ever happens here.

When we turn onto Rte. 45, toward the village of Hafnir, a police officer wearing a mask checks our badges and lets us through the barricade at the junction south of the airport. This was a desolate landscape before—now it looks like my childhood nightmares about the world after a nuclear war, nothing as far as the eye can see but a charred-black, washed-out wasteland and some faint tire tracks running along the coastline in the direction of the ash plume. We drive past a few houses, dark and downcast beneath their sagging roofs, and out in the distance I feel like I can just barely make out Hvalneskirkja, the lovely stone church where beloved poet Hallgrímur Pétursson, whose life would later be memorialized with a much grander cathedral in Reykjavík, was pastor. The little church tries to bear up, lifts its cross to the heavens, *Dauði, ég óttast eigi*, Death, I fear not your sting.

Everything is black and lifeless other than the flashes of lightning illuminating the cinder-gray southern skies, the only sounds emanating from the eruption are claps of thunder. We charge into the gloom and my hands go clammy, my apprehension returns, but I bat it away—what a bunch of emotional nonsense this is. I'm a scientist, damn it, and I've got the most exciting research subject of my career right here in front of me.

We pass through the steam from the geothermal plant, white plumes waving like banners against the black behind them, and just beyond the plant is Reykjanesviti, the lighthouse up on the hill, dauntless and bright, so small in the face of this goliath. It's weathered many storms, but nothing like this.

At the base of the hill, there's a two-story residence, once the home of the lighthouse keeper. Now it's crawling with scientists and media people and best recalls a jolly army barracks. No one's slept, everyone's overexcited and brimming with a mix of anxiety and expectation about the monster just a few miles away. The police haven't declared the area off-limits for no reason: this eruption's unpredictable—it could produce powerful explosions, could muscle its way onto land, new fissures could open up right under our feet. We're placing our trust in the seismographs and the watchful eyes of our guardians at the Met Office.

The Institute of Earth Sciences has set up its war room in what was once a parlor. Computers and seismographs buzz and whir, young Eiríkur is hunched over the microprobe, the table around him covered with carefully labeled sample boxes, ash, and lapilli. Lines and oscillations flicker on the screens, the spectral curves that usually gurgle blue and yellow are now screaming red and purple.

Well, well, well, if it isn't the Big Boss Lady, come to check on her underlings. To what do we owe this honor?

Jóhannes Rúriksson lumbers in, so covered in ash I can barely make out the white of his helmet or the orange of his reflective vest, but there's no doubt who he is—the outlaw gleam in his eyes behind the glass of his mask gives him away. All he needs is a gun holster and spurs.

Johnny Boy, awful to see you, I say. Couldn't you wipe your feet before coming in? And you can take your mask off in here, nothing to fear.

He laughs his deep laugh, yanks off his mask, rubs his gray beard and deeply lined face with the back of his hand.

Oh, Anna, dear. Who'd have thought we'd live to see this? Your dad should be here. I can just picture him out in the tephra rain. He wouldn't've been caught dead in this stupid mask, ha, he'd have just gone out with his pipe—that would've been enough for him.

I smile as kindly as I can. Jóhannes and all the other volcano cowboys hold my father's memory sacred, they practically worship him. To them, he was a gravelly, affable teacher, a legend in the field, fearless and creative. They gave me a framed photo of him a few years back when we held a small conference in honor of what would have been his ninetieth birthday. The photo shows him during the Askja eruption in 1961, about to measure the viscosity of the lava, holding a big poker that he was about to stick into an incandescent wall. He was brandishing a metal shield to fend off the heat and embers, his expression focused, and there was a cigarette dangling from his lips; the hood of his jacket was pulled down to the upper edge of his large-rimmed glasses, his only protection against the tephra that was raining down into the snow around him. The hand holding the poker was clad in a floral oven mitt.

Would you look at him? they gushed, radiating adoration. It's your father, come back to life!

I'm fond of these men and their respect for my father's memory, and I like the photo, but for me, it's not a picture of Dad. It's a picture of a knight charging a mighty dragon, ill prepared and absurdly optimistic in the face of such a superior foe—the person in the photo is not the sober-minded, rational man who raised me. And so I'm constantly forced to set myself in opposition to the cowboys, to make it clear to them that I'm more than the only daughter of their hero, the apple of my father's eye, conceived well past his prime. Not just daddy's little girl, but also their colleague—and boss.

It was a different time, I say to Jóhannes. We're better kitted out these days. And while my father isn't here to see this eruption, I am. So shall we get going?

Jóhannes nods, dunks a cookie into a cup of coffee, and stuffs the whole thing into his mouth in one bite, trudges out, leaving a heap of ash on the floor behind him. I grab a mask, helmet, and safety vest and follow him outside and up the old stairs, cobbled together from lopsided hunks of lava, that lead to the lighthouse. The earth trembles beneath our feet, and dark ash snows down upon us. Jóhannes gives a chivalrous sweep of the hand, gesturing for me to enter the lighthouse first. I narrow my eyes at him and run up the spiral staircase as fast as I can, taking the stairs two at a time. The hatch into the lantern room stands open, and I can finally see it: the submarine eruption just off the coast of Reykjanes.

All the shattered panes have been cleared from the lighthouse windows, and I feel like a strong gust could sweep me over the ledge, but that's just in my head. In spite of the dark cumulus clouds and lightning, the air is still, and there's a mysterious silence suspended over the land; the plume's being swept away from us, south-southwest, it won't do any harm to anyone who isn't traveling by air. The ash continues to fall over the scorched, jagged landscape, waves pummel the shore, the surf crashes, but the fire thrusting itself toward the surface seems to have bested the sea. It boils and bubbles as the tide drags back, gray becomes black becomes white when the water touches the lava and sprays it upward, the lightning bolts dance, and the clouds tumble past, puff up, and collapse into one another in an endless scroll.

I stand there, staring at the leaden pillar. The eruption itself is hidden by the waves, dozens of yards underwater. We need to get close to it, get pictures. I'm struck by an idea: I need a submarine. Last I heard, the Marine and Freshwater Institute has an AUV with a serviceable camera.

The burning heart of Iceland is certainly living up to its name, says a voice beside me. I jump, hadn't noticed the man up here. He's wearing a simple dust mask that covers his nose and mouth, and he's peering at the column of smoke rising from the sea, ash has settled on his eyebrows and the shocks of hair sticking out from under his helmet. He's wrapped his camera in a plastic bag with nothing but the lens sticking out. I stare at him, and he gazes back at me, his eyes glowing green, bright as a cat's.

It's unreal, he says. Here's this full-blown volcanic eruption, and it doesn't make a sound. Like watching a silent movie.

Oh, but it does make sounds, I say. We use special microphones to pick them up underwater. Most of them are at such low frequencies that we don't hear them.

The volcano sings in the deep, he says. That's a lovely thought.

I gape at him, bewildered, and he hesitates and smiles, clears his throat.

Tómas, he says, extending a hand. Tómas Adler. I was in the helicopter with you the other day. When you were talking about Iceland sitting on top of a melt zone. And I was on the observation flight, too, he adds.

You're the guy who almost missed the flight, I say, taking his hand. I'm Anna Arnardóttir.

I know, he replies, eyes laughing above his mask, black streaks of ash around them. You're the woman everyone's afraid of.

What a thing to say, I think, and particularly inappropriate given the circumstances, but it's hard to convey disapproval with a mask on. I turn away and am about to head back down when he stops me.

I'm sorry—I didn't mean to offend you.

Don't worry about it, I'm not offended. I just need to get back to work.

I've been photographing the smoke plume, he says. From here and down there, from the cliffs along the shore. You're welcome to see the pictures if you think you can use them.

Yeah, sure, thanks. Just email me, I say as Jóhannes comes up, puffing like a whale. He leans on the lantern in the middle of the room to catch his breath.

Goddamn stairs, he gasps through his mask. Off so soon?

Yeah, I've got to borrow a submarine.

He looks out toward the plume and furrows his brow.

Looks powerful to me. Could be a three, maybe a four.

I nod. At least a four. With a plume that dark and almost seven miles tall—it's got to be at least three or four hundred million cubic yards. We'll have to wait and see if it makes it onto land, which way the wind blows, how lucky we get.

Tómas Adler points his camera at us, takes a few pictures. Jóhannes snaps to attention, leans back, pulls off his mask, gets a cigarette from his jacket pocket, lights it, and narrows his eyes at the ash cloud. Legs wide apart, hands on hips, he intones out into the blackness:

> Where do you bow your head beneath the suns of
> wisdom gone cold,
> and do you no longer know where mine might
> be found?
>
> Behold, I am the lighthouse, where the wilds
> summon death.

I shake my head and step through the hatch. Only Jóhannes would recite obscure Icelandic poetry at a time like this.

Wait, says Tómas. Let me take a picture of you.

No, I don't want to steal the spotlight from *Herra* Hemingway over there.

Don't you worry, Jóhannes shouts behind me, his deep laughter following me down the steps. I can't be overshadowed, you hear that? Not even by you, Little Anna!

Far be it from me to even try, Johnny Boy.

MT. FAGRADALSFJALL

N 63°53'36" W 22°16'10"

The Fagradalsfjall volcanic system differs in most respects from other volcanic systems on the Reykjanes Peninsula. It is unique in the fact that it is not connected to an actual fissure swarm.

In addition to lava shields, there are 30–40 cones within the Fagradalsfjall system. Six of them, Mt. Skála-Mælifell among them, have a reversed polarity to the surrounding range, and are composed of olivine-rich rock. Radiometric dating shows these mountains to be around 90,000 years old, dating back to the Skálamælifell excursion, a period of significant geomagnetic change which took its name from the mountain. Another notable eruption point in the system is Mt. Festarfjall. A natural dike called Festi is visible in the seaside cliffs at its base; this is the basalt column that birthed the mountain and from which it takes its name.

Kristján Sæmundsson and Magnús Á. Sigurgeirsson. 2013. "The Reykjanes Peninsula." In *Natural Hazards in Iceland: Volcanoes and Earthquakes*, ed. Júlíus Sólnes. Reykjavík: University of Iceland Press.

VOLCANOES ARE BORING

Named after nearby Kerlingarbás Cove on the Reykjanes Peninsula, the Kerling eruption, or Kerlingargosið, was a moderate submarine eruption on the Reykjanes Ridge that began in the early hours of March 7 and continued for six days. Photos taken by an Autonomous Underwater Vehicle (AUV) on the second day of the eruption showed a one-mile fissure stretching southwest, toward Eldey Island.

The eruption was just one and a half miles offshore and generated significant tephra fall and damage to both land and property on the western side of the Reykjanes Peninsula, especially in the municipality of Reykjanesbær, which includes the towns of Keflavík and Njarðvík, the village of Hafnir, and the Keflavík airport. Many structures sustained earthquake damage, and four homes in Hafnir were destroyed when their roofs collapsed under the weight of the accumulated ash. All salmon at the local aquaculture facility died, and Reykjanesvirkjun, the geothermal power station, was inoperable for a time due to damages sustained by its facilities and geothermal fluctuations in the area. Rte. 43 split apart not far from the Blue Lagoon, and the people of Reykjanesbær were without running water for three days.

The ash plume attained a height of seven miles on the first day. Volcanic ash was carried throughout Europe and created significant complications for flights, bringing air traffic to a complete standstill for several days in many countries. The ashfall at the southern tip of the Reykjanes Peninsula reached a thickness of one and a half feet, but averaged two inches around Reykjanesbær and at the Keflavík airport. Groundcover in the capital area was approximately one inch thick, though there was considerable air pollution from sandstorms and airborne particles for months after the Kerling eruption ended.

Anna Arnardóttir. "Kerlingargosið." Abstract, lecture at the spring conference of the Icelandic Geological Society.

The eruption ends as quickly as it began, subsides as though a tap has been turned off, the ash plume fades as it sinks, vanishing under the surface of the sea in a matter of mere hours. The ocean breathes gray for a couple of days, spitting lapilli and dead fish onto shore, but the worst is over. The murmurings of volcanic unrest on the screens at the Met Office wane, police remove barricades and reopen roadways. Reykjanes residents return to their homes throughout the peninsula, begin cleanup by shoveling the ash from their roofs, mucking out their gardens, cleaning lapilli from their drains, sighing over flaking paint and broken windows. Disasters become monotonous after a while—it doesn't take long to get used to the end of the world.

But the world remains gray: The city is gray, every plant is gray, every blade of withered grass is covered in ash. It clings to the streets, to houses and cars, no matter how many times they're sluiced, it wafts through the air, pulls a veil over the sun, settles in hair and on faces. We draw it into our lungs, wipe it from our eyes, swallow it with our dinners, absorb the grayness and try to endure it; we wait for the spring, for the winds that will blow the ash out to sea, the rains that will wash it into the soil, the fresh green grass that will sprout from it, for the world to become new and clean again.

Salka sits by the living room window, drawing in the grime on the windowsill with her finger. I sigh and get a rag to dust the room yet again.

I wanna go outside and play, she says. I bet Máni goed outside yesterday, and I bet he will today too.

I bet Máni *went* outside yesterday, I say. You know you can't do that right now. There's still a lot of pollution in the air, and it's bad for your asthma. Your lungs are sensitive.

She gives me a sulky look from under her dark bangs. Her lower lip has started to tremble ever so slightly.

My lungs are bored.

Do you want to invite someone over to play? Shall we call Máni? Or Hulda?

No. Volcanoes are boring. Eruptions are boring.

I recoil, it's like she's kicked me.

Sweetheart. Why would you say that?

They make everything black and ugly, she mumbles with a hangdog expression. You can't go outside to play or anything.

I sit on the floor beside her and stroke her hair.

You know, eruptions might be a little hard while they're happening, but without them, we wouldn't be here. Everything that is came into being in a volcanic eruption—everything on Earth. Volcanic eruptions created this island we live on a long, long time ago, and Iceland is still being created in eruptions today. They're the reason we're here, our houses and our streets, everything is made from the stuff that came out of those ancient eruptions. Even the atmosphere around the planet— and without that, there would be no life at all.

She traces her finger along the windowsill and then looks at the black smudge on her fingertip.

Mom, does this come from the volcano in the ocean?

Yes, that's the ash from Kerlingargosið.

So the eruption made it all the way here, to our house? Inside our living room?

Yes, you could say that.

But it's messing up everything!

Volcanoes mess up some things while they're erupting, but they also make new land, new ground. They both destroy things and create new ones. Which is why I find them so interesting.

Yeah, but you're a little weird, Mommy, she says, and we both start laughing. She sees an opening. But . . . can't I get a cat, Mom? Then I wouldn't be so bored.

C'mon now, sweetheart, I say, ruffling her hair. Not that again. You're allergic, remember? But how about we bake something?

She beams, and I feel a twinge of guilt over how I've neglected her since the eruption started. She gets to crack the eggs and weigh the sugar and butter; I melt the chocolate and oversee the mixer and the oven. We are entirely caught up in our baking until my husband comes in and hands me the phone.

It's Guðrún Olga. Your mother, he adds, as though I need the reminder.

I take the phone and walk out of the kitchen, I can hardly remember the last time she called me of her own accord, her gravelly voice sounds unfamiliar, low and hesitant, and I let her say her piece without interrupting.

How do you feel? I ask when she's finished, like an idiot. She snorts.

Do you want me to come over?

No, no, don't be like that. Nothing's going to happen until after the weekend. The doctor just called and told me yesterday. Getting hysterical won't help.

Okay then, well, you let me know if you need anything. I can be there in five.

I hang up and sit down on the nearest chair.

What's wrong? asks my husband.

She has cancer, I say. In her lungs. And all over, I guess. She says she doesn't have long.

Aren't you going to go over there?

No.

Anna, sweetheart. She's terminally ill, in shock. You should go.

She doesn't want me to.

I'll go with you.

I shake my head. Sit in silence, staring at the phone, at her name, Guðrún Olga, then put my hand over my eyes.

She doesn't want me, aren't you listening? Not even now, when she's dying. I burst into tears, racking sobs, I'm a fool. He kneels down and puts his arms around me.

Oh, honey, he whispers. Dear heart. I'm so sorry.

I let him hold me and cry on his shoulder. Not out of sadness or sympathy for Mom, but rather sheer self-pity. I cry for me, cry because my dad is dead, because I'm going to lose my mother now, too, without ever really having had her in the first place, without ever really having managed to make her love me. I cry for all of it while Salka's chocolate cookies burn in the oven.

EXPLANATORY NOTE III

YOU CRIED A LOT, AND I HELPED YOU PUKE

I met my husband a few weeks after Dad died suddenly in his sleep, while my grief was so raw and new that I was throwing up multiple times a day, from sheer anguish. It was like I forgot he was gone in between, but then every time I remembered, I'd gag, my stomach would flip and send back whatever was in it. Just coffee, mostly—I couldn't get anything else down.

I'd started attending lectures again at the university, but I hardly took any notice of anything, just stared blankly into space, waited for the next break so I could go out for another smoke, drink another cup of coffee, then go back home and wait for my sorrow to subside. That was the most rational course of action; I'd read up on grief like I would any other illness—I knew it was a project, a process that had to run its course. I tried to believe that with my whole heart and soul, but the sense of loss and loneliness overwhelmed all reason, I felt dizzy at the thought of my bereavement, was seasick with sorrow.

It was on everyone's lips, this grief, the entire department took part in it with me. My professors were Dad's old friends and colleagues who extended their stifled condolences in awkward mumbles, my classmates worried about me. One night, they dragged me to the bar in the basement of the university—I didn't have the energy to protest. Was in no condition to party, either, I blacked out after my second beer, woke up at home the next day with a pounding hangover, wearing a clean pair of Dad's pajamas; someone had put a trash can at the foot of the bed and a glass of water on the nightstand.

I fumbled for a pack of Lucky Strikes in the bedside table drawer and lit one, smoked my cigarette while propped up against my pillow in the darkness and tried to recall what had happened the night before and the face of the person I could hear clattering around in the kitchen, the person who seemed to have slept beside me. I'd retained a few fragments from the evening—a high forehead and serious eyes, a gray suit—I vaguely remembered clinging to him all the way home, trying to kiss him and bumping into his chin, he felt sturdy when he helped me to my feet, I remembered that.

The cigarette hissed when it landed in the water glass, I stumbled out of bed and the world wobbled, my mouth filled with a sour acidity, but I did it—I got up. Put a sweater on over the pajamas, looked in the mirror on the wardrobe door and was met by the sight of a pallid, gaunt wraith, rubbed the sticky black smudges under my eyes, ran my fingers through my hair. Then I opened the door and crept out as silently as I could.

He was facing the kitchen sink and washing up, it seemed like he'd been at it for a while because the three-week mountain of dirty dishes was almost gone, as if by some miracle. I observed the determined countenance of his back; he was wearing gray pants and a white shirt with the sleeves rolled up, his fine, blond hair like a halo where it caught the light from the kitchen window.

I held the doorframe for support with one hand, wrapped my sweater more tightly around me with the other, cleared my throat, making him jump and turn on his heel.

What the hell are you doing?

He smiled cautiously.

Good morning. I thought I should let you sleep. Decided to tidy up a little, didn't think there'd be any harm.

He dried his hands on Dad's apron, he was tall and thin, with a cleft chin and honest, frosty blue eyes. I was infuriated.

What's wrong with you? Is this a thing you do? Sleep with drunk girls and then play house the next day? Were you planning on cleaning the bathroom next? Is this something you get off on?

His smile vanished.

I'm sorry. I didn't mean to frighten you. And . . . nothing happened last night.

You expect me to believe that?

Believe what you want. You were drunk and ill, and, well . . . you cried a lot.

I cried?

Yeah. You'd had a few. I helped you puke, and then you started sobbing and talking about your dad. I just wanted to help.

Sure you did. Thanks for that. But I don't need any help.

So I see, he said with a smirk. Your apartment's a sty.

I looked around. Books, towels, and dirty clothes were strewn across the floor like carcasses, I'd carved out paths to the bed, the bathroom, the kitchen. The table and windowsills were bowing under the weight of withering bouquets from the funeral—roses hanging their brown heads, heaps of ashen lily petals all over the tabletop. The sadness was palpable, like a layer of ash had settled over the whole apartment.

I've had more important things to think about than cleaning. Didn't know where I should start. This is all Dad's stuff, actually—all these papers and books.

Yeah, well. Now we've started.

We?

I looked at him, this pale young man with this strange energy who'd intruded on me, who'd elbowed his way into my dismal, solitary existence and taken it in hand. It made me think of my mother, freezing cold and all alone in her garret, so I swallowed and tried to smile through my malodorous fug.

Want some coffee?

He became part of my life with surprising speed. I tried to maintain some distance at first, asked him to go home in the evening, avoided him at school, but he was determined and quietly dogged and forged ahead. He liked to drag me out for walks—we'd walk around town and try to get to know one another, we talked about our pasts, our parents and friends, about school and the future. I talked about the power of the earth, he talked about principles of the market economy, determined that he was going to be rich and have a beautiful, uncomplicated life.

Look, I'm not saying I'm going to be a millionaire, but I want to live a comfortable life, he said. It's something you learn to value when you've been raised by a single mother.

And he wanted to share this comfortable life with me.

Eventually, I even went to see Guðrún Olga and told her about him, sitting across from her in her little kitchen. She was in an unusually good mood, seemed almost glad to see me.

Well, wouldn't you know it! My girl's got a sweetheart. We should toast to that.

No, no. No toast necessary, I said.

Well, of course we will, she said, getting a bottle of cherry liqueur and pouring two cordial glasses to the brim, handing one to me and raising the other to the light.

Cheers to you and Kristján.

His name is Kristinn, not Kristján. Kristinn Fjalar Örvarsson, I said, pushing the glass away.

Are you in love?

Yes, he's a good man. I like the way I feel when I'm with him.

She laughed quietly and lit a cigarette.

You're not in love. You can't do it. You're like me.

She sat there, thin and dark-haired and aloof as an actor in a French movie, she'd just started to go gray, was pale from staying indoors and smoking too much, and acting like she knew me. She hadn't come to Dad's funeral, although she did come to my apartment the day after and try to console me, but her embrace was cold and stiff, as though she were the one who'd died.

I'm not like you, I told her. I love Kristinn. With all my heart.

She exhaled smoke and looked at me through the fog hanging over the table.

You are exactly like me: you're immune to love. It's okay—it means you have more energy for other things, for your work, this science stuff of yours. People who are immune to love have the chance to be something in life.

Like you? Excuse me? You, who've wasted your whole life alone in this rathole, writing and translating garbage that no one wants to read? God, you're broken. I am nothing like you, do you hear me?

I stared at her with tears in my eyes, vibrating with anger, she looked away and smiled that lopsided half smile of hers, almost apologetically.

I wish you had died instead of Dad.

The words hung in the silence between us, I hardly dared breathe as I waited for her to respond. She just looked down at the table. Then she reached over for my glass and emptied it as well.

Don't be ungrateful, she said quietly. I am your mother, in spite of everything. You should show me some respect.

I have nothing to thank you for except squeezing me out of you. I can't understand what Dad saw in you, how you could've ever been together.

People change, she murmured. We used to talk. About Dostoevsky and Tolstoy.

What? Dad read Dostoevsky?

People change, Guðrún Olga repeated, lighting another cigarette, closing her eyes as she inhaled.

Kristinn and I managed to go to the movies twice and out to eat once before life took the reins and boxed us in, made us an offer, said this is the deal: take it or leave it. I don't know what happened, whether I forgot to take the pill or threw it up, but it was really only as a formality that I told him I was having an abortion. We sat together in my living room—Dad's living room—beneath framed geological maps and yellowing landscape paintings; I talked and smoked, he ran his hands through his blond hair, wrinkled his brow, looked at me with those blue eyes, and I wondered yet again what it was that he actually wanted from me.

There's another possibility, he said. I don't want to pressure you—you're going to do what you want to do, of course, what you think is right. This is your decision. But you could have the baby. We could move in together. Give this a shot.

I looked at him, gaped at him, the idea hadn't even occurred to me. And yet, all of a sudden, I saw the future unspooling through my mind like film in an old projector: images of a beautiful home, a young couple with a child and a bright future, images of ill-timed and staid happiness, of a healthy, normal family.

Are you out of your mind? I stammered. You want to be a dad right now?

There are dumber things, if you think about it, he said. We're not kids anymore. You're turning twenty-one, me twenty-three. What's the worst that could happen? What do you have to lose?

He rose from his chair and sat beside me on the couch, put his arms around me.

I know you're confused, that you aren't sure about anything, he said. But I love you. I have loved you from the moment I first saw you. I want to live with you, take care of you. I want to have children with you. Will you at least give this a chance? Just think about it?

I looked into those honest blue eyes. He was sincere, he meant it. He loved me. What did I actually have to lose? I hesitated, then nodded: I'll think about it.

He kissed me, then took my cigarette, smiled, and put it out in the heaping lava ashtray on the table.

And you'll stop this nonsense. At least while you're making your decision.

He comforted me, you see. Turned on the lights, brought order to the chaos that was my life.

He tidied up.

MA CHE CAZZO STA SUCCEDENDO IN QUESTO PAESE?

We talk about volcanic unrest when we observe anomalous behavior, for instance, increased seismic activity. It's clear that an accurate interpretation of this unrest can make all the difference for situational assessment. What complicates matters for geoscientists attempting to warn of impending volcanic activity, however, is that chains of events that appear to predict eruptions often end without any.

Freysteinn Sigmundsson, Magnús Tumi Guðmundsson, and Sigurður Steinþórsson. 2013. "The Internal Structure of Volcanoes." In *Natural Hazards in Iceland: Volcanoes and Earthquakes*, ed. Júlíus Sólnes. Reykjavík: University of Iceland Press.

The earthquakes start up again in the spring, with no more fanfare than as if they were a common thaw, as if the land were simply shaking off the winter. The Reykjanes Ridge tosses and turns, gnashes its teeth and kicks at its namesake, asphalt cracks like old porcelain and the Bridge between Continents, the tourist site spanning the rift between the North American and Eurasian tectonic plates, collapses under a busload of travelers. They escape unharmed but run screaming onto solid ground, cellphones aloft: *Ma che cazzo sta succedendo in questo paese?* Videos of the calamity go viral, as if the tourism industry can afford that. Peninsula residents groan ruefully, clear their shelves, pack their good china into boxes, take down pictures and wall clocks and stick them in closets. You get used to perpetual shaking, don't even look up when the chandelier starts to jangle, when the cracks creep up the walls of the house.

By May, the source of the earthquakes has crawled up onto land, inched its way along the plate boundary that runs through Reykjanes, north of Grindavík, and set its course for the capital. The quakes stop before reaching the city, dance between the Krýsuvík geothermal area and the Bláfjöll Mountains. The city trembles, the whole of the south-west convulses and spasms.

What a headache, moans the national commissioner. The whole thing is just such an awful headache. You spend all this time preparing for real disasters, and when the day comes, what you really have to worry about is sewage pipes.

He seems downcast and sleep-deprived, has just come from a meeting with engineers from the Road Administration and a major utilities company in the capital, neither of which can muck out the fissures that are opening in the roadways or patch ruptured pipelines fast enough. Whose idea was it to settle on this godforsaken peninsula? he asks, directing the question at no one in particular. The newly appointed Scientific Council is trickling into the conference room—five people plus the commissioner, whom the minister of justice has unceremoniously appointed council chair, all in the name of shorter, more streamlined channels of communication.

Milan boots up his computer and turns on the projector, Júlíus from the Met is here, glowering and muttering into his beard about having better things to do than to sit through this sham of a meeting while the longest earthquake swarm in living memory is passing through the most densely populated part of the country. A slender woman around forty in a high-vis hiking jacket and a beefy young guy in an expensive suit are getting settled in their chairs, and the commissioner introduces them: Sigríður María Viðarsdóttir, executive director of SAF, the Icelandic Travel Industry Association, and Stefán Rúnar Jóhannsson, an administrator at the Ministry of Justice.

Very well, I say, crossing my arms. Before we begin, I want to express my serious misgivings that representatives from a special interest group and a government ministry should have seats on this council. It was originally intended to be an intermediary between the scientific community and Civil Protection authorities; now, the old Scientific Council has, for all intents and purposes, been sidelined, and instead, bureaucrats and lobbyists get to weigh in on the dangers posed by earthquakes and volcanic eruptions. It's a baffling and ill-conceived move.

Stefán Whatshisface clears his throat and affects a tolerant expression, his overpriced suit would be laughable in this makeshift coordination center of ours if he didn't wear it with such genuine self-confidence, like a cat wears its fur.

As far as the ministry is concerned, it's only natural that we should have a representative at a meeting where matters of wide-ranging public interest that fall within our purview will be discussed, he says. And the tourism industry needs to have a seat on the committee because of the high concentration of tourists in the region.

Tourism is still the nation's biggest economic industry, says Sigríður María, narrowing her eyes at me under plucked brows.

It would make more sense to have geothermal consultants from ÍSOR, representatives from the Environment Agency or from municipal Civil Protection committees in the region, I reply. We need to be making our recommendations based on scientific fact and public safety, not politics or the economic interests of one industry. This course of action flies in the face of the time-honored tradition of collaboration between scientists and Civil Protection. The old Scientific Council always got good results.

No one is forcing you to take part, says the commissioner curtly. You've been nominated by the university, but you are, of course, free to excuse yourself if it's beneath your dignity. And the same goes for you, he says, looking at Júlíus. We can always find someone else.

You can forget it, says Júlíus. If this cabal is going to have dominion over our responses to natural disasters, then it's just as well that Anna and I are part of it. He looks at me: Don't even think about it.

And I don't resign, of course. I do my duty, sit through the meeting of the new Scientific Council and then insist on summoning the scientists from the old one to yet more meetings to review the situation when what I should be doing is focusing on the research being done on the forces that appear to have awakened beneath Reykjanes. The meetings of the newly dubbed Natural Disasters Advisory Board are more sparsely attended each time, people think they're pointless. You're just going to take the information that suits you to the Scientific Council either way, says Jóhannes. Little Anna always knows best, isn't that right?

I can't sleep. Two nights in our beautiful summerhouse in Grímsnes should have left me well-rested and rejuvenated, but I didn't manage to sleep at all. Just lay there next to my husband with a restlessness seething inside me, listening for the phone, my fingers itching to take a look at the latest earthquake data that the Met had released. The thrushes don't help, screeching their love songs out into the bright May nights.

We should get a cat and put an end to that racket, I growl on Sunday morning, earning myself a celebratory whoop from Salka. Yay! We're getting a kitty!

You've got to try to relax, says my husband. You thrash around next to me all night, and every time I open my eyes, I see you staring out into the distance like you're waiting for something terrible to happen. Why don't you take a sleeping pill?

Because then I won't wake up if something does, I say, rinsing my coffee mug in the sink. It's no use, I'm going back to the city.

Salka will stay at the cottage with her father—she needs sunshine and fresh air after having been stuck inside this whole gray spring. They've got wifi and are stocked up on food and allergy meds; she won't have any issues with the birch pollen. And yet I have this hammering guilt, abandoning them like this. I hug her to me, kiss her cheek, and promise I'll be back to pick them up at the end of the week.

I drive straight home, sleepy and surly and entirely unprepared to open my front door and walk in on what looks to be the debris from a very successful party—tables strewn with cups, bottles, and beer cans, pizza boxes in the kitchen and potato chips on the floor, my son sleeping on the sofa with a young woman in his arms.

Örn Ögmundur Kristinsson, I say, and he rockets awake.

Mom—you're back already? I, uh, I thought you were going to be gone longer.

What the hell happened here? I ask, looking around.

I just had a few friends over . . . I was gonna have everything cleaned up by the time you got home. Mom, this is Líf, he says, fumbling for his boxers and gesturing in the direction of the girl who's confusedly gathering up her clothes, one item at a time.

Hey, she says, trying to smile, she's pretty, with short blonde hair and a ring in one nostril. And some conspicuous trinket in her belly button, I see, looking away.

What are you thinking? Can't we go out of town for a weekend without you destroying the house?

Mom, listen, just give me a sec and I'll take care of it.

You'd better, I hiss and storm downstairs. They were partying down here, too—someone has been lying on the handwoven blanket on the master bed and left a beer bottle on the night table. I make a quick inspection of the house, no one seems to have gone into my office, nothing's been broken or ruined, and yet, I still feel like everything is dirty, like our home has been tarnished, anger wells up inside me and I stomp back into the living room. The girl is on her way out to a taxi, and my son is turning in a slow circle, dazed and unkempt, like he has no idea where to start, but at least he's got clothes on now.

Where did you get the idea that you could throw a party without asking us? I shout at him. You're not sixteen anymore.

Hey, I'm sorry. It wasn't supposed to happen like this, he mumbles, brushing his dark hair from his forehead and looking at me with his puppy-brown eyes. There weren't that many of us—we were just going to get a pizza. And I was going to have everything cleaned up before you got back.

This isn't about cleaning up, this is about trust. This is our home, your little sister's home. This isn't the place for your drunken conquests.

It's not a "conquest," he says. Líf is my girlfriend. Or close enough, he says, looking somewhat doubtfully at the door she's shut behind her.

You're almost twenty-four, you live in your parents' house, and you act like a teenager. Totally irresponsible. You aren't in school, you don't think about the future. All you do is work some menial job so you can live like a rock star. You don't do anything around the house, do nothing but fool around.

I thought this was my home, too, he says. If I'm not welcome here, I'll leave. No problem.

Maybe you should. Fly the nest finally.

I regret the words as soon as they come out of my mouth, he jerks back, like I've hit him. This is going all wrong. I don't want him to leave—not like this.

Öddi, sweetheart, I say with a sigh. I didn't mean that. Of course you'll live here as long as you want. But maybe it's time for you to make some decisions about what comes next. Enroll at university in the fall.

I'm not going to university here, he says through clenched teeth. I'm going to Italy.

I stare at him. To Italy? Why?

He clears his throat and squares his shoulders.

I applied to school in Milan. I'm going to be a set designer.

A set designer? Are you serious?

He looks at me and nods. Dead serious.

Set design? And live on what exactly? I think you might still be drunk, kiddo.

I'm not a kid, Mom. And this is what I want to do.

This floors me.

Örn, honey. You're so smart. You could be a good student if you just gave yourself the time, applied yourself. You could be whatever you want. Don't throw that away, don't waste your time on nonsense.

You should hear yourself, Mom. I'm going to school, not running away with the circus.

I shake my head unhappily. This is such an irrational choice, sweetheart. You can't make a living like that. There's no security, no future. I thought that you were working at the smelter so you could save up for your education, get into a good school abroad—MIT or someplace like that. You said you were going to think about it, find yourself.

I did, Mom, and this was what I came up with. This is what I found.

Theater?

I shake my head sadly and start picking up cans and bottles. My son gives me a wounded look.

What's the matter with you, Mom? You're acting like I'm throwing my life away. I'm not. It is possible, you know, to live a different life than you and Dad. You don't have to, like, study law or geology or engineering and have a wife and kids and mortgage before thirty. There are other things in life. Things that matter too.

I pick the stub of a hand-rolled joint out of a saucer from my good china set and hold it up to the light. Like this? Is this what matters? Sailing from one party to another and smoking pot? Is this the life you want?

Don't be like that, Mom, he says, shaking his head. You're so judgmental. If someone isn't exactly like you, if they don't meet all the demands you put on yourself and everyone else, then they must be out of their mind. One huff away from an overdose or some bullshit. But it isn't like that, people live all kinds of lives, they thrive, they're happy even though being "rational" isn't their end-all, be-all. You have to give other people a chance, even if they're different than you. You have to show just the slightest bit of tolerance.

I hand him the trash bag. Here, I'll give you a chance, alright. Here's the chance to clean up all on your own. I've got to go try and be of some use. Monitor these earthquakes, work for this home that you're so unimpressed with. I want everything in order when I come back.

There are other things in life, he shouts after me as I close the door. The world is made of more than stones.

THE CREATION OF THE
WORLD—OR ITS DESTRUCTION

Tómas Adler holds an exhibition of his photographs at the end of May, about two months after the Kerling eruption ends. Spring has arrived in Reykjavík like a miracle, bright grass piercing through black ash; the golden plover, whose arrival harkens the end of winter, and the common snipe, its nickering cousin, trill amongst heaps of lapilli with cheeky optimism, but the slightest puff of air stirs up the ash again, suspends it across the sky, a dust cloud hanging over the city like sadness in an old house. No one wants to hear a word about the eruption, everyone is sick of gray grime on their walls, in their scalps, their nostrils. Pressure washers and vacation packages to Spain are sold out, and meanwhile, interest in this tedious eruption is at an all-time low.

So I go to the opening out of both professional interest and empathy—the Institute of Earth Sciences at the University of Iceland is also feeling the determined disinterest of the nation, our phones have long since stopped ringing. We've got plenty to keep us busy, charting and analyzing the tephra fall, measuring faults, and fine-tuning our earthquake data, but we're getting fewer and fewer inquiries from the public, the heroes have hung up their capes and are back to hunching over their computer screens, their halos given way to mundane bickering about graphs and particle size over cups of tepid coffee, academic scuffles in scuffed indoor slippers.

Tómas's photos are displayed on the walls of a downtown art space, its bright galleries reverberating with the guests' chitchat and clinking glasses. The prints are large and low res, entirely different from what I was expecting. They remind me of the first photos of the Surtsey eruption, taken by astonished fishermen in the 1970s. At first, I think they're black and white, but then I notice neon smudges on each image: red shovel handles, spruce twigs, flecks of blue sky. These are color photographs of a black and white world, coal-gray and white ash plumes, collapsed houses, tire tracks across a black landscape, a terrible evil welling up from the sea.

It's beautiful, don't you think? he asks, suddenly beside me, looking at a photo with his arms crossed. Everyone's so tired of this eruption because of the ash and the grime, but I wanted to celebrate its beauty, to show it in all its magnificence.

He shakes my hand, his grip is firm and warm. He's unshaven, with streaks of gray in his thick dark hair. His eyes are extraordinarily green, his expression open, his joy infectious.

Really precise and informative photos, I say and smile. They're good depictions of the eruption. Congratulations. And thanks for the invitation.

Precise and informative? You're funny, he says with a laugh, but it's a warm and earnest laugh, not derisive. I can't help but laugh with him.

Sorry, I'm a scientist—I get stuck there sometimes. I think they're really beautiful, although I don't know anything about that stuff. Beauty and artistic value and all that.

Much appreciated, and don't apologize for yourself. You're remarkable. I'm so glad you came, he says. Come, I need to show you something.

He leads me through the white expanse and into a side gallery, which is full of smaller photos. They're sharper than the images in the main space, and their subjects are very specific: a broom leaning against the wall of a house, ash-gray sheep being herded into a cart, a dead seagull, half-buried in the sand. And pictures of people: little kids in neon snowsuits playing in the middle of blackened desolation, a grim-faced woman carrying a suitcase out to a car, Jóhannes Rúriksson, eyes narrowed at the eruption and a cigarette between his lips, and then there's me. In three or four pictures: Drawing on a whiteboard in the coordination center, holding a palmful of lapilli by the Reykjanesviti lighthouse, ash in my eyebrows, my expression severe. Surrounded by my fellow scientists in all but one, which was taken aboard the Coast Guard's Bombardier. In that one, we're all facing the windows and look-ing out, a measured professionalism on everyone's face but my own. My expression describes wonder, fear, and profound rapture. My eyes are wide open, my left hand on my chest, fingers resting on my collarbone.

We consider the photo.

What do you think? he asks shyly.

I don't answer, I don't know how I feel. Offended, shocked, and—flattered? Could that be?

I nearly got in touch and asked your permission to show it, he says. But then I just didn't, was so afraid you'd say no. It's my favorite photo in the whole show.

Why?

Look, he says, extending his hand, touching the picture. Do you see how the light is coming through the window and illuminating your face? Like a holy icon, like you've had a revelation, witnessed the resur-rection, the creation of the world—or its destruction.

His fingers caress my cheek in the photo.

You're such a pro—certain and intelligent and dependable. But in that moment, I felt like I'd glimpsed behind all that, like I'd seen you as you are. How spellbound and vulnerable you are against those forces—just a human being in the face of nature. And you're so beautiful.

I give him a surprised look and he gazes back at me, sincere, the laughter gone from his eyes. One moment passes, then two, three, it seems like he's about to say something else, but then my husband wends his way into the gallery, catches sight of me, and walks over to us with a smile. He puts his arm around me and kisses my cheek, apologizes for being late, holds out his hand and congratulates Tómas before his eyes fall on the picture.

Hey, that's a great picture of you, he says. Fun to see you *in action.* What do you say we buy it? Is it for sale?

Yes, says Tómas. They all are.

Great, says Kristinn. Nice to support a starving artist too. How much is it?

I'm surprised at how embarrassed I am for him.

With one stipulation, I interrupt. If we buy it, I want to take it right now.

Tómas looks at me, his expression inscrutable. Then he crosses his arms.

Very well. But you aren't paying for it. I'm giving it to you.

Nonsense, says Kristinn. Of course we're buying it—we've got the money.

No, says Tómas. It's my gift. To Anna.

We stare at one another, not saying anything. My husband looks at both of us in turn, uncertain, then perks up.

Okay, then, we'll buy a different picture. One of those big ones out front. What do you say, Anna? How'd you like to have your eruption in the living room at home?

Tómas takes the photo from the wall and hands it to me.

With my compliments, he says. I hope I haven't upset you.

I shake my head, not saying anything, but take the picture. We go back into the main gallery and choose one of the large photographs, one where the gas thrust region of the eruption column is clearly visible and the white part of the umbrella region is well-delineated from the gray, just like you'd see in a textbook diagram.

My husband pulls out his credit card, and Tómas sticks a red dot on the wall over the title of the photo to show that it's been sold. But you can't have this one right away, he says, I have to keep something for the show.

Where shall we hang the picture of you? asks Kristinn when we get home. I shrug. Don't know. Maybe here in my office, or maybe I'll hang it up at work.

Then I take it downstairs to the laundry room and put it in the bottom of a drawer in the linen cabinet, hidden under a stack of tablecloths and napkins.

THIS MAGMA INTRUSION IS GOING TO HAVE A NEGATIVE MARKET IMPACT

This is a really unpleasant position to be in, repeats the commissioner, looking at Júlíus and me like we're responsible for the whole thing. There's really no way to say what will happen next?

We're sitting around an oval meeting table in the coordination center, people clutch their coffee mugs, and a plate of grayish pastries and wan doughnuts is arranged in the middle. The tension is palpable.

If I'm understanding you correctly, there's nothing to specifically indicate there will be another eruption, says Stefán, stroking his shiny tie. It's vital that we don't fuel unnecessary fears amongst the public.

I look at him—after our meeting in the spring, I felt like I got him. He's barely thirty, but his hair's already thinning, he's got his initials embroidered onto the cuffs of his custom-made shirt, he looks at this stint on the Scientific Council as his ticket to advancing through the ranks of officialdom. He's as methodical as Júlíus is temperamental, as starched as Júlíus is rumpled, and they seem to have a physical aversion to one another. The seismologist opens his mouth to answer the bureaucrat, but I send him a warning look and he thinks better of it, keeps his mouth shut.

Sorry, but it really is difficult to say what will happen next, I say, smiling my most courteous smile. The magma could make its way to the surface and erupt—probably in a mafic fissure eruption. But most likely by far is that this will be a magma intrusion, as we saw happen in Grindavík in 2020. That's what the crustal deformation and earthquakes indicate.

What's a magma intrusion? asks Sigríður María.

The term "magma intrusion," or "igneous intrusion," generally describes magma that's moving up toward the earth's crust; it's an eruption that doesn't breach the surface. Instead, the magma forces its way between the uppermost strata of the earth and forms a bubble on the surface. What we call "uplift."

Sigríður María shakes her short-clipped blonde head: This is all so complicated and jargony. I'd give anything for another eruption like Eyjafjallajökull. First the pandemic and then the Kerling eruption and now this. We can always market a photogenic volcanic eruption on land, but not this ashbomination out in the ocean. And the damn earthquakes scare the tourists away. This magma intrusion is going to have a negative market impact.

I'm sorry, what? I say. A negative market impact? What's wrong with you? The earth and its forces aren't some ad agency. You can't just order up a marketing campaign that suits the tourism industry. We have no control over this chain of events, the only thing we can control is our response to it. We can try to act rationally to ensure people's safety.

Milan looks at Júlíus. Speaking of people's safety: Where do things stand? What does the Met read from the seismic activity of the past few days?

Júlíus stands and takes position in front of the map on the wall, his brown argyle sweater straining across his stomach.

It's similar to what it's been over the previous weeks, the unrest is continuing here along the transtensional plate boundary that runs through the peninsula, he says and points. Over the last few days, there have been fewer earthquakes at Mt. Fagradalsfjall, but there have been more of them here, under the Trölladyngja volcano, and we've also seen uplift along the Krýsuvík volcanic system—but really, these are minor changes. The peninsula is always all aquiver, but the quakes rarely go over a three.

Stefán interrupts: That's good news, right? If the earthquakes aren't changing, there's not much danger of it erupting again.

Júlíus looks at him with undisguised contempt.

They aren't abating, either, he says. The land is rising and falling, and the recorded activity is moving in an easterly direction, toward the city. I don't know what good news you see in that. But there's nothing that specifically indicates that the magma will breach the surface, he says with a shrug. For now, at least.

Stefán grips the table and looks at him stiffly. If I'm understanding the two of you correctly, there's nothing that conclusively indicates that the earthquakes are increasing or that there's an eruption on the horizon. That means, in my mind, that there's no special reason—now, at this moment in time—to change the preparedness level.

I shake my head and turn back to the commissioner. I want to, yet again, register serious misgivings about representatives from the ministry and special interest groups being a part of Civil Protection's Scientific Council. The purpose of these meetings is to give a scientific assessment of the situation, not to spin a version of the truth that suits the government or the travel industry.

The commissioner lifts his hand.

We've been over this, he says. If the pandemic taught us anything, it was that we shouldn't make any decisions about the safety of the general public without also taking the economic impact of those decisions into account. The economy is part of public safety. Stefán is heading up the ministry's review of the Civil Protection system, and I have a clear mandate from the prime minister to be guided by both public administration and the nation's economic welfare.

Stefán gives a cheery smile and strokes his tie: All I'm doing is sharing the ministry's perspective. The government has serious concerns about where things stand at present. It's bad enough that you've declared an Uncertainty Phase because of all these earthquakes, although granted, you haven't put us back at Alert Phase and ruined everything all over again. The economy can't withstand any more blows.

We're not doing this for our amusement, I say. We have to ensure public safety. Most of the nation lives right here, in and around the capital, and it's also where the majority of the tourists are.

People's security also involves having work and being able to support themselves, says Sigríður. If we set limits on free enterprise and scare away the tourists, we'll lose all the jobs that have been created—all the work we did to resurrect the travel industry will've been for nothing. We were just getting back on our feet when you declared the Uncertainty Phase, and since then, tourist numbers have decreased by almost forty percent. The few travel companies that survived are dying like flies, and the city's full of empty hotels. If you lot continue to ratchet up the hysteria, we're going to have another crash—no question.

I can hardly believe my ears.

Hysteria? I don't know if you missed it, but for two months, we had an enormous phreatic eruption happening not twelve miles from our international airport. Do you think it's our fault that tourists are hesitant to come here? The responsible thing for us to do would be to close the borders instead of filling airplanes and the city with tourists. If we had to clear Reykjavík, we wouldn't even be able to evacuate all the residents.

Wouldn't be able to evacuate? Why?

I look wearily at Stefán, then Milan, who takes pity on me.

The escape routes out of the city are too narrow, he says. Almost two hundred and fifty thousand people live in the southwest region, and that's not counting tourists. If everyone tries to get out at the same time, the roads will be pandemonium. He shrugs. And where are all these people supposed to go? To Akureyri? To Selfoss? There isn't room for them. We can, at most, clear a few neighborhoods. Hopefully, that will suffice.

Hopefully?

Hopefully, say Júlíus and I in chorus.

This isn't a satisfying answer, says Sigríður. It's bizarre that Civil Protection's Scientific Council would declare an Alert Phase for the entire southwest of Iceland on the basis of nothing but speculation.

The national commissioner clears his throat. I agree with Stefán and Sigríður María. It doesn't sound like there's any reason to resort to such drastic measures. We can't forget that there are a lot of interests at stake—foreign exchange earnings, Iceland's reputation as a tourist destination, the GDP, people's standard of living.

Júlíus is still standing next to the map of Iceland, his face now beet red under his scruffy beard. Really—what is the *matter* with you people? he asks in a loud voice. Do you think this is just about putting the right spin on things? And foreign exchange earnings and GDP? What do you think is going to happen if there's a major earthquake or eruption and the public realizes that the nation's top officials and scientists said nothing about the possible danger?

He grabs a red marker and scrawls a big circle on the map.

Here! Lava flowed here eight hundred years ago. And here! And here, and here too! You've built whole communities on this lava! Schools, nursing homes, apartment buildings! Do you know how long eight hundred years is in geological time?

He snaps his fingers. That long! The blink of an eye. For the first time in history, we have a chance of measuring and understanding what's happening under our feet, to take rational measures and save what can be saved, but now these godforsaken politicians have to weigh in, feather their own nests. Stakeholders and special interests—everything's always about goddamn special interests.

He falls silent, breathing heavily, with a little spittle in his beard. The rest of us are staring at him, and he swears, throws the marker on the floor, shoves his computer and papers into his backpack, and storms out, slamming the door behind him.

Milan looks at me.

Jæja. Well, Anna, what's the verdict?

I swallow.

The geoscientists on the Scientific Council recommend that Civil Protection declare an Alert Phase due to the risk of a major earthquake or eruption in the southwest region.

Very well, says Milan, looking at his boss. The national commissioner presumably accedes to this verdict?

The national commissioner looks at me, Stefán, and Sigríður in turn, then clears his throat.

As the senior official in charge of Civil Protection, I don't see any reason to lift the preparedness level to Alert Phase or to change Civil Protection's contingency plan in the southwest for the time being. The Uncertainty Phase will stand, but we'll continue to closely monitor developments and be ready to change this assessment whenever necessary. It's important that everyone involved in the management of Civil Protection demonstrates responsibility and proactivity in equal measure, so as to avoid arousing fear and distrust amongst the general populace.

He gives me a hard look: I trust that everyone will abide by this decision and conduct themselves accordingly.

You're aware of our responsibility, I say. This decision will hinder all preparations for, and responses to, any disasters.

The national commissioner nods. We'll reassess and change our approach as needed.

He looks over the group. Any questions?

No one says anything. Stefán smiles like he's just won a hand at poker.

Meeting adjourned, says Milan, standing up.

EXPLANATORY NOTE IV

AN ADVENTURE BOLD

As far back as I can remember, there was always a mirror hanging on the wall over my mother's desk, the glass becoming spotted and brown from her cigarette smoke as she translated Tsvetaeva and Mayakovski. This strange old ornament is haunting me this spring, now that Mom is sick; I'm strangely aware that its fate depends on me. Should I give it away, throw it out, keep it? It's nothing to look at, worthless outside of being a nostalgic curio, a laughable example of Soviet decorative arts. The frame is made from a cheap tin alloy, an embossed relief shows laborers with sledgehammers and farm girls with lambs and bushels of corn, a tank, a satellite, a balalaika, and at the very top perches the star with its hammer and sickle, symbols of the workers' utopia.

I became obsessed with this mirror the first time I saw Mom after she moved back home to Iceland. I remember little of our reunion except having stared at this strange object, longing to touch the pictures, as if they would tell me what had filled her days over there, abroad. I remember nothing of Mom herself, whether she gave me anything or what she said to me, but I was also only five years old. All I remember is the blend of anxiety and excitement I had over getting to see her, the letdown, and this mirror.

Later, a very few times, she let me look at it and touch the pictures, when she was in a particularly good mood. My visits to her house were short and awful, I'd try desperately to please her, to get in her good books, but never with any success. I felt like an outlier, like I was bothering her. She wasn't mean to me, quite the contrary: she always asked how I was doing in school, and I gave her the longest answers I could, enumerating my classes and teachers, trying in vain to fill the miserable silences that would follow. We had nothing to talk about, she almost always forgot to buy anything for me to eat, and, after a few minutes of this oppressive disconnection, would get to her feet, put a record on the phonograph, and sit down in her office to work. Find something to amuse yourself, she'd say, and I was ten—albeit an unusually mature ten—before it occurred to me to ask not what was the matter with me, but really: what was the matter with Mom?

We were sitting at the kitchen table at home, Dad and I, under the window with its checked curtains, eating beef patties topped with fried eggs, one of his specialties. He was looking stubbornly down at his plate and collecting green beans on his fork, as if they were the answer to my question.

People are so different, he said after a pause. Your mother is an unconventional person.

I considered this for a moment.

Is that why she doesn't want to live with us?

Pfft, yes, perhaps, he said. That could be it. And we can't live with her. She needs to be alone.

I had photos of us together, me a newborn in her arms, the three of us together at my christening. Dad was starting to gray, and she looked for all the world to be his daughter, scrawny and wide-eyed as a kid taking her first communion under her long dark bangs. The picture had been taken in our living room, with the big bookcases in the background, I was staring out into the blue with a serene, sheepy expression, my christening gown almost reaching down to the floor.

She used to live here, right?

Yes, right after you were born. But it just didn't work. She got sick.

But if she were sick, shouldn't we have taken care of her? Couldn't she be cured?

It's not that kind of sickness, Stubby.

Dad sighed and set aside his fork and knife, clasped his hands under his chin, and looked past me and out the window. He had his orange apron on, and his sleeves were still rolled up after he'd finished cooking. I thought he seemed kind of tired.

She's always been locked in a battle with life, you see. Had unrealistic ideas about things, lived in something of a dream world. Poetry and novels—nothing else ever gets close. In the end, she stopped being able to tell the difference between imagination and reality. She—she got lost and never found her way back.

He took off his large glasses and polished them with the corner of his apron, peering myopically out the window.

She isn't a bad person, your mom, he said. She did what she could. But she couldn't cope with living with us. So it was best for you to stay here with me.

He took a big swig from his glass of milk and returned to his dinner, seemed to think the matter was closed, but I wasn't finished.

But if she isn't bad, then why is she the way she is?

What way is that?

Why doesn't she want to be my mom?

Anger subsiding, my voice wavered, and Dad looked up. Then he reached his big hand across the table and took mine.

Do you know, I think there's nothing she ever wanted as much as to be your mom. She tried the best she could, and she just couldn't manage it. It wasn't her fault. And you can't be mad at her. That would be irrational. We must be grateful to her.

Grateful? For what exactly?

For bringing you into this world—she gave me you.

He squeezed my hand and smiled warmly, then stuck his fork into a slice of beet.

There now, Stubby, finish your dinner.

We never talked about it again, but it was around that time I stopped calling her Mom. I'm not sure she ever noticed.

I went through a period where I tried to understand her, read books for people who had parents with mental illness, but they didn't answer my questions. Guðrún Olga hadn't been violent toward me, the worst she ever did was leave me in the care of a reserved scientist who loved me and worked hard to get me to adulthood in one piece. Other than more than my fair share of secondhand smoke, scientific articles, and processed meat, I had less than nothing to complain about in my upbringing.

I am with her when she dies, listening to her last, wheezing breaths. It's summer, and the sunlight pours through the window, even though it's close to midnight; she hasn't been conscious for days. Earthquakes continue to convulse the southwest, but they arouse little interest these days, least of all in the palliative care ward. Loved ones and nurses straighten pictures of angels on the walls and collect flower petals that are shaken from lilies in crystal vases before resuming their vigils at the ends of beds, just as I'm holding mine at the end of Guðrún Olga's. The morphine running through her veins is alleviating her suffering, but it's also relieved her of the last dregs of her waking life, the chance to open her eyes and see me, say goodbye to me. Ask me for forgiveness? Admit her love for me and repent, now in the final stretch, almost half a century later, for having rejected me? I should mourn this final chance to be her daughter, but I feel nothing but restlessness. There's so much work to be done, and yet here I sit. At the bedside of this woman who might as well be a total stranger to me.

She's settled all her affairs; she allowed Kristinn to draw up an affidavit after she was diagnosed and signed it in her delicate, unwavering hand: No cancer drugs—no chemotherapy or surgeries—just plenty of morphine.

And the old lady knows best. By the time she finally goes to the doctor, the cancer has spread from her lungs into her organs and pancreas. Three inoperable cancers in one crone, she says with a cough. Not too shabby.

I don't try to talk her into a course of treatment, it's her decision. But I make an effort to visit or talk to her every day, without exactly knowing why. As before, she shows me limited interest, she wants to finish her translation of "The Tsar Maiden" by Marina Tsvetaeva and revise her old translation of *Anna Karenina*—a whole cultural sphere rests on her stooped, gaunt shoulders, she works like a racehorse until the morphine slows her down, her handwriting becoming disjointed and the lines tilted, leaking off the pages like melted candle wax.

Why are you doing all this? asks my son. Why bother putting yourself out for a woman who never bothered herself about you?

Oh, Öddi, sweetheart. She's all alone, I'm her only family. I have to do my duty.

This is, perhaps, not an entirely honest answer, but it will have to do. My son's an adult now, I've grown accustomed to that idea, but I don't think he's matured to the point of understanding that this isn't exactly about her, but me. This is how I get even with her, by doing better by her than she's done by me. No one could say I haven't done my due diligence, that I haven't fulfilled my obligations.

And so I do. I'll be damned if I don't stand up on my hind legs, wet her dry lips, raise her headboard, read to her, and type up the final handwritten pages of her manuscript.

And then she draws her final breath, and I don't even notice, sitting there and absently watching the curtains flutter in the open window. Don't notice until the nurse comes in and takes her pulse, I just sit there, gaping and exhausted from having spent the last three months watching her die.

She's gone, whispers the nurse, and I see that she's right: the woman who could not be my mother has left the body in the bed. It reminds me of a withered leaf in autumn, the empty and uninteresting husk of an intelligent, eccentric person. I should probably cry, the circumstances call for that, but I can't. I feel like this small, dead body has nothing to do with me, it's unthinkable that it once enclosed me, protected and nourished me all those months before I was born.

Do you want close eyes? asks the nurse in somewhat stilted Icelandic, and I stare at her like an idiot, why on earth would I close my eyes?

Her eyes, she says with a warm smile. Not yours.

Oh, right, right, I stammer and paw clumsily at her face, my fingers stroking her forehead, across her fine brows and her eyelids, dry like butterfly wings, run them across her blank, dull eyes.

I stand over her and stroke her emaciated cheek, touch her face for the first and last time, and suddenly, my tears are falling on her breast. The tears take me completely by surprise, it's irrational, Guðrún Olga doesn't deserve my tears, nor my prayers. And yet, here I stand, crying at the foot of her bed, praying for her with every fiber of my being, praying to a god I've never believed in to look after her, forgive her, take her to a better place.

Poppycock.

We hold a small, sparsely attended funeral, I sit next to my husband in a little chapel beside the cemetery, Salka and Örn are at home. I didn't see any reason to make them take part in this lonely, depressing ceremony, no one should die like this, no one should live like this, alone and friendless. The only other mourners are a few colleagues from the university and the Russian Cultural Association; a brusque man around sixty gives my hand a limp shake and introduces himself as my mother's publisher. He gives his condolences and then asks when he can have the last pages of her translation—someone has to take over her life's work, pick up where she left off.

She chose the music herself: Waltz no. 2 by Shostakovich, a Russian folk song, a battle hymn played on a slightly off-key organ.

Together we murmur lines from a poem by Jóhannes úr Kötlum:

> As sun sets in ocean stream
> our hidden grief does us compel
> to hold their memories, death but a dream
> an adventure bold in which they dwell

and I start shaking. Kristinn puts his arms around me, holds me close, and I cry into his jacket, cry with great, heaving sobs, like a child.

She did her best, he says. She didn't have an easy life, but she's at peace now.

I know, I sniffle. I don't know why I'm so sad.

Because you cared about her, in spite of everything, he says. You did right by her. You've been a good daughter, so strong. I'm proud of you.

I squeeze his hand, so fortunate to have this good man of mine. To have a life partner, someone who walks through life at my side, stands by me in good times and bad.

Do I feel doubts creeping in? A worm wriggling into my heart?

No, I think not. I'm satisfied.

My mother is dead, and I am not her. I share a happy and secure life with my good husband and beautiful family.

My grief gives way to gratitude, happiness brings tears to my eyes.

The next day, I go to her apartment and look upon my inheritance. It could never be said that Guðrún Olga was a materialistic person. The Russian Cultural Association will take a few books, and others I'll foist off on the university, but the majority will end up in a dumpster. The few pieces of furniture will meet the same end, too worn and tobacco-smoked for anyone to be interested in them. I can't imagine keeping anything but a faded watercolor of Red Square in Moscow and the few pictures that show the both of us together, forced smiles and bell-bottom jeans.

And that ugly mirror. I mean to take it to the charity shop, but in the end, I keep it out of a sentimentality that I can't even explain to myself. I take it home, but it doesn't fit in anywhere on our pale-painted walls, amongst our tasteful contemporary possessions. I don't think it belongs in my home office, so it ends up on the wall in my office at the university, in amongst the bookshelves and maps. Hangs there, gathering dust, patient and silent. It reflected my mother's face for so long as she sat working at her desk that I almost feel like she's still lingering in it, I see her appear there sometimes, her mouth curling into a scornful sneer.

CRÊPE DE CHINE

Get yourself something nice, you deserve it.

My husband puts his arm around my shoulders and presses his nose into my hair. A dress or a jacket or a nice sweater—you need it.

He's in a good mood and happy to be with me, just the two of us, downtown, for the first time in months. We work too much, he says, we hardly see each other except in the dead of night. You have to cultivate a marriage, you can't let it get choked off by weeds, it's work, like running a business, and I feel like I hear an accusation in his voice even though he works almost as much as I do. He thinks I'm being distant, as I am sometimes, distracted, I don't hear what he says, I miss whole evenings sometimes, he rambles about this or that and I nod, agree with everything without hearing a word he's saying.

Where are you? he asks sometimes. Where'd you go? And then I snap out of it—oh, sorry, I'm just tired, I say—but he's right, I was worlds away, in my father's arms reading about the strata of the earth, up in the Bombardier watching the cumulus clouds break through the ash plume, in the bowels of the earth, down in the darkness, thinking about expansion and movement and pressure. I've always tended toward it, this distance, but after Guðrún Olga dies, it gets worse, like a dam collapsed and my attention poured out, my thoughts can no longer be accommodated in their old quarters.

But today, it's summer and the sun is shining, our little downtown is almost charming with all the flowers blooming and people out and about. And I am present, attentive, and amiable, we eat lunch and drink white wine at an outdoor café sheltered from the north wind, then wander up Bankastræti and Skólavörðustígur like we're twenty years younger and in love the way you only can be at that age, the alcohol simmering pleasantly in our blood. I don't want anything, don't need anything, but I give in and go into a shop, it's nice to let yourself be tempted every now and again, to try on something that's a little too expensive and daring, to look at yourself in the mirror and feel like you could be an entirely different woman, exotic and elegant, feel that rush of euphoria and dopamine when you hold out your credit card and pay.

And he's right, I've been too numb and distracted for personal upkeep. My hair has gone gray at the roots, my nails are bitten down to the quick, and my clothes are hanging off me, shabby and felted, a woman has to make an effort to look decent, it doesn't just happen of its own accord—not anymore.

I enjoy trying on clothes in the shop—dresses, skirts, and blouses, filmy organza, crinkly crêpe, silk, muslin, poplin, I'm mesmerized by the names of the fabrics, every material has its own texture, density, and characteristics, just like the rocks and stones I handle at work. The woman in the mirror turns around and gives me a contented smile, she's wearing a red summer dress that's a little too expensive, a little too risqué, but it goes well with her dark hair, falls prettily around her waist and stomach, doesn't make her breasts look too big. I glance around for my husband to see what he thinks, but I don't see him anywhere until finally, I catch sight of him through the window, he's standing on the sidewalk outside the shop and talking to a short woman in a gray jacket. I can only see her back, but she's holding his arm, speaking emphatically, and their heads are bent toward one another. He smiles in embarrassment, nods, and squeezes the woman's hand in parting.

Who was that? I ask when he comes back into the shop.

Just a work thing, he says, checking me out. Nice dress!

A client?

He looks away. Pfft, she really fought to get here, it's just her and her son, they needed a little help with their asylum application, nothing big. Are you going to get the dress? Or that one, that one's really lovely, he says, pointing to a prim, dove gray shirtdress hanging in the dressing room.

My dear husband. Kindheartedness is his Achilles' heel, it tangles him up wherever he goes. He tries to stick to tax law, guiding monied clients through our labyrinthine tax system, it isn't easy to be rich in Iceland, looks after companies' earnings and manages high-yield estates, but then a little guy crosses his path—grim fate, injustice, human rights violations—and he blindly flings himself down legal dead ends so he can extend a helping hand, right wrongs. Asylum seekers, down-and-outs, victims of sexual assault—casualties of the system—his secretary is in a constant struggle to ward off pro bono work that yields nothing but tearful clients in the waiting room, emergency calls in the middle of the night, but not a króna in the coffers, it's no way to run a profitable law practice, no way to secure a tranquil life.

I look at the dresses. You know, I think I'm going to pass on both. They're too expensive. And I don't need a dress.

One hardly ever *needs* anything. But we have the money to buy ourselves things we don't need.

I kiss him on the cheek, entwine my fingers behind his neck, and look into his eyes.

You're a good man, you know that?

He squirms and shakes his head, I go into the dressing room and put my old clothes back on, leave both dresses hanging there.

Come on, I say. Let's go get a coffee.

Two days later, I come home from work and find a shopping bag on the kitchen table, a paper bag with the label of the shop on

Skólavörðustígur. There's a dress in the bag, wrapped in crinkly tissue paper. *To Anna, from your admirer*, it says on the card, written in Kristinn's elegant, orderly handwriting. I pull apart the paper, expecting the red silk dress, but instead, I find the shirtdress, dove gray, prim.

I try it on, look at myself in the mirror, it fits me perfectly, is suitable for a woman of my age and position. I love it—really.

EXPLANATORY NOTE V

A GEOLOGICAL MISUNDERSTANDING

and heather and moss
burn
in mythological fire.

Matthías Johannessen, "Wrestling with the Mountain"

We live in enlightened times and as such, have the privilege of being able to use scientific techniques to make sense of phenomena that were once completely incomprehensible to us. Our forefathers had no choice but to resort to superstitions and lore to try and solve the riddles the world put before them: the progress of celestial bodies across the skies, the changing of the seasons, life and death.

The earth's forces were no exception; there are so many of them, and they've gone by so many names. Typhon was the monstrous father of storms who caused earthquakes by thrashing his hundred heads in the underworld; Vulcan stoked the fires under Mt. Etna and Vesuvius—the Romans cast live animals and even children into bonfires to keep him from roving around the world, laying waste to it. Plato wrote of the flaming river Pyriphlegethon, which ran through the bowels of the earth and would sometimes well up to the surface; the goddess Pele created the Hawaiian Islands and protected them from the encroachment of the ocean and the winds. As a rule, I don't go in for religion or any other superstitious nonsense, but I can't help but envy the Hawaiians their beautiful and powerful fire goddess, black ropes of lava draped over her shoulders like glowing braids and garlands of flame encircling her brow. They also understood the generative power of volcanic eruptions and their battle against erosion; Pele was forever fighting her sisters—the sea, the wind, and snow.

By comparison, the mythological explanations that came into being here along the plate boundary on the other side of the planet are not particularly convincing. The jötunn Surtur guarded the fires of Muspelheim with a burning sword—as if such a realm needed any further protection—and the earth shook when a venomous snake dripped its poison on Loki's face. Strange tales that originated in mainland Scandinavia, where earthquakes and volcanoes were seldom-seen wonders.

I think it's a point in our nation's favor that from the very beginning we never really embraced these mythologies but have approached volcanic eruptions with an ice-cold empiricism. They came and went—twenty, thirty times a century—spewed their black plumes of smoke, cast clouds of ash and glacial floods across the countryside, laid arable land to waste, amassed new mountains and islands, killed sheep and horses. And the nation would heave a sigh, shake the sand from its hair, and then carry on with its daily exertions: corralling sheep and catching fish, spinning yarn and weaving, composing the odd couplet, surviving. The eruptions rarely reached mythological proportions, most occurred far from human habitation, and the strongest were simply filed away with the many instruments that Almighty God used to chasten his sinful children, became interchangeable with other disasters—winters of starvation, plagues.

*Then a man came running up and said that there had been
a volcanic eruption at Ǫlfus and it was about to engulf the
homestead of Þórroddr goði. Then the heathens spoke up:*

It is no wonder that the gods are enraged by such talk.

*Then Snorri goði said: What were the gods enraged by when
the lava we are standing on here and now was burning?*

I'm put in mind of this scene from *Kristnisaga*, which tells the story of
Iceland's conversion to Christianity and is a narrative I've always found
surprisingly contemporary. I can picture the powerful chieftain, Snorri
goði, standing before me, wearing his parka and narrowing his eyes
behind his big glasses at the dolts around him, shaking his head and
knocking out his pipe: Poppycock. Snorri was standing on 8,000-year-
old lava when he pooh-poohed superstition; his forefathers had sailed
across the ocean 130 years before and washed ashore on this land, which
isn't really a land at all, but rather, a hunk of the ocean floor that protrudes from the sea, formed by a hot mantle plume on a plate boundary,
amassing century after century and eruption after eruption.

All of which is to say that Iceland is not really a land, as we tend to
conceive of these things, but a geological misunderstanding—it came
into being out of sheer chance and will continue to exist for as long as
the plume rises from the earth's mantle, like hot air rising from subway
tracks flipping up the skirt of a woman's summer dress as she walks over
a grate in a bustling foreign metropolis, just for that instant before she
gasps and pulls down her hem.

It's exactly like that, just a bit slower.

THERE'S NOTHING MORE BEAUTIFUL THAN A PRETTY WOMAN WHO KEEPS HER MOUTH SHUT

The magma begins to release water when the pressure drops. It increases significantly by volume and transforms into foam, like champagne fizz when the cork is popped (releasing carbon dioxide, CO_2, not water vapor).

Freysteinn Sigmundsson, Magnús Tumi Guðmundsson, and Sigurður Steinþórsson. 2013. "The Internal Structure of Volcanoes." In *Natural Hazards in Iceland: Volcanoes and Earthquakes,* ed. Júlíus Sólnes. Reykjavík: University of Iceland Press.

The summer is windy and chilly, dust sticks to cars and windowpanes, children sneeze soot when they come home in the evenings. Ash blows across lanes and lawns, drags a gray filter over the sun, the sky is dull and colorless. We all hope for rain, warm showers to rinse away the drab monotony, to summon back a world of color.

We need a pick-me-up, and at the end of June, Jóhannes Rúriksson, professor of volcanology, my colleague, competitor, and friend, celebrates his sixtieth birthday with pomp and circumstance—a band, an open bar, a two-hundred-person garden party in a tent.

We're running late, Kristinn is held up at work and I'm painting my nails coral pink and mixing myself a gin and tonic while I wait for him at home. There's a peculiar restlessness simmering inside me, I change out of my dove-gray shirtdress and into pants and a blazer, add a little eye shadow, put the dress back on, drum my fingers on the kitchen table and send him a message: You close?

On my way, he replies and then comes home half an hour later, sweaty and stressed. Sorry, love, the meeting ran late. Big client, really important for the firm.

He changes his shirt, puts on a blue suit, I watch him getting ready. Time has been kind to my husband: his hair is only starting to thin, and there's the odd gray hair in his well-manicured beard, but it suits him. He's tall-statured and broad-shouldered, sunburnt from his cycling and cross-country skiing, no beer belly or wine drinker's nose, his clothes and shoes bearing witness to taste that is both well-off and refined. He's tired from his day and sighs as he runs his fingers through his hair.

You don't have to go, I say. I can go alone, no problem, if you want to take it easy tonight.

I want to go, he says. I want to be with you. We've hardly seen each other for four months.

Are you going to want to leave before midnight, like last time?

No, of course not. Don't be like that.

He kisses me on the cheek, holds me at arm's length and meets my gaze.

You look lovely. Shall I call a cab?

I nod, smile in anticipation.

They're already into speeches by the time we get there, guests tipsy, peals of laughter drowning out the speakers, and the party planner suggests a short intermission. The evening air is calm and the rowans are in bloom, grass peeks from beneath the ash, and my heels sink into the soft soil. I curse under my breath for not having worn more sensible footwear, a woman of my age should know better than to wear dancing shoes to a garden party in Iceland.

I put my gift on a table that's there for just that reason. I'm pleased with it, managed to dig up a copy of *The Annals of Mývatnssveit*, a beautiful leather-bound volume chronicling the local history and place names around Lake Mývatn up north, only two hundred copies published in the 1930s, almost impossible to get your hands on—the perfect gift for an old country boy.

And here he comes now, swanning over, taking my hand in his, swaying a little when he kisses it. He's drunk on wine and good company, his eyes are sparkling, and his beard tumbles over his red silk shirt, unbuttoned to the middle of his chest.

Little Anna, darling, welcome! Am I glad to see you! How lovely you look in that dress, you should wear dresses more often. Women should be womanly, show off their beauty. And keep their mouths shut. It's like I've always said: There's nothing more beautiful than a pretty woman who keeps her mouth shut.

My husband gapes at him, scandalized, but I know Jóhannes and don't walk into the trap he's laid for me. Just laugh: You old bastard, when you keep your mouth shut, you're the best of a bad lot too. Happy birthday—today you can get away with saying anything you like, but only today! How you doing? Having fun?

Well, I'm inching ever closer to the brink, but there's nothing to do but just keep going, he says. Come on now, friends, drink up, drink up!

He carves a path to the refreshment table and hands us glasses of champagne, I just manage to get hold of mine before it sloshes all over me.

See what I gave myself for my birthday? he says, rolling up his shirtsleeve. Isn't it beautiful?

He's gotten a volcano tattooed on his strong, sinewy forearm—tongues of red fire, a plume of smoke standing straight up in the air.

Hekla, '91, he says, closing his eyes for a moment. Your first eruption is like your first time with a woman, you never forget it.

I laugh, but my husband rolls his eyes.

Why does he always have to be so over the top? he whispers in my ear.

Aw, he's fine, I say. He's just had a snootful. Just a bit drunk.

My husband smiles: He gets away with saying things you'd never tolerate from anyone else. You're weirdly protective of him.

Don't be silly, I say and look around for my coworkers. We smile and say hello in lowered voices so as not to interrupt the speeches, which have started once again. Sip our wine in silence, listen to laudatory and slightly long-winded recitations of the birthday boy's exploits, his scholarly articles and perilous climbs up Grímsvötn and Kilauea, his adventures on Eyjafjallajökull; amongst his colleagues, Jóhannes Rúriksson always leads the charge, going where no man ought to go after a series of unlikely detours, a flask of whiskey and a cigarette never far from his hand.

You're always telling heroic stories about yourselves, says my husband. And you treat Jóhannes like he's Indiana Jones.

He is Indiana Jones. Or he thinks he is.

The speeches are over, Elísabet toasts the birthday boy, we raise our glasses and beer bottles, hip hip hurray four times, and then my husband follows the stream of people into the house and over to the buffet. And then he's standing there, looking at me like he knows something about me that other people don't.

Tómas Adler isn't wearing a suit, he doesn't look like he's at a party at all or like he's the least bit concerned about what other people think of his ratty appearance. He's rather tragic, actually, ragged jeans and an old leather jacket, his hair sticking out like he's just woken up. He's holding a glass of wine and looking at me with a big smile on his unshaven face, as if he's overjoyed to see me.

Hi, he says. What fun to see all of you in your finery, I've only ever seen you lot in your hazmat suits. It's not every day you encounter volcanologists wearing ball gowns.

It was the baseline requirement tonight, to wear something nice, I say, and I regret it immediately; he points to himself and laughs.

I'm sorry, I say. I wasn't trying to knock you. You're plenty dressed up.

No, I'm really not, he says. But I ran into the birthday boy stocking up on champagne at the Vínbúð and he dragged me to his party, wouldn't hear of anything else. And so now here I stand, like a vagabond, I don't know a soul, and I'm almost as drunk as the host.

I sincerely hope not, I say, and we both look at Jóhannes, who's doing a Greek circle dance with his doctoral students, barely keeping his balance on the hops.

Are all volcanologists like you and Jóhannes?

How are me and Jóhannes?

Harder than the mountains you study?

I start laughing: You're putting Jóhannes and I in the same category? He's the cool guy. A little too cool, really. I'm just a normal middle-aged woman from the suburbs.

Tómas looks at me: No, you're not. You are a very unusual woman. More hardcore than all of them put together. How'd that happen? How'd you decide to become a geoscientist?

It was a pretty straight shot. My dad was a geoscientist, this job runs in the blood.

And then, all of a sudden, I'm talking about volcanoes and the shaking of the earth, telling him about my dad and the chunk of lava from Hekla.

He wasn't actually educated as a geoscientist, I say, but an astronomer. Specialized in the corona of the sun. The outermost layer of the sun's atmosphere. He was mesmerized by it, dreamed of unlocking its mysteries. Why the corona is so much hotter than the surface of the sun itself. He talked about it often, read up on it and studied it. It was basically his sole interest, outside of volcanoes.

I could've answered that, says Tómas with a solemn expression.

Answered what?

Why the corona is hotter than the surface of the sun.

Oh?

Because it is the sun's hot kiss. The sun kissing the heavens.

I stare at him, flabbergasted, he looks back at me and a smile spreads across his face and then we both start laughing, such a deep sort of belly laughter that it dislodges something in my breast, brings tears to my eyes. His eyes tear up from laughing, too, they're strangely green, his nose on the large side, he's a little younger and shorter than I am in my high heels. We laugh and talk and get another glass of wine, then another and another, and then my husband is there, courteous but curt, he wants to go home, though he doesn't say it. Tómas excuses himself and disappears into the crowd; the clock strikes ten, and the band plays their first song. I try to drag Kristinn out onto the dance floor, but he's not in the mood.

Go dance with your friends, he says. I'll wait.

It's hard to dance when someone is waiting for you, you've got to have downed more than a few glasses of wine to not care that someone's standing on the sidelines and watching you and waiting for the clock to strike again.

I dance with my coworkers, "Dancing Queen" and "Heart of Glass," with the birthday boy, who nearly suffocates me with his after-shave and red silk shirt during "Sweet Home Alabama," and then I dance with Tómas Adler. He smiles shyly but moves with confidence, he takes me in his arms and spins me in a circle. I'm probably a little too drunk, dancing a little too close, I kick off my shoes so I won't be taller than he is, his hands are warm, his eyes are green and laughing, his neck smells of soap.

Alright now, the car's here.

Suddenly my husband is standing in the middle of the dance floor, no nonsense and stone-cold sober with my coat over his arm, I let go of Tómas Adler and allow my husband to put my coat around my shoulders. Then run out to the taxi with dance thrumming in my blood, my hips, my abdomen. Kristinn kisses me in the taxi on the way home, puts his hand under my dress and strokes my thigh.

You're drunk, he says. I've got to get you into bed.

It's not even midnight, I say. I knew you'd drag me home before midnight.

You're a woman of a respectable age, in a respectable position. You've no reason to be out after midnight.

Then he kisses me, and I let him, even though I'm a bit irritated with him, with myself for having not sent him home and kept on dancing. But he's right—what business does a middle-aged university professor have out in the world after midnight, other than to get too drunk, embarrass herself, knock herself off her academic pedestal?

We open the front door without a sound, sneak down to the bedroom so as not to wake Salka, he takes off his tie and hangs his shirt on a hanger, I heave a sigh of relief when I remove my shoes, free myself from my nylons. We touch each other with care and tenderness, the way it's only possible to touch someone after you've made love to them for decades. Every inch of our bodies familiar, every touch evokes the same reaction as always, like playing the same instrument, plucking the same strings for half your life; a tremor courses through my body at almost the same time that he lets out a muffled cry and collapses on top of me, and it's like coming home.

THE DOOR WAS OPEN

Natural disasters *here* aren't necessarily natural disasters *there*. Natural disasters *now* won't necessarily be natural disasters in ten years. Natural disasters are nature's reactions to imbalance and her way of regaining her balance once again.

Páll Imsland. 2013. "Reflections on Natural Hazards." In *Natural Hazards in Iceland: Volcanoes and Earthquakes*, ed. Júlíus Sólnes. Reykjavík: University of Iceland Press.

She's sitting at the kitchen table when I come home, as if nothing could be more natural.

I open the front door with my elbow, loaded down with shopping bags, and jump when I see her. She's sitting at the kitchen table with her legs crossed and her hands in the pockets of a tatty faux-fur coat with a leopard print, smiling at me.

Good afternoon, I say quizzically. Who are you?

Then I wait a moment, a few seconds, wait for an explanation, for this strange woman to explain what she's doing in my kitchen, but she doesn't answer, just looks at me and smiles broadly, as if she's so pleased to see me, as if nothing could be more normal and pleasant than for her to be sitting at my kitchen table.

Sorry, can I help you? I ask.

No, I think not, she says then, her voice deep, raspy, and tinged with irony. The question is rather: Can I help you?

I stare at her, lost for words, when suddenly a light bulb goes on. Oh God! You're the interior designer! We had an appointment at four!

She nods: Bingo.

God, sorry, I say unhappily and put the shopping bags down on the kitchen counter, hold out my hand. I completely forgot, things have been insane lately.

No problem, no worries, she says and stands up without taking my hand. I'm not in a rush.

How'd you get in?

The door was open.

Yes, of course. I'm always nagging at the kids to lock up after themselves . . . can I offer you a coffee? Seltzer? Tea?

No.

She smiles a bit condescendingly, taking me in, looking at me like she already knows everything about me, just another respectable suburban woman, but she doesn't. I take off my overcoat and hang it in the closet, put my shoes on the shelf with toes out and stick the laces in them. Take my time, let her wait.

Well then, I say. I wanted to ask you about the curtains. In the living room, and paint for the walls.

She walks into the living room ahead of me, her hands still in her pockets. I follow her, trying to read her expression from the line of her back. I've always thought of interior designers as delicate creatures dressed tastefully in linen, but she's obviously not that kind of woman. She's of an indeterminant age, her hair is mussed and dyed with prominent dark roots, it just brushes the shoulders of her shabby fake fur. She's wearing tight black jeans, she's skinny, around my height, strides across the white oak parquet in scuffed lace-up leather boots, narrows her eyes as she takes in my home.

We bought the sofa about ten years ago, it's gone a bit gray and uninspiring, but I'm really fond of it. I wanted to have it reupholstered but then found out it would cost twice the amount to have it recovered than it would just to buy a new one—absurd, right?

She doesn't answer so I continue: We've felt a little exposed here in the living room since they put in the walking paths just there beyond the edge of the garden. So many people use the area around the lake. We'd like curtains, but nothing too heavy or grandmotherly, you know, no sheers. No vertical blinds, either, just something classic, simple, and elegant.

Of course, she says and smirks. Something classic, simple, and elegant.

And then there are the walls, they've always ranged from white to beige, but we're a little bored with them, I want to paint them a nice color. Change it up a bit. We thought you might have some ideas. Maybe we could paint one wall gray?

She turns around and gives me an appraising look: Are there any other rooms I need to see?

No, I don't think so. We're just thinking about the living room.

This room is so . . . simple and elegant that it tells me next to nothing about you. I need to have a little more to work with.

She walks toward the window: The view's fantastic, obviously. And I totally get why you don't want to pull focus from it, but we could maybe do something a little more personal, a bit more . . . you.

Me? This *is* me. This is my living room.

Okay, she says with a sigh. So, it's all really nice, very classic. But it's missing the dot over the *i*—a little character, if you get me.

I look around my living room, somewhat offended on its behalf. Maybe it isn't in keeping with the latest style, but it's tasteful and simple, the furniture Danish modern, nice pictures on the walls, Iittala candlesticks and Omaggio vases on the tables, a glossy black piano and a light-colored throw rug, certifiably produced by skilled adult weavers in a socially responsible workshop in Pakistan, I have nothing to be ashamed of.

The bedrooms are downstairs, and then there's just my curiosity cabinet, my office.

She turns around, and her eyes are shining: Curiosity cabinet? That sounds good. May I see it?

I hesitate, then lead her downstairs through the bedroom wing and up the steep stairs that lead up to my office. She stops in the doorway and looks around, then strides in, crosses her arms and nods, smiles with satisfaction: Now we're talking.

I raise an eyebrow: Talking about what?

Here, says the interior designer, casting out her hand, here we've got character.

You call this character? I hardly let anyone in here, it's just a bunch of old junk.

That desk is a treasure. I'd bring that up to the living room. It's a bit cramped in here, but in the living room, it would be the epicenter, the focal point, it would draw attention to itself, liven everything up. The rugs, the photos—here's color, here's life.

We'll think about it, I say, and hold the door open to show her out of my office, I'm almost affronted. I thought interior designers were supposed to help you beautify your home, give professional advice about buying paint and curtains, not order you to move around your old worn-out furniture, fill the living room with tacky, dusty sentimentality.

And about the walls, she says when we're back up in the living room, I'd suggest something bold and unusual. Red.

Red?

It's the only option, she says. Bloodred. The walls, the ceiling too. Something organic, she says, striding across the floor so that her fake fur swirls around her. Something powerful and bloody. Your living room is the beating heart, the bleeding pericardium.

I station myself in the middle of the room and cross my arms: I'm afraid that's out of the question. These aren't the kind of changes we have in mind.

She looks at me, unibrowed and pretty-eyed, far too much eyeliner around her big dark eyes, her eyeshadow smudged and caked in the creases of her eyelids, her red lipstick smeared around her lips. She smells of cigarette smoke and a heavy, sweet perfume.

You know what? she says. I'm not gonna be able to make this work.

What do you mean?

There's an imbalance in this house. I can't fix it. You have to choose.

Choose what?

You have to decide which woman you are. The one up there in your office or the respectable, sensible one down here in the living room.

Anger surges through me, but I calm myself, fix a cold and courteous smile on my face: You know, I'm afraid your ideas aren't going to work for us. My apologies.

She shrugs, smiles slyly, and walks toward the front door. I follow her out: Have a nice day. You're welcome to send an invoice for the consultation.

Then I close the door gently behind her, stand completely still for a moment and try to regain control of my heartbeat, the storm raging through my mind.

The gall! Who the hell does she think she is?

I go back up to my office.

It's filled with the furniture and landscape paintings from Dad's apartment, his well-worn sofa and easy chair upholstered in ripped green leather, his desk, as big and heavy as a grand piano, the deep dark bookshelves full of long-obsolete scientific texts I can't bring myself to throw out, leather-bound tomes that smell of printer's ink and smoke and are filled with my father's fingerprints. Just a lot of sentimentality, nothing else, in no way befitting this lovely, light-filled space, designed, as it was, to capitalize on the vantage and view over Elliðavatn Lake,

Heiðmörk Nature Preserve, and the Reykjanes Peninsula beyond that, preferably while reclining on a minimalist Italian leather chaise and polishing off a martini. Instead, I've filled it with rubbish, filing cabinets, and a tired old globe that opens and can be used as a minibar but which I use to store a little electric kettle and box of my favorite tea, Twinings Earl Grey, emergency supplies for when I'm too caught up in my work to allow myself the time to walk through the house and make a cup in the kitchen.

◆　◆　◆

Did the interior designer stop by? asks my husband after dinner. Wasn't she supposed to come today?

No, she didn't, I say. But you know what? I'm not sure she's the right designer for us.

Oh? No problem, it's up to you, he says and starts filling the dishwasher. We have a beautiful home, maybe there's no real reason to change things just for change's sake.

No, I say. We have a lovely home, we don't need to change a thing.

I'm not even sure myself why I don't tell him what happened earlier, about that vulgar, unmannerly woman. I'm not in the habit of lying to him—but it's like I feel guilty. As if our conversation was some kind of sordid secret. I shake my head as I clear the table, wring out the dishrag, and wipe the table down. I find one garishly dyed hair on the kitchen table and throw it in the trash, as if it was never there.

HELL'S CRACK REPAIR

Activity on the Reykjanes Peninsula alternates between periods of eruptions and rifting on the northeast-southwest fissure swarms, and periods of earthquake activity originating along the north-south fissure. During the last eruptive phase, the eruption activity moved between volcanic systems at intervals of 30–150 years. The eruption activity is characterized by fissure eruptions that may continue for several decades, but with intervals between eruptions. Eruption episodes of this kind are called fires.

Kristján Sæmundsson and Magnús Á. Sigurgeirsson. 2013. "The Reykjanes Peninsula." In *Natural Hazards in Iceland: Volcanoes and Earthquakes*, ed. Júlíus Sólnes. Reykjavík: University of Iceland Press.

In truth, we know nothing. We can put forth a hundred different hypotheses, support them with scientific arguments and geochronological facts, but life is as impossible for us to predict a week out as it is months or years. Was the Kerlingargosið eruption a unique, isolated event, like the submarine eruptions on the Reykjanes Ridge of late, or does it herald a new phase of uninterrupted volcanic activity on the Reykjanes Peninsula? Are the earthquakes around Mts. Þorbjörn and

Fagradalsfjall an indication that we'll be seeing an upsurge of activity in other volcanic systems northeast along the peninsula, one after the other, while the crustal plates break apart, like a zipper opening the earth? Or do the quakes just stem from changes in geothermal heat? We don't know.

You use explosives for this kind of research?

Milan sounds like he's asking if I like milk in my coffee. The jeep lurches over the uneven tracks like a giant insect, and I ramble as I try to make out the guideposts peeking out of the ash, forced to stop occasionally and back up so as not to drive off the roadway and get the car stuck in a crevice. He's sitting next to me and listening, cool as a cucumber, showing no indication that he has any doubts about my driving, and I'm thankful to him for that, I've grown accustomed to the men I work with holding on to the handles above their doors for dear life when I drive these virtually impassable roads.

Not often, I say, throwing it into reverse and wrenching one of the front tires back out of a hollow before we stutter forward. Seismic reflection surveys are generally used to examine the structure of the earth's crust, they're less useful for observing the way the land is deforming, how it rises and subsides. As a rule, they're too expensive and unwieldy, so we usually resort to other methods. The Met's established a pretty good system of devices for measuring earthquakes, and we get new InSAR radar images from satellites every week. And we have GPS readings, of course. The only reason the usual methods aren't working this time is because the ash layer from Kerlingargosið has impeded the results.

Then what are we doing here now?

The land has risen around eight inches since the New Year, and at the same time, it's sunk a few *miles* to the west of here. Iceland GeoSurvey believes these changes aren't a result of a magma intrusion at all but rather an increase in pressure caused by fluid phase transitions at the injection wells at the Svartsengi and Hellisheiði power plants.

What?

The Met office thinks that the crustal deformation and quakes aren't a result of the magma moving but rather changes in the geothermal system because of the activity here in the southwest. And Jóhannes Rúriksson intends to disprove this by blowing up a few little charges and then measuring the reflections. It's an old-fashioned method and kind of a long shot, but at this point, we can't rule anything out. And I think it's best to keep an eye on him when he pulls out the dynamite.

The banks of Djúpavatn Lake are usually grass green this time of year, the Móhalsadalur valley a soft oasis of moss in the middle of a volcanic wilderness, but not this summer. Reykjanes has become a singed brown wasteland, the mountains protrude from it like chipped teeth, and the only vegetation that appears able to withstand the cycles of ash is the occasional lupin, sticking its violet tongue into the sky. The weather map shows cloudless skies above this area, but the sun is barely visible, the southwesterly wind swirls up fine ash and draws a gray veil over the land; it's everywhere, in scalps, eyes, and nostrils, it slips through the jambs of our car doors, through the zippers on our Gore-Tex jackets, under my bra, my skin turning red and raised as under a rough kiss.

The jeep crawls across blackened landscape until we reach the shelter the Institute of Earth Sciences erected to protect its equipment—a small, orange, and absurdly cheerful shack that stands stiff-backed on the hillside and looks out over the lake and Trölladyngja Volcano in the north, Sveifluháls Ridge in the southeast. A knot of people in yellow vests stands on the plain to the north of the hillside, their white helmets shining like light bulbs against the blackness. I park the jeep next to the shelter, and we step out, pulling on dust masks, yellow vests, and our legally mandated helmets.

The techs barely look up as we approach, they're gazing down at a rift where Jóhannes is arranging a piece of tube in a crevice. He grins when he sees us: Well, if it isn't our honored guests! The delegation from the exalted Scientific Council. You guys got here just in time for the banquet, we're shaking up our last cocktail now.

He takes a red cylinder from a bag beside him and drops it down the tube, slaps the dust from his hands, and lights a cigarette after climbing out. Now we're getting somewhere, he growls through his beard.

The shack is crammed with computer equipment and instruments, and we arrange ourselves in front of a screen and wait while Jóhannes informs the people on duty at the Met and one of the techs begins to disengage the safety.

Alright, let her sing, says Jóhannes and starts the program, makes a check next to a point on the map on the screen, and hits enter. We sit and listen, there's a low churning sound in the distance, like a stomach rumbling in the next room.

Milan looks at us, surprised.

That's it?

Yep, I say. It's not like it is in the movies. No giant box with a plunger to push down, no mushroom cloud.

He smiles: I'm from Sarajevo, remember. I'm used to a bit more noise.

These little poots will be just fine for us, we don't want to hurt anyone, says Jóhannes, opening tables and images on the computer. He scratches at his beard, looking concerned.

What now? Anna, I don't see a goddamned thing.

No, you wouldn't right away, I say, scanning the image that appears; it's your typical lava and palagonite as far down in the bedrock as the eye can see.

Damn it to hell! Jóhannes can't conceal his disappointment.

Alright, you knew this was a shot in the dark, I say. And even though we don't see any sign of magma intrusion, there's also nothing that indicates changes in the geothermal area. And now we've ruled out Mt. Trölladyngja for the time being, so we can focus on other areas.

The magma's here, growls Jóhannes. I'm sure of it. I can feel it in my bones. We're just not looking in the right place, or else we didn't go down deep enough. It could be much deeper.

Or somewhere else entirely, or a hundred years in the future, I say. We don't have any data that shows anything other than everything exactly as it should be. We've got to base our assessment . . .

. . . on facts and scientific conclusions, yeah, yeah. Jesus, woman, you're like a broken record, says Jóhannes. I know. But it's also very possible that it's there and we just haven't found it. These quakes aren't normal, new fissures are opening every day, you can see the shift in the landscape from how the groundwater's rerouted.

Where else could the magma be? asks Milan.

I shrug. Basically anywhere. There are five systems on the Reykjanes Peninsula, and that's not counting the systems out in the ocean. Farthest out, we have Reykjanes, then Eldvörp and Svartsengi, where the Blue Lagoon is, then comes Fagradalsfjall, and now we're in the Krýsuvík area, which can actually be subdivided into three fissure swarms— Trölladyngja to the north, Sveifluháls, and then Krýsuvík itself, which is right next to Kleifarvatn Lake. The fifth system is the Brennisteinsfjöll Mountains, and Mt. Hengill is often counted as part of that, although strictly speaking, it isn't on the Reykjanes Peninsula. Reykjanes is actually just one long row of volcanoes that could go off whenever and wherever.

So right now, you're looking for . . . the place the magma's stored?

A magma chamber? No, there aren't any magma chambers under the systems here on the peninsula. For that, you'd need a central volcano, like Hekla or Katla, or Öræfajökull. What we have here is just a primitive fissure system, but the earth's crust is a lot thinner here than it is almost anywhere else, just three to six miles thick, so it isn't hard for the magma to reach the surface when the crust spreads apart. It only rarely surfaces—usually it forms a submarine intrusion.

Jóhannes grins: You could call it Hell's Crack Repair. The devil doing some home improvements with a caulking gun.

Milan looks at the computer screen, at the image the dynamite charge reflection has produced for us.

This is all fascinating, he says, wrinkling his brow. But it hardly gives us cause to change the preparedness level.

I shrug: Maybe it changes nothing, but it also doesn't confirm the Energy Authority's theories about geothermal heat being the culprit. We've no reason to think anything but that we're contending with a magma intrusion and plate spreading. I think we should announce an Alert Phase just to be on the safe side.

How long might that phase last?

Impossible to say. A week or a year, maybe even a decade.

Milan shakes his head: Then we change nothing. People stop paying attention to the preparedness level if it's in effect for too long. We have to wait for something to change.

Damn it, says Jóhannes. The peninsula is kicking off. I can feel it, down to my bones.

We'll wait and see, I say, standing up and dusting the ash from my pants. Your bones aren't enough to change the preparedness level. We're going to need to find this magma if we're going to talk any sense into the Scientific Council.

NEGRONI

Olivine is a magnesium iron silicate with the chemical composition $(Mg^{2+}, Fe^{2+})_2 SiO_4$. It forms the majority of the earth's outer mantle and is the most common mineral on the planet by volume. Once on the surface of the earth, it erodes quickly and vanishes.

Kristján Sæmundsson and Einar Gunnlaugsson. 1999. *The Book of Icelandic Minerals*. Reykjavík: Mál og menning.

Welcome! Come in, let me take your coats.

Nice to see you.

Thanks for having us, gorgeous place!

What a great location!

Hey, man! New haircut, eh?

So nice!

What a pretty dress, where'd you get it?

The guests start to show up around seven, not too early, not too late, the living room fills with warbling conversation. The men are fit and sunburnt, their temples gray, their beards neatly trimmed; the women are tastefully made-up, sleek blowouts and pastel manicures. They want hoppy beer, they accept Italian cocktails in cut-crystal glasses.

It falls to me to greet them and show them into the living room, my husband's standing watch over the grill with three digital thermometers in the prime rib.

Why don't we have something simpler, I'd asked, something we know will come out well? What's wrong with grilling a leg of lamb?

But this is his cycling club, they train together for the summer race, and I've come to realize that they're locked in constant battle with one another, and not just over their wildly expensive leaf-light carbon-frame bicycles. The competition revolves around houses and cars, jobs and annual income, charisma, abs and golf handicaps, their wives' waistlines and their children's grades. And grills—they buy complicated Webers and Landmanns, coal and gas, I'm shocked when I see the receipt from the butcher: sixty thousand krónur for one piece of meat? Have you lost your mind?

We have the money, he says. It's okay to give ourselves permission, just this once, it'll be fun to try something new.

But it doesn't seem like he's having all that much fun now, standing there worrying over the grill and trying to take all his friends' conflicting advice with equanimity: Keep it closed, it would've been better to use coal on the right side, pour more water in the metal tray, keep it open. Careful, it's starting to burn on the end there, do you have another beer?

The men stand on the deck, full of mirth and gravitas, beers held aloft, while the women inspect the living room, clink their glasses, babble, and stroll around on their stilettos like ornate, oversized wading birds. I've met them before, but I have trouble distinguishing one from another; the chipper loud one is called Elín, or Emilía, she's the HR manager at some insurance company, one's a flight attendant, another a physical therapist. A marketing manager, a lawyer, a nutritionist. Alda, Lísa, Gurrý, Aníta Rún, they chat about golf courses, chia seeds, and TV shows, people I don't know. They ask polite questions about my work, I mumble something about satellite images and earthquake measurements, encounter their blank stares and suggest, in my desperation, showing them the house. The group trails behind me, through the living room and into the kitchen, down to the bedroom wing as I sweat profusely. All of a sudden, I can see my home through the eyes of the interior designer, the white walls and light-colored furniture, all so terribly pale and impersonal, the paintings like they've each been chosen for a movie set. My house is unfamiliar to me, dull and gray as a shed skin, I lead them through the bedrooms but feel like I'm impersonating someone, pretending I live here and unexpectedly finding myself playing host in a house I don't know.

What's in here? asks one of the women, already halfway up the stairs that lead to my office.

Oh, that's just my home office, it's a dreadful catchall, I say, too late to stop her. They follow her up, stand in a knot considering the bookshelves, the old Persian rug, the mahogany desk under the picture window looking out at the lake and the wood, Mts. Hengill and Keilir. I don't invite guests in here, I didn't give myself a chance to tidy up, the round table with the carved feet is covered with books and maps, one of the old filing cabinets is half-open, papers overflowing from their folders. Salka is sitting on the floor with Dad's old rock collection, she doesn't pay us the slightest bit of attention, she's organized the cubby contents around herself and is peering at a beautiful piece of zeolite through a big magnifying glass.

Salka, sweetie, what are you doing? You know you have to pick up after yourself, put the right rock back in the right cubby.

She looks up with a focused wrinkle between her eyebrows: I'm trying to figure out if this is Iceland spar or rock crystal.

God, how cuuuute, says one of the women and sits on her heels next to Salka, putting her glass down and starting to root through the box. A little geoscientist, just like her mommy. Do you like playing with the pretty rocks?

Salka stares at her, piqued, she isn't playing a game. Iceland spar is a kind of quartz, rock crystal is a calcite. It's important.

It's okay, sweetheart, I say. It's zeolite, see? All you have to remember is to count the corners of the crystals, three on spar, six on rock crystal. You'll get it.

This is a fantastic office, says another of the women.

It's my burrow, I say, with an apologetic smile. I like to work at home sometimes.

I don't tell them that sometimes, my husband complains that I'm in here all night, all weekend, instead of watching Netflix with him, going for a bike ride, out to dinner, to the movies or a concert, a book club, meeting up with my girlfriends. I don't tell them that I don't actually *have* any girlfriends, no book club to speak of, that I only go out with my workmates, people who understand what I'm talking about, are concerned about the same things I am, who hike glaciers and volcanoes with me, who can read the layers of the earth and stones like dime-store thrillers. That by all typical standards, I'm a rather dull workaholic, married to an understanding man who bought this fine house with this big office so that I'd be happy and have peace to do my work.

Fab, says the first one and stands up from the floor, tottering a little on her heels and bracing herself on the desk, her eyes swim a bit as she looks at me. Aren't you lucky? You got it all. Great husband and wonderful kids, beautiful house, cool job, it's all just perfect. Isn't it?

She laughs her shrill laugh: Isn't it just perfect, girls?

Alright now, Gurrý, says her friend, taking a hold of her under one arm, maybe we should sit down and have a glass of water, babe.

Dinner comes out well, the three thermometers deliver a roast that is suitably browned on the outside and 140 degrees Fahrenheit inside—we serve it with herb butter and green Italian sauce; baked potatoes stuffed with spinach, butter, and Camembert; asparagus with brown-butter almonds, dill, and capers; a salad of orange, fennel, and black olives—Kristinn does the carving, I refill the glasses, and the guests groan and moan and sigh with pleasure.

Everything's perfect, but I still can't shake off this strange feeling, that my home has become foreign to me, that I'm one of the guests sitting and chatting and laughing around the dinner table, dabbing beef fat from my lips and polishing off my wine, Châteauneuf-du-Pape 2015.

They're all gone by midnight, the babbling and the laughter gone silent. We collect coffee cups and cognac glasses and fill the dishwasher, what doesn't fit will have to wait until morning. The front door opens and in comes Örn, straight off the night shift, exhausted, with a dark shock of hair hanging over his eyes.

What exactly is going on here? he thunders. Where did you two get the idea that you could throw a fancy dinner party without discussing it with me first?

I tut and give him a hug: Hilarious, funny guy. You're on thin ice, I haven't entirely forgiven you yet, you know.

I know, he says, and kisses me on the head. But you've made your peace with me not going into geoscience, right?

You're a grown man, I don't know what I can do to steer you away from this nonsense. It's something you have to decide for yourself. You'll go to Italy and see where it leads you. Worst-case scenario, you'll learn to cook and make a decent negroni.

His smile fades. I'm dead serious about this, Mom. I'm not going to party or whatever. I think I could be good at this, I've got so many ideas.

Three precious years, I say, shaking my head. To design stages. I design stages, too, you know. To preserve human life and prevent property damage. It isn't impossible to be a bit practical.

Anna, says my husband. Give it a rest. You're not going to talk him out of this. He has to make up his own mind, you don't control him. He claps his son on the shoulders. I'm just happy you've found your niche, buddy. The time's come for you to choose a direction, stop this gadding about. And you can always change your mind, do something else if you end up thinking better of it.

Örn shakes him off: Neither of you are taking me seriously! You think it's not work, but just wait. I've got all this experience from the smelter, I know machinery and metals and all that kind of stuff, I know what I'm doing. And I'm going to be a name, I'm going to work in theaters all over the world and make beautiful things.

I'm sorry, says his father. I didn't mean it like that. It's exciting, I'm sure you'll do great.

I look at them standing across from one another, the same height but strangely dissimilar in every other way. Örn is powerfully built where his father is wiry; he's dark, unkempt, and unshaven, his somber eyes burn with passion as they meet the watery blue mildness of his father's. Örn is my son, the grandson and namesake of my father, with science and fire in his blood, I can't fathom how he can walk away from such an inheritance.

Alright, guys, I say. We're not going to solve this tonight. I take off my apron, tie its strings together and hang it on a hook, when suddenly, this odd, unfamiliar feeling rushes through me once again.

I'm going to bed, I say, but on the way, I look in on Salka. She's lying curled up like a ball of yarn under the duvet, her dark locks flowing over her white pillow. I can just barely see her breathing, but her black lashes are fluttering over closed eyes; my baby is dreaming. She's holding something tight in her fist, I gently loosen her grasp, it's a piece of olivine the size of a matchbox, bright green, the crystal so smooth that at first glance, it looks like bottle glass. A shard of eternity that was borne up out of the deep and wound up in my father's rock collection, now lying in my daughter's palm and powering her dreams, warm and soft to the touch, like a living thing. I wrap her fingers back around it and kiss her little fist, sleep now, Stubby, sweet dreams, I love you.

THE EUROPEAN RESEARCH COUNCIL

To: Anna.Arnadóttir@hi.is
From: tomas.adler@gmail.com
Subject: Photo Nr. 13 of Kerlingargosið

Dear Anna,

Takk fyrir síðast, so nice to see you, talk to you, dance with you. I want to let you know the exhibition is over, and you're welcome to pick up your photo. I can also bring it to you, if that's more convenient. Then maybe you could show me where you've put the other picture, the one I took of you in the plane? I hope you like it, that it didn't upset you. I love it.

Yours,
Tómas

I read the message again, want to write back, but I don't know what I should say. Close my email, then open it again, run my fingers through my hair, surprisingly nervous. Nice to dance with you, he wants, he hopes, he loves, the picture of me. Maybe I could show him where I put it, lead him down to the laundry room, dig it out from under the Christmas tablecloths in the linen cupboard.

I jump up, walk around my office at the university, turn on my heel and go back the other way. Catch sight of myself in my mother's old mirror, see reflected there a dancing woman at the moment her body takes control. The laborers grin and the farm girls chat and giggle; the woman's in her forties, she's wearing comfortable, practical slippers and clothes befitting a college professor, the shelves behind her bow under the weight of scientific journals and scholarly articles she's annotated, and yet she glows, dances like she's fifteen years old with a head full of happy nonsense when what she should be doing is going over the new models of possible magma movement under Mt. Fagradalsfjall.

Tómas Adler, says the face in the mirror with a snort. What's the matter with you, woman? Get your head in the game.

There's a knock, Elísabet swings the door open and sticks her head through the gap, gives me a searching look over the top of her glasses.

What? she asks curiously.

What? I ask in return.

Her breath catches: Did we hear back?

About what? I ask, frowning.

The grant from the European Research Council?

No, why?

You're shining like the sun. So rosy-cheeked, I thought maybe we'd finally gotten word from them.

No, I say, hiding my cheeks in my hands and flopping down in my desk chair. I've just been going over the earthquake data from Mt. Fagradalsfjall. It occurred to me I should look at it alongside the data from the quakes during the Krafla Fires.

We both peer at my computer screen, and Ebba's saying something, but my mind drifts back to the email, how on earth should I respond?

It's like the nature of the plate boundary is transforming before our eyes, she says, poking her pen at the newest earthquake data from Krýsuvík. The peninsula's behaved like a transcurrent fault for centuries, inched along this narrow earthquake belt, but it looks like the activity's changing. The whole thing could break wide open.

And start an eruption on land? Or not, I say and shrug. These earthquake swarms are just coming and going, the land rises, then falls, it's all anomalous.

Something's got you worked up, says my friend, looking at me. I can feel it. What's your feeling about this?

I smile at her.

Feelings don't count here, Ms. Elísabet. You of all people should know that. We're reading the instruments, monitoring the data, measuring earthquake amplitude, surface movements, changes in surface tilts, gas emissions. There could be an eruption here wherever, whenever, but not without the instruments picking up on it. And they don't give a damn about our feelings.

Not without the instruments picking up on it, she sighs and nods. It's just such a terrible feeling, not being able to forecast this with any more precision. Do you know how many phone calls I get a day from ministers, government agencies, reporters, airlines? Everyone's waiting to hear something. The tourist industry is only just getting back on its feet, and then there's all this uncertainty. It's such an enormous responsibility we have.

And it all comes down to you, I say with a smirk. You've got to take those phone calls, while the rest of us get to work in peace.

She stands up and opens the door: Best let you work in peace, then. But let me know if you come across anything interesting. Some crumb I can throw them, appease them for a time.

Sure thing, I say. You'll be the first to know.

The door closes, and I keep looking at my computer screen, at the tables and data progressions, the diagrams. I close my eyes and feel some movement behind them, feel the land rising and falling like waves on the open sea, the embers streaming out of the mantle and forcing their way up under the earth's crust, the magma tossing and turning like a fetus at full term, pressing on the membrane encasing it and searching for a way out.

Just a feeling, nothing I can put my finger on, nothing to base an argument on. I grab a pen and scribble on a scrap of paper:

$$\tau = \gamma \frac{\eta}{\mu}$$

I look at the equation, beautiful in its simplicity. It isn't complicated, volcanic activity is simply a matter of time, the pressure exerted on magma, and the resistance of the surrounding rock.

Then I sigh, close the tables and open my email, read the message from Tómas Adler once more. Type out a short, dry reply. Takk fyrir síðast, nice to see you, too, I might be able to come by your studio to pick up the photo later. Then press send.

Time, pressure, and resistance—that's all there is to it.

KÓPAVOGUR

Tómas Adler's studio is in an old industrial building in Kópavogur, tucked in amongst junk sellers and auto body shops; it takes me a long time to find the right cul-de-sac, the right door. They're all unmarked, no doorbells, so I bang on the door a few times, no one answers. I hesitate for a moment, then take the handle, it's unlocked, stick my head through the gap and call: *Halló?*

The vestibule is crammed with winter coats and loud music, there's a motorcycle helmet hanging on a hook. I knock on the inner door, it opens like a shot, and Tómas Adler looks at me in utter astonishment before a smile stretches across his face:

How wonderful! I wasn't expecting you! Welcome, come in!

He's got a wolfish look about him, face unshaven and hair tousled, he's wearing a holey T-shirt for some metal band, didn't see my email but seems genuinely glad to see me. I extend my hand at the same time he moves to kiss me on the cheek, we bump into one another, laugh, and greet each other with a handshake, a kiss on both cheeks, I blush furiously and look away. He runs a hand through his hair and invites me into the cacophony:

> These cliffs have been awake
> for a thousand years
> Look into the stone,
> and you'll see their tears

Bubbi Morthens's voice echoes through the room. I remember this song from way back, another life, but I don't say so, focus on putting one foot in front of the other, edge along behind him and into the apartment in back. His movements are quick and agile, they remind me of a dancer's, his shoulders are strong, he has paint smudges on the back of one hand.

It's a raw space, unfinished with a painted concrete floor, there's a worktable in the middle covered with photographs. Everything against one wall is in disarray—a clothing rack, cardboard boxes, tool bags, metal shelves laden with paper and junk, an unmade futon tucked in a corner. Projectors and tripods stand about the room like bewildered guests at a cocktail party, the walls are papered with photographs, drawings, and maps. The light streams in through the windows along one side. I catch my breath; Reykjavík appears from a new and unfamiliar vantage, I can see the green south slopes of Fossvogur and Öskjuhlíð, church spires, construction cranes and the glinting sea.

Fantastic view, I say, trying to push aside my agitation.

Yes, not many people appreciate the beauty of Kópavogur, he says with a smirk. I won't apologize for the mess, I like being able to look at what I'm working on, that's how I get all my ideas. It gets a bit chaotic sometimes. But I know where everything is, unbelievable as that may seem.

You have nothing to apologize for, I say. I'm bothering you at work.

He turns and smiles at me: You're not bothering me in the least. You could never bother me. I'm happy to see you. Shall we take a look at it?

He walks toward a stack of big placards leaning against one wall and pulls out a photo.

Not bad, he says, lifting it up to the light. Maybe not the best in the show, but it gives a good sense of what it was like. How did you put it again? Precise and informative?

Tómas points to the lighthouse, a small, white exclamation point in relief against the black ash plume: That's where we met, remember?

I nod but barely look at the photo. My heart hammers and my hands shake. He doesn't notice, he's contemplating the photo and furrowing his brow, the light plays in his eyes, fine smile lines deepen, and a little scar appears on his forehead, the trace of some unknown incident in the past, I have to stop myself from asking what happened. He's oddly unphotogenic, the pictures I've seen of him on the internet don't look anything like him, show him solemn and a bit big-nosed, no laughter in his eyes, his beautiful, restless energy doesn't come through the lens. He's meant to stand on the other side of it.

He looks at me and sees me looking at him, sets the picture back against the wall, runs his hands through his dark locks, suddenly nervous, boyish. Would you like some coffee? he asks.

I nod, can't form the words.

Tómas pours coffee from a checked thermos into a green mug, our hands touch when he passes it to me, his eyes meet mine, and then I plummet, plain and simple, lose all direction, lose my balance and fall into him, drawn into him as into a black hole, completely out of control. I don't even make the conscious decision to relinquish control, to let myself fall, my body isn't obeying my commands, my mind's silent but my heart shouts for joy. I reach my hand out and touch his face, he closes his eyes and leans his cheek into my palm, we're both trembling, as if we've been rocked by the same shock wave. He opens his eyes, they're gleaming, no laughter now, he takes my hand and pulls me to him as if to dance with me. Our bodies touch—cheeks, shoulders, chests, stomachs, hips—we embrace, wrap ourselves around one another for a fraction of a second, an eternity. We breathe in deeply, together, our heartbeats in sync, once, twice, three times, then I tear myself from him, run out, stumble over the shoes in the vestibule and land on my knees. Scramble to my feet and push open the door, start the car and back it out of the lot, drive away as if pursued by demons, but I'm not getting out of this so easy. My heart beats wildly in my chest, I can hardly catch my breath, tears are streaming down my cheeks. I don't know if I'm crying from sadness or joy or terror, and it doesn't matter. I am in love with Tómas Adler, my life as I know it is over, and I haven't even kissed him.

EXPLANATORY NOTE VI

BÁRÐARBUNGA

On July 3, 1972, the ERTS-1 satellite was launched from the Vandenberg Air Force Base in California. NASA put it into orbit around the earth to shore up its geographical data and at the same time get a look at military bases on the other side of the Iron Curtain. Over the next eighteen days, ERTS-1 flew over Iceland ten times; each time, it took five pictures of the country. The satellite provided Icelandic scientists with their first-ever opportunity to view Iceland from space with any kind of accuracy, 570 miles in the air, and at the end of January 1973, it captured an image that caused my father to drop his mug, which shattered on the floor of the University of Iceland's geoscience building with an earsplitting smash.

The photo revealed an enormous unknown volcano under Vatnajökull. The domed, benign-looking Bárðarbunga turned out to be the biggest, most powerful volcano in Iceland, her caldera 2,788 feet deep and filled to the brim with glacial ice. And underneath it all bubbled an enormous magma chamber responsible for some of the largest lava fields in the highlands.

It was, in all likeliness, this sudden attention that roused Bárðarbunga from her tranquil slumber, she woke as the satellite drifted overhead and snapped its photo. Bárðarbunga actually had a lot to answer for, back in the gray mists of antiquity—torrents of glacial run-off from her caldera had surged over great distances, carving out both Jökulsárgljúfur and Ásbyrgi Canyons, a destructive power equal to that of several short-range nuclear blasts. But after the settlement in the eighth century, she'd behaved herself for the most part, only erupting along fissures up in the unsettled wilderness where no one would be bothered, keeping quiet as a church mouse once people started measuring earthquakes, up until her picture was taken from space and she revived and started rumbling anew. Since then, large quakes have been common at Bárðarbunga; she erupted along the Gjálp ridge in 1996 and at Holuhraun Lava Field in 2014. But she's biding her time, an enormous powder keg sitting atop the burning heart itself, directly over the mantle plume where it rises up under Iceland.

And up above, we unwittingly putter about—we nurse, teach, and write, we build buildings, fry meatballs, brew coffee, plant woods, harness hydropower, and pave roads as if all this scratching at the surface meant anything in the face of the forces that rumble in the depths below us.

It's just a question of time, pressure, and resistance.

AESTHETICS: PLAGIOCLASE, MAGNETITE

You could say that the melt zone in the mantle where magma forms is the burning heart of Iceland.

Freysteinn Sigmundsson, Magnús Tumi Guðmundsson, and Sigurður Steinþórsson. 2013. "The Internal Structure of Volcanoes." In *Natural Hazards in Iceland: Volcanoes and Earthquakes*, ed. Júlíus Sólnes. Reykjavík: University of Iceland Press.

Ghastly, says Jóhannes, reaching over the gunwale and prodding a dead trout. The farther we go out into Kleifarvatn Lake, the more of them there are, floating, pale bellies up. Jóhannes looks at the sky in agitation: There's something sinister in the air, there's going to be an eruption, I can feel it in my bones.

It's easy to feel it in your bones when every single instrument in the area is broadcasting as much, I say, but I've got to admit, he's right—the sky is ominous, thick with silence and the stench of sulfur, even the Arctic terns are mute. The stillness suspended over the lake is ruptured only by the rattling motor, it breaks on the jagged hillsides and sends ghostly echoes across the water's surface, we all want to wrap up this expedition quickly, although no one has said it—before the CO_2 meters in our breast pockets start to wail.

Damn, we need new gear, says Úlfar, the engineer from Iceland GeoSurvey, lifting the float out of the water and shaking the gauge that hangs from it. This one's busted.

No wonder, the sulfuric acid readings were maxed out when it stopped sending data yesterday, I say. We didn't bring a new gauge; the lake's become dangerous.

We take a sample, our third of the outing, but Úlfar's hands are shaking so much he drops the vial in the lake and, in the end, we just turn the boat around and head back toward land.

Who the hell's that, Jóhannes is asking when a big motorcycle rumbles onto the site. The police should have barricaded the area by now.

The rider steps off the bike and takes off his helmet, takes a camera out of a bag and holds it up in front of his face, the flash glitters, chip, chip, chip, like a celebratory chant from the shore.

It's Tómas Adler, says Jóhannes. The photographer. I met him at Kerlingargosið, he took some pretty snazzy pictures of me. And the eruption. Even invited him to my birthday party. You two know each other, right, Anna?

I can't get a word out, sit like a condemned woman on the thwart as the boat carries me closer to land, yard after merciless yard, Tómas drops his camera from his eye and smiles at me, that shining, lopsided smile.

Well, fancy seeing you here, he says when we reach the shore, he's greeting all of us but looking at me, holds out his hand to help me onto dry land. I look away, don't take his hand, jump out unassisted on shaky legs. My hands ache to touch him, oh, God, why is he here?

Ooph, that was one of the worst outings I've ever gone on, says Úlfar with a sigh. The lake could blow at any time—and that stench, man!

How'd you get through the barricade? asks Jóhannes. I thought the police weren't letting anyone through but us.

As if that would stop me, says Tómas, pulling a Civil Protection ID out from under his safety vest. I managed to convince the national commissioner it was important to document the measures being taken here from the start, I'm allowed to enter and photograph restricted areas as I see fit.

Milan Petrovic couldn't have been too thrilled with that, says Jóhannes. He refused to allow media past the barricades.

I'm here at my own risk, says Tómas, smiling cheerfully. In the end, Milan said I could fall into a volcanic fissure for all he cares, if that's what I really want.

The ground shakes under our feet and everyone starts, we listen, but the shaking subsides, doesn't seem to augur anything else.

Can we get a move on? says Úlfar, looking around. This is a disturbing place. The sulfur smell is making me sick.

He's right, the reading on my CO_2 meter's been going up. We need to get out of the valley before the hydrogen sulfide settles and turns this place into a death trap.

You all take off, says Tómas. I'm going to get a few more shots, the colors here are incredible.

I look at him, leaving him behind is out of the question, such inane exuberance and failure to grasp the looming danger here. I'm positive he didn't have the sense to bring a CO_2 meter or TETRA radio with him, I feel a desperate protectiveness, long to lead him away by the reins, save him from every danger.

We've still got to take a sample from Grænavatn, Green Lake, I say as curtly as I can. It's in a volcanic crater, full of sulfur. You're welcome to come with.

He looks at me, surprised and happy, you'd like me to?

It just occurred to me that it might make a good subject for your photographs, I mumble. The water's, you know, green.

He smiles from ear to ear: Gracious lady, your wish is my command.

I flee into the jeep, and we drive out of the valley, into the geothermal area, Tómas hard on our heels on his motorcycle.

Welcome to hell's kitchen, says Jóhannes when we get out of the car, plumes of steam are rising up into the air around us as if geysers are straining to break through the earth's crust above them. Keep that boy on a leash, Jóhannes says to me and points at Tómas, who's flitting around with his camera in front of his face. We don't want to lose him in a crevice. As much as that might please Milan.

This is incredible, Tómas enthuses, clambering up on a big boulder and taking aim with his camera. The last time I was here, it was a beautiful blue-green, but look at it now: it's like a dragon's eye.

It's true, the lake is picturesque, the sulfur's turned it an incredible poison green. Úlfar and Jóhannes carefully pick their way down the bank with sample vials and gauges, the ground shakes under our feet again. Tómas totters on top of the boulder.

Careful, I say, a little too loudly.

Could it erupt right here, underneath us? he asks, jumping down, breathless and wriggling with excitement.

Absolutely it could, although that hasn't happened in a long time, I say. Most of the eruption fissures are to the north and west of us here, where the new lava is. Grænavatn is in a volcanic crater that was formed in an eruption six-hundred-some years ago. It didn't produce a lot of lava, just stones and steam and a terrific amount of noise. The blast tore gabbro up from the eruption channel, it's all over the ground here.

Gabbro, he says. What's that?

I look around for a suitably smooth piece of rock, pick it up and brush the dirt off it.

It's not a volcanic rock, but a plutonic one. Basalt, like lava, and yet very different. See how speckled and pretty the color? The shards in it are much bigger than in your typical gray stone because it solidified deep in the earth.

Those speckles are minerals?

Yes, the white's plagioclase, a silicate mineral, and the black cubes are magnetite. The crystals have had a long time to form and the minerals to develop down there.

Eternity nurtures its depths, he whispers, moved, and looks at the stone and then at me. There's a Galician poet who was translated into Icelandic—Blanca Andreu—do you know her work?

I shake my head no, I'm not much for poetry.

Not much for poetry? Woman, what of beauty? asks Tómas.

> now I ask myself what might become of this fire
> and the ashes, its night

I snort.

I don't want for beauty. Science is full of it.

Of beauty? You're joking.

Just look around, see how beautiful the world is. What poetry could capture the movement of magma through the depths, making its way up to the surface? Look at the plumes of steam, the colors and the light, feel the earth shaking under your feet, what poem could come even close to that?

He shakes his head. Without poetry, we're just brute beasts on a trembling earth. It's what makes us human, it gives us a higher purpose. It shows us the beauty that's in the world and allows us to describe it. I'm not a poet, I don't know a thing about verse or diction, but I try to think about my photographs as poems. I want them to show something other, something more than what's actually in them, I try to uncover the beauty hidden in the material world. That's my poetry, he says, holding up his camera.

And this, I say, holding up the stone, is mine. Plutonic rock from the depths of the earth. To me, gabbro is all the poetry and aesthetics I need.

Jóhannes is back and thumps a bucket full of gauges and sample vials on the ground.

An eruption in the offing, the earth shaking, and here you both stand, debating aesthetics and poetry! What would your father say, Anna Arnardóttir?

Poppycock. But he would have agreed with me about the beauty of gabbro.

I won't be easy until I'm back home, says Úlfar darkly, getting into the jeep. This hellmouth is on the verge of exploding.

Tómas shows me the stone he's picked up.

Now I have some of your poetry.

Suit yourself, collecting rocks, I say and trail the others toward the car.

He reaches out: Anna, wait. Looks at me and hesitates, then says: I've thought so much about what happened the other day, at my studio. Can't stop thinking about it. I hope you don't have any regrets.

I look at him, don't say a word.

He continues: I don't know what you meant by it, whether it meant anything to you. But it meant a lot to me. Something happened—that much I'm sure of. We both felt it, right?

Finally, I manage to stammer:

Not here.

Come over. To my studio. Now. Please?

I look down, he can interpret it however he wants that I nod, say no, I don't know. Then I get into the car with the others without looking his direction.

Jóhannes and I don't write up a site report on the way back to town. He's been inspired by our conversation about beauty, rambles about geology and poetry, I sit in silence and try to tamp down the hot, anguished joy that's spreading through my body like a disease, my ears ring, my lips tingle, my cheeks are hot and my heart hammers in my chest, hot currents flowing into my fingers, down into my womb.

I hope, desperately and sincerely, that my workmates don't look over and see what's come over me, glowing like a ball of fire in the back seat.

I needn't worry, Úlfar is staring silently out the front window and gripping the steering wheel tightly, the car is jostling over the uneven road, and Jóhannes has his eyes closed, intoning Einar Benediktsson's ode to Hekla at the top of his lungs:

> From her shoulders she shrugs her ice-gray brocade,
> raises to the heavens her fire-sharp blade.
> Doomsday in the vastness of her crown.
> On her brow danger and splendor.
> On the land in a flash her sword crashes down.
> Pastures and farms laid waste in flaming cascade.
> Iceland's burning heart beats within her.

CAN SOCIOPATHS
FALL IN LOVE?

A central volcano is a site, most often a mountain, that erupts over and over. Central volcanoes mature over time, and it's thought that their lifespans can be up to a million years. On the Reykjanes Peninsula, there are four fissure swarms that are crisscrossed by geothermal systems: Reykjanes, Svartsengi, Krýsuvík, and Brennisteinsfjöll. At first, these may look like central volcanoes; it's only the low-lying mountain ridges that demarcate the underlying plate boundaries.

Sigurður Steinþórsson. 2016. "What's the Difference between Volcanoes, Volcanic Systems, and Central Volcanoes?" The Icelandic Web of Science.

Effusive eruptions can be beautiful and peaceful events if the amount of magma is moderate and the location fortunate; incandescent fountains of magma bursting out of eruption vents, newly formed lava creeping across the land, productive and efficient as a crew of German road engineers. But they can also turn into terrifying disasters like the Skaftá

Fires of 1783, when the earth vomited poison gas and nineteen square miles of lava and snuffed the life out of the better part of the nation. In the beginning, it can be hard to say which phenomenon you're dealing with, whether in the next moment you'll be pulling out your camera and waxing rhapsodic, or fleeing for your life.

And I'm guilty of unforgivable optimism in the beginning, I underrate the danger, choose to put my faith in the sense of security that's baked into my comfortable, routine life. I believe no natural force could upset my equilibrium, destroy my beautiful garden, light my birch trees aflame and poison the lake where loons swim on bright summer nights with their chicks on their backs. I lack the imagination to envisage my home in ruins, the white oak floors brown, the Danish furnishings soot-covered and scorched.

Could I have staved this off, saved our fortunate, mundane existence from these calamities? I don't know, all I know is that there, in the beginning, I'm convinced that I'm in control of the situation. That I'm standing before an interesting little problem and have all the tools I need to unravel it: experience, knowledge, and a bottomless cache of logic. What an exciting, yes, and even fun idea: to try and take this task on, examine it from all angles, use tried-and-tested science to break it down and figure out its component parts. When you take everything else away, I'm a scientist. You will know the truth, and the scientific method shall set you free.

But oh, how simple I am. Simple and stupid and ignorant of the forces that stand against me, like an infant facing down a weapon of mass destruction. Trudging ahead, armed with childish curiosity and optimism, butterflies in my heart and a glint in my eye, I accept the challenge, allow myself to be tempted, accept the invitation and go to Tómas Adler's studio, we stand in front of one another and look each other in the eyes before he reaches out a hand, touches my face, runs his thumbs over my lips before kissing them. The kiss is unfamiliar and aggressive, the thrill both shakes me to my core and completely disarms me.

We make love on his futon, frantic, like we're drunk. Fires are burning in the depths of the earth, and my world is on the verge of ending, but I'm oblivious to the danger, too consumed by my self-centered passion to think about it. My body trembles with new pleasures, nothing exists in this world except for my lover. He is a wonderous, unknown land, I drink him in, enraptured by his body, his skin, the smell of him, sobbing with unforeseen, physical joy.

Afterward, we embrace, breathless and overcome, our legs are intertwined, and I am sincerely bewildered: Is this what love is, when you really get down to it? I'd always believed it was just puffed-up sentimentality, a conflagration that only waylaid soppy, weak-willed people. And now, here I lie naked at the foot of this stained futon, undone and overrun, elated, guilt-stricken and anguished, five missed calls on my phone, two from the Met Office, two from my husband, one from Salka.

I put down my phone, stand up on shaking legs, and look for my clothes, blunder around in my underwear, hands shaking so much I can barely fasten my bra, it's like I'm in withdrawal, my joy fading like a wine buzz.

Tómas reaches out his hand and strokes mine, his eyes dewy and green as olives.

Are you okay? Are you sad?

No. I'm too awful a person for that. I think I must be a sociopath.

I love you, he says. Even if you are a sociopath. Will you marry me?

I am married, remember? I say. I have a husband. And a family.

But you love me, he says. You said so. That's got to change something.

I swallow, hard, feel like I have some big mass stuck in my breast, a fist where my heart should be.

No, it changes nothing. Nothing when it comes to my marriage.

Anna. *Ástin mín.* My love.

He looks at me, sad and vulnerable, I look away, can't meet his eyes.

I have to go.

I slip into my shoes, put on my jacket, pause before going out the door.

Don't call me. Don't write me. Do that much for me. We're going to act like this never happened.

OVEN-ROASTED CHICKEN, END OF THE WORLD

A memory (hazy)
a nightmare
long forgotten:
A mountain devoured a man

Ingibjörg Haraldsdóttir, "Magma"

And then life goes on, as if it never ended. The car starts, the streets lead me to the right place, the house key fits in the front door lock as if nothing's happened. I put my shoes on the rack with their toes facing outward and stick the laces into them, hang my coat in the closet, and walk into the kitchen, where my husband's chopping onions and listening to the news on the radio. He smiles when he sees me: Hi, how was your day, dear?

And I don't tell him the truth. I don't tell him that the world's ended, that life as he knows it no longer exists, I've already transformed it into a lie. I just stretch the corners of my mouth, each in their own direction, and show him my teeth; this is what's called a smile.

I lie when I give him my cheek and kiss his in return, I let him put his arms around me and squeeze my waist, his familiar scent blending with the smell of onions, I love him so very much. And yet, I'm still in that other place, that other life, the new one—I know my old life is over, that the world is no longer as it once was, that nothing remains but a crackling, desiccated husk.

It was fine, I lie, and my voice sounds almost normal. We went out to Krýsuvík to see if anything was happening out there.

He gets concerned.

I hope you took precautions. Couldn't it go off at any moment?

No, not immediately. Don't worry about me, I know what I'm doing.

I hope so. You've got to be careful. Those colleagues of yours have a tendency to take leave of their senses.

You know me, I don't take any risks.

I know, sweetheart. I trust you completely. You'd never do anything irrational. I'm just worried about you, don't want you to go falling into a fissure. I don't know what I'd do without you.

He puts his arms around me, presses a kiss onto my forehead.

My brilliant wife, I'm so proud of you. Here, grab a knife, we still have to peel and dice the potatoes.

I wash my hands, tie an apron around my waist and stand beside him at the kitchen counter, our knives chopping in time on the boards, chock chock chock. We cut up potatoes, onions, carrots, fennel, and celeriac; we peel garlic, pick thyme and rosemary leaves from their stems, squeeze lemons and zest them, season the chicken and place it on a bed of vegetables, stick the whole thing in the oven, we don't need a recipe, we know it inside out.

Oh, hey, he says then, smacking his forehead. I forgot to tell you that the picture arrived this morning. From that guy, the photographer. He sent it by taxi.

Oh yeah?

My voice becomes small and pinched.

Come see, it's waiting for you.

We go into the living room, he removes the thick butcher paper from around the picture. Leans it up against the wall and looks at it, pondering for a moment, then turns to me with a smile.

It's fantastic, Anna. It's going to look great in here. It'll fit perfectly on the main wall. He's good, that guy.

I should say something, or else just die, turn into a pillar of salt and blow away in the wind, but I don't, I just smile, stiff and lopsided: Yeah, it's pretty nice.

He gets a drill, a tape measure, and a level, marks the wall and hangs the picture, grave and competent, then puts his arm around my shoulders, happily regarding the fruits of his labor.

Really, it's great, he says, kissing me on the forehead before hurrying back into the kitchen to set the table.

I linger behind, gaze at the picture, it's a meter and a half tall and just as wide, the smoke plume from Kerlingargosið printed on canvas and stretched into a frame. It's made it onto the wall of my tasteful living room, ash-gray clouds of destruction now hang over my sofa, and I hate this picture with my whole sad and deceitful heart, I long to rip it to shreds and stamp it into a pulp, sweep the ribbons from the house.

But, of course, I don't.

I have become two women. One of them walks around the house as she did before, collects socks from the floor, changes out the towels in the bathroom, runs a hand over my daughter's head and asks whether she should practice her piano, empties the washing machine and chats with my husband, listens to him talk about his job, about the case he thinks he lost in the Court of Appeal; the other woman lies in the arms of another man on a shabby futon, their lips touch, he strokes her cheek, she closes her eyes and smiles, her heart sings for joy at the same time that it bursts from sadness.

I love you, says my husband and wipes off the kitchen table, I love you, says the man I love and kisses me on the neck, I've loved you from the first moment I saw you, fell in love with you on sight that day in the helicopter.

You're the end of the world, you destroy everything, I say, and my husband turns around from the oven and looks at me surprised: What did you say?

It's not the end of the world if you lose a case, I say, hastily separating the two worlds, becoming his wife once again, acting as though life goes on.

And go on life simply must. That was a momentary lapse, an accident, a shameful blip in a beautiful and bounteous marriage. I will never see Tómas Adler again, I'll never again let him distract me. I'll set this incident aside and sequester it in my mind, in a locked chamber of my heart. My feelings are irresponsible, irrational, I will make the effort and stop this nonsense; I am a responsible, grown woman, I make morally correct decisions.

I care deeply about my family, my husband, my home. I am happy. I live a good and comfortable life. I'm not going to let anything ruin that. Not even love.

SIX-HUNDRED-THREAD-COUNT SILK DAMASK

I wake with a start when she strokes my hair, runs a finger along my cheek. She's sitting on the end of the bed, redolent of cigarettes and a heavy, sweet perfume, patchouli and sandalwood; I can make out her smile in the half light and am filled with an unbridled fear.

What are you doing? I stammer, sitting up in bed and pulling the blanket to my chin. You'll wake my husband.

Don't worry, she whispers. He biked fifty miles yesterday, he's sleeping the sleep of the just. Meanwhile, here you lie, wide awake.

She runs a hand over my duvet, fondling the stitchwork along the edge and looking around, teeth glinting.

Spare no expense, you two, she whispers. Everything so simple and elegant. Six-hundred-thread-count silk damask on the bed, an orthopedic mattress with customizable head and foot, nice blackout curtains—it's all perfect, really.

She slips a hand under the blanket and pinches my thigh, hard: But there's something missing, isn't there?

That's it. I leap out of bed, throw on a robe as I storm out of the bedroom, dash, swearing, up the stairs and into the foyer, open the front door.

Out! Get out, now, I mean it! Leave me alone!

She takes her time walking down the hall in her lace-up leather boots, red dress, and fake fur coat. Lights a cigarette and takes a deep drag, looks at me through her heavy black eyelashes, an ironic smile playing on her lips.

Have you made up your mind?

She presses herself close to me and her eyes burn, her breasts are hard as torpedoes, her teeth sharp and yellow in her smirking mouth, tobacco smoke wafts around her, I can't catch my breath. She shoves me out of the way and walks out into the summer night, I wake up shaking like a leaf in bed, clammy with sweat, gasping from the nightmare. My husband mumbles something in his sleep and puts his arm around me, I lie still and try to regain control of my breathing, my uncontrollable panic.

She's gone and yet, she's everywhere, it's like she's taken up residence in the walls, her eyes are watching me from the mirrors, it's as if the whole house moves and breathes with her.

TO LOVE IS TO LIVE IN CONSTANT FEAR

To: tomas.adler@gmail.com
From: Anna.Arnardottir@hi.is
Subject: Re: Picture nr. 13 of Kerlingargosið

This has to stop. I can't see you again.

I have a good husband and family, I haven't done right by them, I've behaved irresponsibly. I'm not going to further endanger our happiness.

If I've given you cause to think that we've more than a superficial connection, I apologize—this was a fling, a poorly thought-out dalliance that unfortunately went too far.

I'm asking you: Don't write me, don't call, do not get in touch with me again.

Anna

The six fissure swarms are marked in red on the geological map of southwest Iceland that hangs over my desk. The fissures are short, parallel lines stretching north-northwest, from the tip of the Reykjanes Peninsula all the way east to Lake Þingvallavatn; they cluster around a largely pristine area in the middle, a raised, angry-looking scar on the land. I focus on them, breathe in deep and swallow the sob in my throat, I'm not going to start sniveling, not here at work, not over this foolishness. I close my eyes, grit my teeth, and press enter, send off this loathsome message, open my phone with fumbling hands and look up his name: Tómas Adler, photographer. Block his number, remove his name from my contacts, my life.

Okay. It's done.

I force myself to open the latest earthquake data, yet again. Work is healing, and science should be dependable in the midst of this illogical sadness, but today, it doesn't work. The program compares the quake data to what we're getting from the satellites, calculates the tension in the earth's crust, and under normal circumstances, the model should indicate where the magma has started accumulating under the surface, but these numbers aren't behaving like they ought to. The land rises and then falls again, then rises again somewhere new and on the entirely opposite end of the peninsula, as if there's an enormous beast tossing and turning under the surface and pushing it up in different places whenever it rolls over. The conclusions are illogical, it's maddening.

I shake my head dejectedly, I'm on the verge of giving up. Anytime a decisive pattern appears to be taking shape, I hold my breath, thinking now we've got it, now we've found the magma chamber, but then the swelling subsides, the land falls, and everything goes back to the way it was until a bulge rises in another volcanic system, somewhere else on the peninsula. We know that we're dealing with a chain of events similar to what occurred before the Krafla Fires, but Reykjanes refuses to bow to this well-supported hypothesis, it simply will not allow itself to be managed. Our projection model is deficient.

Like me. Sadness and guilt flood my mind and displace my thoughts, push them out of their logical channels and into some unfamiliar bog that's riddled with dead ends and wrong turns, lose them in desire-tinged morasses and tangled dreams—I've got to shake off this senselessness, got to focus on improving the model.

The computer emits a series of soft clicks, my heart leaps for joy, happiness flows through me, just for a moment, before my agony sets in once more. An unopened envelope appears on the screen, an email from Tómas Adler. I look at it, hesitate, grit my teeth again, grope for the mouse, and move it, unopened, into the trash, change my settings to Block This Contact. Create a trash filter to sieve love from my life.

Despair flows through me like a shock wave, I stand up from the computer, walk around my office, throw my arms around myself and convulse, rock myself like a child and fight back tears. My craving for him is like an addiction, he's like a drug, I just have to get through the first days, and then I'll be free. I just have to think about something else.

I stop in front of the mirror and consider myself in the spotted glass. Love is consuming me like a disease; my cheekbones protrude, my eyes are larger and darker than usual, like deep wells under my dark hair, which has started to fall out in wisps, coiling atop of the white sheets of paper on my desk. The woman in the mirror could be my mother, eroded by smoking, isolation, and poetry. I stroke my drawn face and throat, put a hand under my shirt, hold my belly. It's accommodated two healthy, beautiful human beings but is now as thin as a drumskin stretched between my hip bones; I'm so full of desire and anxiety and shame that I can't keep anything down. I lift my blouse and look at myself in the mirror, the fine stretch marks like filigree around my belly button. In the beginning, they were red and raised, but over time, they've gone grayish white, like spar. I turn in the mirror and look at these traces, threads that run in vertical parallel lines around my middle like a silver belt. I've had them so long that I've stopped noticing them. Almost a quarter of a century, long enough to bring up two kids, get myself through my doctorate and embark on a successful academic career, enter middle age. At first, the marks engendered shock and misery, I'd found it strange enough to watch my body bulge, strip me of power, and although that really didn't happen, it did disorient me. Moreover, I didn't feel a connection to the phenomenon that had taken up residence in my body, it grew and thrived inside me, distended me, left behind these jagged red fissures, seemed to be trying to break through my skin. I'd become the shell encasing another living being, a creature that would, in the fullness of time, explode my body from the inside out in order to enter the world.

It was actually always foreign to me, this body, at best, it acted as a suitable stand for my head. I thought of myself as an intellectual being, reading, thinking, perceiving, I went through the world armed with information, logic, facts, arguments—it was traumatic when my body bloomed and puberty transformed me from a serious and scrawny kid into some kind of walking target with breasts and waist and hips. I was genuinely always surprised when I caught sight of myself in the mirror, that this woman should be me. The greedy glances of men did little for me, it was as though my body stood between them and my intellect.

But then this little spark caught flame and divided itself once, twice, three times, and I never suspected what was in store for me.

What's the worst that could happen, asked Kristinn, sitting there on the sofa all those years ago, before he took my last cigarette from me and snuffed it out. What do you have to lose?

And, of course, my mother was the worst that could happen, I was terrified that she was right, that I was like her, incapable of love. That I'd reject my child like she'd rejected me. But I didn't say it, didn't let the father of my child into that dark corner of my heart, just looked at him and nodded: I'll think about it.

And so, think I did, as my body stripped me of power, inflated me, demanded spinach, pears, pistachios, vomited constantly, brought me to tears and robbed me of sleep, but no counterarguments were forthcoming. In between gagging over the toilet bowl, I read electromagnetics and classical mechanics, tried to teach myself to think like a scientist while my body took me over, turned me into a calving heifer.

The triumph of the flesh over the mind reached its climax when this automated, productive machine disgorged my progeny on its bloody, slimy conveyor belt. A handsome eight-pound, eight-ounce boy, I held him in my arms and looked at his tiny face, his fingers, his shock of hair, sticky with vernix, tears streaming down my cheeks. I loved him, oh, how I loved him, how relieved I was to feel this overwhelming love flooding through me, but it also paralyzed me, filled me with despair. How was I supposed to raise this little person, protect him in a world that was such a horrible place?

I cried because love is the most magnificent, most awful thing that happens to us, it turns the world upside down, robs us of our sense of security and fearlessness, it's a crevasse that opens beneath our feet, an abyss, the terror of losing someone we love. And sitting there, weeping with my newborn child in my arms, I understood: To love is to live in constant fear.

I drag my fingertips across my stomach and look at the map on the wall above me. Think about red fissure swarms and silver-white stretch marks, life roiling under the surface, and all of a sudden, it's as though a blinding light flashes before me, I can see it, and yet it can't be. It defies all logic.

I tuck in my blouse, wrench the door open, and call: Ebba, can I have a word with you?

Elísabet comes in, squinting at me, a concerned expression on her face. Did something happen?

I just had a really strange idea. It's nothing, I'm sure, but I want to run it by you.

What?

What if—I pause and try to put into words this light-filled image that's blossomed in my mind—what if everything we thought we knew about the Reykjanes Peninsula was wrong?

What do you mean?

What if there aren't a bunch of small volcanic systems, like we've always thought? What if it's one big system with many egresses? That's why they're acting so bizarrely, the magma is flowing between them—what if that's why we haven't managed to find it?

Ebba looks at me like I've lost my mind, I drop into my chair and bring up the 3D map of the Reykjanes Peninsula.

We've been looking for mafic magma intrusions under each system. But what if there's a big magma chamber somewhere else, like under Krafla except much deeper, let's say around six miles. And the chamber has . . . side streets . . . under every volcanic system, and the magma erupts through them in turn? Like . . . udders on a cow . . . and the systems on Reykjanes are the teats?

Like udders on a cow? Are you for real? asks Ebba. This flies in the face of everything we know about the Reykjanes Peninsula. Everyone knows that these are clearly demarcated systems that erupt one at a time. None of them have volcanoes that are developed enough to have their own magma chambers.

I know, I say, rubbing my forehead. It just came to me all of a sudden. Maybe I'm talking nonsense. I just don't get it; everything indicates that there's going to be an eruption—the earthquakes, the geothermal activity, the land movement—but we haven't been able to find the right spot, or the magma chamber.

Ebba shrugs: Then maybe Iceland GeoSurvey's theory holds water. That the land is rising and falling due to changes in the geothermal system, not in a magma chamber.

GeoSurvey has geothermal heat on the brain. Their scientists wouldn't retract their theories even if an eruption started right under their noses. And what about the fact that all the lava that's flowed on the peninsula since the ice age glacier vanished is of a similar composition? It's all basalt, which, if you think about it, could mean that it all came from the same magma chamber.

But Anna, there's not a trace of felsic rock until you reach Hengill. And mafic magma evolves and turns felsic in magma chambers.

I know. You don't have to tell me.

The earth's crust is, at most, six miles thick under the peninsula, where would this mysterious magma chamber of yours even fit?

No one knows for sure how thick the earth's crust is under Reykjanes. There're as many theories on that as there're scientists who've researched it.

Can you base a hypothesis on such vague clues? Can you demonstrate it, run the numbers? Update the model?

I shake my head: No, the model doesn't encompass this. No model does, not unless we alter the whole premise, everything we know about volcanic activity in this country. It was just a feeling that came over me, totally out of the blue. I can hear how improbable it is just saying it out loud.

She looks at me strangely: A feeling?

Don't mention this to anyone, please. I'd be mortified if anyone got wind of this. It was just a spur-of-the-moment thought.

She shrugs: No reason we can't discuss it, try to do the calculations, maybe it would help us clarify the big picture. You could take this to the Advisory Board, get their take?

And become a laughingstock? No, thanks. I'm just going to ask you again not to breathe word of this to a single person, Elísabet. We've got to just keep monitoring all the systems. Increase our surveillance, keep an eye on every spot where an eruption could potentially begin. It could happen anywhere.

But if you're right about this, she says thoughtfully, if this . . . feeling . . . of yours turned out to be correct, then the systems on Reykjanes are much more unpredictable than we've thought.

Forget it. Please, I say. Forget I said anything. I'm just mixing myself up, there's no science behind it, no calculations, nothing.

More unpredictable and much more dangerous.

Keep it to yourself, Elísabet Kaaber. Or I'll never speak to you again.

EXPLANATORY NOTE VII

KRAFLA 1975–84

There's little doubt that the inflation and deflation of the Krafla area is connected to movements of magma. Gravity changes combined with the vertical movements require the transfer of material at least as dense as magma.

Bryndís Brandsdóttir and Páll Einarsson. 1979. "Seismic Activity Associated with the September 1977 Deflation of the Krafla Central Volcano in Northeastern Iceland." *Journal of Volcanology and Geothermal Research,* vol. 6 (3).

Volcanic eruptions don't happen out of nowhere, without any warning or advance notice. They always have antecedents, clear and logical causes. Every eruption stems from specific conditions under the earth's crust, and it's the volcanologist's job to analyze those conditions, decipher the clues, and try to anticipate the imminent chain of events. And the location of these events is a matter of vital importance.

Just before Christmas 1975, an eruption began at Mt. Leirhnjúkur, near Krafla. It only lasted twenty minutes, and it left nothing behind but a few foul-smelling mud springs spitting gravel and rocks into the air. Geologist Sigurður Þórarinsson was struck in the head by one such stone, stunning him a little. Afterward, what upset him most was how close he came to being remembered as having lost his life in the smallest, most unremarkable eruption in Icelandic history.

He was devastated, said Dad, shaking with laughter. We started wearing helmets after that.

The smallest, most unremarkable eruption in Icelandic history turned out to be the beginning of the Krafla Fires, which would go on to erupt, at intervals, for just under a decade. They had, however, surprisingly little impact on life in the country. Krafla is located in the back of beyond, you might say, and the nation quickly got used to the idea that the hinterlands were just perpetually on fire. Lava flowed over the grazing land of a few farms in the area of Mývatn and disrupted construction on a geothermal power plant—one of the Bjarnarflagsvirkjun power plant's boreholes actually erupted during the third of the Fires' eruptions, in September 1977, like a chimney rising from hell, spewing incandescent lava many yards into the air. Or that's what we *think* happened, because no one was there to see it when it first started.

That is to say that this particular eruption began five and a half miles to the north, at Krafla itself. Every Jón, Dagur, and Helgi—geoscientists, farmers, and countryfolk—hurried out to the volcano to witness the spectacle, which turned out to be a splendid, tidy little eruption that lasted a few hours. But while everyone was admiring this pageantry, nearly all of the magma underneath the surface was flowing down toward the village before bursting out in a real eruption right under the power plant.

We were in the entirely wrong spot, said Dad, cleaning out his pipe with his pocketknife. Everyone on shift went up to Krafla and left the control center in the basement of Hótel Reykjahlíð completely unmanned. A farmwife named Guðný was the one who informed us about the eruption, she'd been frying doughnuts in the kitchen when her kids came in and told her that the earthquake monitors were going berserk, they'd been playing down there when the eruption began, prescient little tykes. I swear, I don't know what we were thinking, he said, shaking his head. But it taught us a lesson, that much is certain. Volcanoes are unpredictable. An eruption in one place doesn't preclude the possibility of another one somewhere else.

I was almost five weeks old when the Krafla Fires began and had been christened Anna, in honor of my paternal grandmother and Anna Akhmatova, my mother's favorite poet, two birds with one stone. Dad was a man of his generation, he left his wife and baby and went north to research. He put forth the first theories about rift-zone activity in the Krafla area, described the way the land rose and fell, diverged, shook, and ripped apart again and again, how the magma flowed up out of the mantle, into the chamber in the earth's crust, and then out of it again in bursts. His writing is concise and neutral, but when I read the articles today, it seems to me like he's describing a body—a living, bleeding, breathing earth. I look at the tables over his measurement results and see before me a relentless beating, the blood flowing into the heart and out of it again, the veins dilating and contracting once more.

The messages were first delivered via the only phone on site, located in the control room of the Krafla power plant, a few weeks after the first eruption. They were then conveyed over to Leirhnjúkur Crater, not far from Krafla herself: some kind of family emergency, illness or accident, but no one in Reykjavík would pick up the phone. Dad swore, shuffled his feet and racked his brain with the phone receiver in hand, but in the end, it was clear to him that he had to leave Krafla and go back south. I don't know what thoughts were running through his mind in the jeep on the way to the airport in Aðaldalur Valley, where a supply plane was waiting for him—something about the pros and cons of single life weighed against marriage and having a child in your fifties, I expect—but south he flew to find me safe and sound and sleeping in a rocker with Solveig, our downstairs neighbor. My mother had been checked into the hospital's psychiatric ward.

The birth had taken a toll on her, my father told me apologetically sometime later. It wasn't your fault, Stubby. Back then, they thought it wasn't advisable to visit people in the hospital, least of all psychiatric patients.

He didn't like to talk about it much, but this I know: that when he came to pick her up at the hospital, she was gone, had simply packed her clothes into a suitcase and books into a box, rented a room in a guesthouse, and bought a plane ticket to Stockholm; she took a ferry from there to Saint Petersburg a few days later and didn't come back home until just before my fifth birthday.

I think about this sometimes, the fact that both my parents abandoned me in the first few weeks of my life. My father could use the accepted gender roles of the time as a cover; my mother lost her mind. But she did do me the favor of sending Dad back home to me, forcing him to shoulder the responsibility he'd clearly found as absurd as the idea that she'd expect him to start laying eggs. Solveig and a long line of housekeepers and nannies of varying degrees of tenderness helped him bring me up, but he was my sun, the center of my universe. I didn't actually miss her, I was a daddy's girl.

The burning heart under Krafla beat twenty times. Fifteen of those beats saw considerable lateral magma movement under the surface, three much less, and two even less still. Nine of the biggest reached the surface and turned into eruptions, one a year on average. These events were my father's primary area of focus while they were taking place, his legacy in geological history, and he mourned the Fires when they ended, unexpectedly and quickly.

AND THEN THERE'S ALWAYS THE POSSIBILITY WE GO TO BLACK

It's important to realize that models seldom give an accurate picture of reality, but they are helpful in understanding it. Which is why all models need to be taken with caution.

Ólafur G. Flóvenz. February 12, 2020. Internal memo, Iceland GeoSurvey.

I'll almost be relieved when this thing finally starts, ha. Be nice to get it over with.

The national commissioner stretches nearly to the point of bursting the brass buttons off his expansive chest, he's smiling from ear to sunburnt ear, seems likely that when he got the call, when a 5.0 magnitude earthquake rattled through the capital region, he was drinking a few beers and grilling, as is to be expected on a sunny summer night.

Get it over with? Do you think there's a particular reason to celebrate the fact that an eruption might be starting just a scant few miles from the capital?

Júlíus from the Met Office narrows his eyes at the tipsy and highest-ranking Civil Protection official in the country. The Scientific Council has convened in the coordination center and is trying to come to a consensus on when this much-augured event will finally come to pass.

Let's go over it again, says Milan in his soft-spoken way, running a hand across his gray buzz cut. Anna, what's the situation at present?

The situation's this, I say, opening my laptop and connecting it to the screen. The quakes and land rise that have been inching forward and backward along the Reykjanes Peninsula seem to be reaching their apex just east of Sveifluháls Ridge, between the Krýsuvík and Seltún geothermal areas. These developments could, of course, come to an end without an eruption, it could be harmless lateral magma movement, but our latest models indicate it's likely that the magma will break through to the surface. And if things continue apace, this could occur within the next few days.

Would you review the scenarios that you all think are the most likely?

There are three. The first anticipates a magma intrusion, the second a minor eruption, and the third a medium-sized fissure eruption. Based on our mathematical models, the earthquakes, land uplift, and historical precedent, we think there's an up to fifty percent chance that we'll have a rather small Hawaiian fissure eruption, probably in the vicinity of Krýsuvík. If this is the case, the lava would flow south along the water catchment area and toward the sea. The models predict that we'd have a maximum of four days to act before the lava would be anywhere near Rte. 427, which runs along the southern coast of the peninsula, as you all know. The magma in this area is always mafic, which is good news, although we can never entirely rule out the possibility that we'll end up with some felsic garbage.

Felsic garbage? Mister Silk Tie from the Ministry of Justice looks at me uncomprehendingly. What happens then?

Then we could end up with a phreatic eruption. The magma will acidify and become more viscous as it accumulates, such that if it's been biding its time under the crust, it has the potential to erupt explosively, even though magma on the Reykjanes Peninsula is generally mafic and tends to have a low viscosity. Mafic and low viscosity: that's by far the likeliest outcome. But then we also need to allow for the possibility that the lava will come into contact with a considerable quantity of water, particularly in the hot spring area at Krýsuvík. We must always be prepared for some explosive activity, although I think it's unlikely that that would characterize this eruption. With all this in mind, I think we should plan for a fissure eruption of a medium size, just to be on the safe side.

But is that enough? asks Júlíus. Shouldn't we plan for a major eruption, just to be absolutely sure?

There's nothing in the data that points to this turning into a significant disaster. Even taking into account all the known variations in this equation, we can still expect a rather small and harmless eruption, I say and shrug. But, of course, it's always better to be prepared for all eventualities.

Milan is thoughtful: We've been at Alert Phase since last week, because of the earthquakes. The question now is whether we should keep it there or go up to Emergency Phase.

The national commissioner laughs derisively: Emergency Phase? Now? Are you sure you don't just want to go straight to Black?

Black? questions Sigríður María, wrinkling her freckled brow. What does that mean?

Black is the fourth level. We don't talk about it a lot publicly, says Milan. It encompasses our contingency plan for circumstances that threaten the safety of the nation. Nuclear attack, foreign invasion, life-threatening disasters.

What happens if we go to . . . Black?

We'd potentially need to evacuate the entire southwestern region. Move the better part of the nation out of their homes in order to guarantee the safety of the general populace.

The director of the Travel Industry Association looks at us in turn, blinking her ice-blue eyes.

Move everyone out of their homes? Where would they go? Didn't you say it's impossible to evacuate the capital area? That there isn't room for city residents elsewhere in the country?

That's absolutely correct, says Milan. But we have an emergency plan, of course. We'd need to get people to Akureyri and form an air bridge to transport them out of the country. We have standing agreements with the other Nordics and Canada, but hopefully, we won't ever have to activate them. No one wants to move two-thirds of the population to refugee camps in Esbjerg or Tromsø. Or Gander in Newfoundland if an eruption were to prevent eastward air traffic.

No, says Stefán. That would be a bit much. If the geoscientists think this'll be a rather small eruption.

The problem is, we don't know for sure, I say. All the data points to this being a traditional little fissure eruption with a comfortably slow lava flow, but we're having a hard time determining where the lava's coming from. And the Krýsuvík swarm runs almost all the way into the capital area.

Alright, alright. Are you university types always so optimistic?

The national commissioner scratches the back of his neck and smiles at us, he wants to get back home to his grill. If you all think that the most likely outcome is a minor effusive eruption, why not just stay at Alert Phase for now? Wait and see what happens?

I think the best thing would be for us to go to Emergency Phase, says Júlíus. I think we should evacuate the area around Krýsuvík and put Rtes. 41 and 427 on around-the-clock watch. This isn't the time to be taking unnecessary risks.

Milan looks at me: Anna?

I look at the map and the recent series of seismic events yet again before replying: Everything seems to be by the book. I think we should stay at Alert Phase and wait for developments. There's no point in announcing an Emergency Phase too early—people will stop paying attention to it.

The national commissioner smiles, relieved, and stands up from the table: Let's say that, then. It's good to still have a card up our sleeve.

FAGRADALSFJALL SHAKES
AND SO DO WE

Over 1,700 earthquakes have been measured at
Fagradalsfjall since last night. The strongest occurred at
11:36 p.m. and had a magnitude of 5.1. Numerous after-
shocks have been measured, the strongest of which were
4.6 at 5:46 a.m. and 4.3 at 6:23 a.m. today. In addition,
22 earthquakes of a magnitude higher than 3.0 have been
measured since midnight. The strongest earthquakes were
reported to have been felt as far as Akranes to the west and
Vík in the south. This wave of seismic activity is ongoing
and likely connected to impending lateral magma movement or the eruption that Civil Protection has advised may
occur in Krýsuvík.

The Icelandic Met Office. "Seismic Activity at Mt.
Fagradalsfjall."

Mt. Fagradalsfjall shakes, and we shake with it. We shake and we wait for
this long-foretold eruption, the land shakes and houses quiver enough
to make glasses and chandeliers rattle, horses bolt and dogs howl, cats
hiss and crawl under the furniture. The whole capital shudders, panes

shatter in the windows of the old church in Grindavík, a few wine bottles tumble onto the floor and shatter in a little coffeehouse near the harbor, Rte. 427 splits apart, and the utility companies are in a constant battle to keep the water on in Keflavík and Njarðvík. Our tightly woven net of seismographs projects each palpitation onto the Met's earthquake map; they are constantly, perpetually writing out—almost in real time—swarms of red circles, indicating an earthquake occurred less than four hours ago, and green stars, indicating those quakes had a magnitude of 3.0 or higher. But people have grown accustomed to all this commotion, they hardly look up except to glance around and mutter, that was a big one, before turning back to their grilling and hedge clipping.

It's the height of summer vacation season, and people make their getaways: to Alicante and Tenerife, to summerhouses around Lake Þingvallavatn, to the countryside farther north. I encourage my husband to make such an escape, go to our summerhouse, but he doesn't want to, it won't be any fun if you don't come, too, says Salka.

And although I hesitate to even admit it to myself, I'm relieved to have an excuse to not be home, seek solace in my work from morning till night, hunch over models and run calculations late into the evening.

My beloved, hardworking wife, you can't save the world if you kill yourself working, says my husband when I stand up from the kitchen table, thank him for breakfast, and tell him not to wait on me for dinner, I've got to work late.

This is just for the moment, I say, putting on my raincoat. You know how it is. We'll do something as a family when it's over.

When what is over? I ask myself in the car on the way into the city. Tómas is still there, a hard, painful knot in my stomach, a hitch in my throat, his scent still fills my nostrils, I can still feel his skin on mine. I'm waiting to recover from him, like an illness, I tell myself over and over again that it's just going to take some time to get him out of my system. It's like detoxing, I intone, I've got to be able to stop loving because I managed to quit smoking. The sadness will subside, the longing ease with time, and in the end, I'll stop feeling like I'm sitting at the bottom of a deep well, denying myself a glimpse of the light.

It's been weeks since I shut him out, ordered him to forget me, and yet, here he is, standing outside my office door on this rain-drenched Tuesday in July. The rain is gratefully received, it rinses the ash from the walls of our homes and down into the grass, it pelts the glass roof of the earth sciences building at the university like a thousand fingers on a drumskin. The university is empty but for the geoscience department, which buzzes with activity, seismographs, and a steady flow of foot traffic. I'm expecting a group of foreign scientists and stand up when I hear a knock at the door, open it with my widest smile, and then it's him who's standing there, and I almost fall over from surprise and happiness, and then I'm furious, that he should have the gall! He smiles, but there's no laughter in his eyes. It's almost like he's taken off his hat and is holding it apologetically over his heart, but it's not a hat he has in his hands but rather a thick paperboard folder.

What do you want?

These are the photos, he says and hands me the folder, he's speaking loudly, as though to make sure that the students in the hallway will hear him.

What photos, damn it?

He lowers his voice: Anna, please. Please let me talk to you. I have to talk to you. You don't answer my emails, you don't pick up the phone. We have to talk.

I open my mouth to say no, we have nothing to discuss, to tell him to leave and never come back, but all of a sudden he's come in and closed the door; he extends his hands to me, and the world vanishes. Nothing exists except this dizzying void and we two in the middle of it, in this kiss, this embrace. It drowns out the weak voice of reason that's whining its reedy protests, my steadfast will snaps like a twig in a glacial flood. I fumble for his belt buckle, he yanks up my skirt, and we make love—no, we rut like animals on my desk, on top of my printouts of earthquake maps, drawing compasses, and glow-in-the-dark highlighters, his head knocks into the desk lamp, a button pops from my blouse and flies through the dusty air of my office to land on the bookshelf with a click.

Fagradalsfjall shakes and so do we, the two women I've become; one is weeping with pleasure, the other with horror, thinking about her husband and her children, her colleagues and the foreign visitors, hoping that our moans can't be heard through the thin walls, that no one will have any business that brings them through the unlocked door.

He lets out a half-smothered cry when he comes, and I cover his mouth, shh, ástin mín, quiet, they'll hear us, I'm taken up short by the tenderness in my voice. He closes his eyes, when he opens them again, they're brimming with tears.

I'm sorry, he says then, almost like he means it. Because I'm crying, too, out of happiness and anguish and mortification, push him off of me with trembling hands, pull up my underwear and tights, smooth my skirt, slip into my shoes and stumble to the mirror, try to fix my hair. The face in the mirror is pure turmoil, its eyes deep hollows of despair.

Anna, he says. Talk to me.

Right, because that always goes so well, I say bitterly. Our conversations always end like this. You are destroying me. You're destroying my happiness.

It's not real happiness, he says. You're living a lie.

He's standing in the middle of the room and tucking his shirt into his jeans, full of puppyish self-confidence, he wants me to throw everything away and follow him. I want to murder him.

How dare you say such things to me? I asked you to leave me alone, I told you to stop writing, stop calling, and you didn't respect that. You pursue me, day after day, week after week. You show up here at my place of work and put my security and my whole life at risk, you . . . you're stalking me!

Stalking you? What? He shakes his head. Did I rape you too?

You don't respect my boundaries.

Boundaries? What are you talking about? You love me and I love you! I can't live without you, and you can't live without me. Look at the two of us! We can't control ourselves. You're no better than me!

Tómas, this is madness. I'm married. I have a good, kind man, wonderful kids, I love my family, I live a good life. Why should I throw all that away?

Because it's a sham, and you know it. You play your part so well that you've started to believe it yourself. You love me, not him. How can you stay married to him?

You can talk. You, who have nothing to lose, you don't have a wife, you don't have a family. Squat in that storage shed of yours, living your broke bohemian life, thinking *of course* I should throw everything away to share that with you. You've got nothing to offer, you own nothing—not even a car!

He laughs. Not even a car! Is that the problem? That I'm not rich enough for you?

No, of course not, I say, hiding my face in my hands. You're just so . . . irresponsible. Like a teenager.

He shrugs: But it's never boring, right? You're not thinking about money when we're making love. Love doesn't need a car, it can fly.

Oh, give it a rest, I'm serious. I can't let my life and my family's fate be ruled by feelings. This isn't like me, I'm a rational person.

He shakes his head and laughs: Anna, you aren't *just* a rational person. You effervesce and crackle with feelings, they boil up inside you, shoot out in all directions. That's what I love about you. I love how passionately you love, how you fly into a fury, how you tear up when you're happy. You *don't* in fact let yourself be ruled by rationality, and what's least rational of all is that you believe, in all sincerity, that you are not an emotional being. It's so absurd it's heartbreakingly beautiful.

He walks up to me and strokes my cheek, takes a lock of hair and tucks it behind my ear. I try to shove him off, tell him to go, but my words turn to sobs, my hands come to rest on his chest, I can't push him away.

What made you like this? he asks. Why are you so afraid to love?

And what can I say? That I've always thought that love was a positive and generative force, something that brings people together, brings them happiness? You just have to make an effort, just a little, to be considerate, and behave like a human being, share your terms and feelings, and then everything'll be fine? My husband and I are friends, we wish each other well, what more can a person ask for? Is that not the recipe for a happy life, a successful marriage? Why isn't that enough, why can't that be love, I ask in despair, and then I have my answer:

Because love doesn't give a damn about concepts like goodness and fairness and justice. You can live in harmony with God and men for decades, have children and a beautiful home, pay down your debts, cultivate a garden, bake bread and invite friends over for dinner, live a lovely and secure and happy life, but then right when you think you've overcome the biggest hurdles, right when you've started thinking about retirement, pensions, that's when love appears out of nowhere and shows you its true nature. And love's no kitten, oh no. It's a searing-hot supernova, with fangs and claws and a tail that it whips around, leveling everything that crosses its path. It's a comet that comes crashing into earth, throwing it off course, changing its axial tilt and reversing its polarity, flipping the entire world upside down so that suddenly our well-trod paths simply no longer exist but rather end in the void, and now I'm plummeting in outer space, falling, falling, falling, and nothing can catch me except the man I love, the man with the green eyes and the lopsided smile, my love and my lover.

I touch Tómas Adler, I run my fingertips along his smile lines and stubble and the spot behind his ear that's surprisingly soft, I kiss his lips and tears course down my cheeks, because this beautiful world is so new and unfamiliar. The old world stands in crumbling ruins, everything that I held most sacred has been destroyed and it was me myself who ruined it, trampled it underfoot and dishonored it, betrayed all that I'd lived and fought for.

My home, my family, my children. My beloved, kind, good husband.

Poets can prattle on about love, but I know her, I've seen her at work. Love is nothing but a natural disaster.

This was the love that came for me.

KRÝSUVÍK

N 63°53'43" W 22 °03'22"

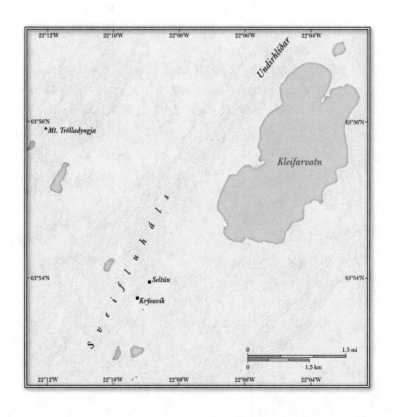

The Krýsuvík system is approximately five miles wide and at least 31 miles long. It contains two eruption and fissure swarms, which take their names from the Sveifluháls ridge and Mt. Trölladyngja, respectively. The third eruption site, at the Krýsuvík geothermal area, differs from the others in both the kind of volcano present and the level of volcanic activity. Namely, the Krýsuvík system has the makings of a central volcano.

Almost directly northeast of Reykjavík, this system's fissure swarms are clearly delineated by ravines and fault lines. A new residential neighborhood built there this year extends into it. The capital area gets both hot and cold water from fissure swarms in the Krýsuvík system.

Kristján Sæmundsson and Magnús Á. Sigurgeirsson. 2013. "The Reykjanes Peninsula." In *Natural Hazards in Iceland: Volcanoes and Earthquakes*, ed. Júlíus Sólnes. Reykjavík: University of Iceland Press.

A PERFECT LITTLE TOURIST
ERUPTION

Effusive eruptions are known as *flæðigos* or *hraungos* in Icelandic. There are two kinds of effusive eruptions. These are either eruptions along fissures which range from several to dozens of miles in length or, on the other hand, *dyngjugos*, or lava shield eruptions, in which the magma predominantly issues from a single eruption vent. Jets of white-hot magma clumps will spew dozens or even hundreds of yards up from the eruption vent, but the ash plume for an eruption like this is, for the most part, composed of volcanic gases and steam.

Kristján Sæmundsson and Magnús Á. Sigurgeirsson. 2013. "The Internal Structure of Volcanoes." In *Natural Hazards in Iceland: Volcanoes and Earthquakes*, ed. Júlíus Sólnes. Reykjavík: University of Iceland Press.

The volcanic eruption at Krýsuvík heralds its arrival with the protocol and advance notice befitting a foreign diplomat. The magma travels with intense seismic activity for around half a mile before the eruption opens right next to the tourist area at Seltún, just before dinnertime on

Thursday, July 16, and begins completely by the book, ceremoniously and courteously, almost as if apologizing for creating this disturbance and making the reasonable demand that the area be closed to the public at a moment's notice.

We are nearly able to count down to it like a space launch, we watch the land swelling up and the water table drop; the hissing heads of new hot springs pop up around the visitor center; one of them opens right underneath the café, the eruption jet shooting straight up out of the hot dog vat, but everyone manages to vacate in plenty of time, sullen drivers shuttle away all the tourists. The earthquakes occur in regular bursts, which then ease off and turn into the mumbling of volcanic unrest, the rumbling baritone of the volcano.

The spectacle doesn't disappoint expectations; it looks beautiful and dignified from the surrounding vantage points—even from the capital. Glowing red jets spew into the bright summer sky, and black tongues of lava crawl slowly and determinedly southwest, away from the city and toward the sea, exactly as the models predicted. This is almost too good to be true: the only man-made structure that appears to be in imminent danger is a couple hundred yards' stretch of Rte. 427.

A perfect little tourist eruption, says the director of the Tourism Industry Association as we stand together on a mountainside to witness it in all its glory. The size, the location—we couldn't have gotten any luckier.

Sigríður María warmed up on our hike up the mountainside, she's taken off her fleece, crossed her muscular, sunbrowned arms over her neon-pink athletic shirt, and is veritably glowing with satisfaction. And it's easy to be moved by this eruption on such a beautiful summer day: bloodred columns of lava shooting into the sunshine; heat shimmering, mirage-like, from the surface of the black lava, willowy and glinting like quicksilver; the surrounding valley is emerald green, and to the south, the sea is the bluest of blues. The grandeur of it strikes the Scientific Council dumb, a sight like this makes you realize just how beautiful the earth is and how small you are in relation to it, we're all equal here, all living creatures, from *Homo sapiens* to the ground beetle scrabbling through the grass, our entire existence is but the blink of an eye, an insipid film on the surface of our mighty mother, who's opening herself to us in all her awful majesty.

Nice spot for a viewing platform, says Sigríður María. Enough room for a parking lot and a gift shop.

Have you taken leave of your senses? I ask, shocked. A mile from the eruption site?

She turns to me, sizing me up with her ice-blue eyes. Travel agencies can barely keep up with the bookings, and the hotels are finally filling up. This eruption is coming at the best possible time, it's exactly what we need to get the jump on other tourist destinations post-pandemic. People want to experience something unique, unlike anything they've ever seen. Venice and the Acropolis are old hat, while a volcanic eruption on the outskirts of Reykjavík—that's something new and exciting. The Keflavík airport is open, airlines are lining up out the door, our tourists are getting a direct hit, straight to the bloodstream. Passengers on the flight from the US can book a stopover sightseeing tour to the eruption and a glass of champagne at the Blue Lagoon, they'll be tempted to stay a night. We'll resurrect the tourism industry, thanks to the Krýsuvík eruption.

This has all happened without incident so far, says Milan. But you need to speak to your people. We've had a number of reports that the barricades aren't being respected and tourists are being taken all the way up to the edge of the lava.

The current area restrictions are absurd, says Sigríður María, furrowing her plucked brow. A six-mile radius? The eruption isn't the least bit dangerous, just something nice for our tourists to look at. And we've got to be offering something more than a sightseeing tour that stops six miles away. We can't sell the eruption like that. People pay to feel the heat, to come into contact with it. They want to experience it, not just see it.

This isn't an amusement park, I say. Volcanic eruptions are some of the most dangerous and unpredictable events on earth, we have to show them respect.

Not an amusement park, eh? Except for you scientists? You ignore every closure, all of you, whole busloads of you and your blue-eyed students and foreign guests, parading around like kings and lapping up the attention. But when the tourism industry wants a bite of the cake, suddenly you're worried about safety and civil protection.

We're professionals, I say. The eruption might change its behavior without warning, the average Joe can't read the conditions and foresee that. And I frankly see no reason to let the general public so far into the eruption area.

Money! shouts Sigríður María. We are going to rake in the krónur, create new jobs! Iceland is going to be the most sought-after tourist destination in Europe. And we can vastly increase our earnings by allowing people to get all the way up to the eruption, letting them experience it. Helicopter tours, weddings, Michelin-star restaurants on the edge of the lava, steak and lobster grilled in its glowing embers, site visits guided by leading scientists—the possibilities are endless.

It's a valid perspective, says Stefán, unzipping his parka. And wouldn't you know it: he's wearing a suit underneath. We can't forget the people who live here. This could mean thousands of new jobs. The Krýsuvík eruption could breathe new life into the economy, just like Eyjafjallajökull did after the crash. We can't restrict our possibilities without reason. This eruption won't last forever, and the nation needs to capitalize on it as long as it's able. What we earn here is part of the GDP, and we can certainly use the revenue. I'll remind you that the Kerlingargosið eruption cost us at least three billion krónur, and the pandemic three times that.

He looks at us like we're personally responsible for these expenses and are obliged to repay him, preferably with interest.

We need to seize this opportunity, he adds.

Júlíus from the Met Office shakes his scruffy head, he's wearing a holey *lopapeysa* under his brightly colored windbreaker and is the only one who doesn't seem particularly enthused by the eruption.

And so what if a few tourists are killed along the way, eh? Just the necessary trade-off for jobs and money, am I getting that right?

There's no danger! shouts Sigríður María. This eruption is zilch! Nothing! Nada! You've all said so yourselves!

This isn't an emergency situation as it stands, I say. But that could change. The eruption could move to a new location. Ravines could open, the earth could literally swallow people. Lava could come into contact with groundwater, creating explosions and burning ashfall.

Júlíus lifts a quivering finger: Do any of you remember the eruption on White Island in New Zealand? Seventeen dead, whole families wiped out, and dozens in the hospital with severe burns, disfigured from the burning ash that rained down upon them. And all because some mercenary travel company decided to ignore geoscientists' advice and make a profit off of those unfortunate tourists. Seize the opportunity.

That obviously wouldn't be good for the tourism industry in the long term, says Stefán thoughtfully. It would reduce our earning potential. Maybe this Doomsday prophet has a point.

I shoot Júlíus a warning look, don't want him to lose it and storm off, abandoning me with politics and GDP.

But the main danger is gas pollution, especially carbon dioxide, I say. We've been lucky up to now, the levels have been low so far, but again, that could change. And if it does, we may be forced to evacuate a large part of the capital area if the wind direction isn't on our side. The 2014 Holuhraun eruption occurred in the middle of the central highlands, and we still had to order people all over the country to stay indoors for a time. Don't you remember that blue haze that hung over the capital area? The sulfur pollution in Höfn reached twenty thousand micrograms per cubic meter, which is the most pollution we've ever measured in a populated area in Iceland.

The Holuhraun eruption was, of course, much bigger than this, says Milan. Is there reason to be concerned about that much gas pollution now?

I shrug: We don't know. Don't have a clue. But you wouldn't want to be sitting up here with a group of foreign tourists on the edge of the lava when clouds of hydrogen sulfide or carbon dioxide form. It's hard to sell tourists anything if they're dead.

This shuts them up.

You're always so negative, says Sigríður María after a moment. All of you. Icelandic nature has always been dangerous and unpredictable. That's what makes it so exciting.

But then there are the jobs, says Stefán thoughtfully. We have an ethical obligation to use every opportunity we have to create new jobs. We've got to be able to reach an agreement, create a stronger system for monitoring the area so we'd be able to evacuate on short notice.

He looks at Milan, Júlíus, and me.

Economic issues are also civil protection issues, he says. We all have a responsibility to utilize our land in a lucrative and logical way.

And in the end, we give in, allow the viewing platform and bus tours to the eruption site. Nearly a billion krónur toward increased surveillance of eruption sites throughout the Reykjanes Peninsula, additional funding for the Met Office, the Institute for Earth Sciences, and Civil Protection, more gadgets and more employees to monitor them. This is the most logical thing for us to do under the circumstances, I know that—everyone profits from this arrangement—but there's still something in the back of my mind, warning me like a muffled alarm cry, something telling me to get away from here as fast as my feet will carry me.

EXPLANATORY NOTE VIII

REYKJAVÍK DOLERITE

Reykjavík dolerite forms the bedrock under the better part of the capital area, all the way from Engey and Viðey islands in the Kollafjörður bay north of the city to Álftanes peninsula in the south. Its origins are unknown. Most of the fissures and faults in the capital's bedrock are connected to the Krýsuvík fissure swarm, which runs northeast around Elliðavatn and Rauðavatn lakes.

Árni Hjartarson. 2005. "A Tunnel in the Capital Area." Iceland GeoSurvey, report on behalf of the Icelandic Road and Coastal Authority.

We were together when the Krýsuvík eruption began, we were holding hands and felt the land swell and shake beneath our feet, when it opened up with something like a sigh and sent a comely little plume of ash into the sky. Fountains of lava spurted out of the fissure, shyly at first but then picking up speed, cheerful red splashes of untempered earth. He was open-mouthed, like a small child, and I was moved, even though I knew what to expect.

An eruption can start almost anywhere on an eruption belt at any time—generally, in this volcanic arcadia rising out of the sea we call our country, at three-to-five-year intervals—and yet it's like our senses reject what they're witness to when the earth opens and fire gushes from its depths. It's as though we're witnessing a miracle, a supernatural wonder that changes the way we look at the world, despite the fact that a volcanic eruption is the most primordial, most natural phenomenon on our planet. Other than giving birth, that is, birth being the other supernatural miracle that we witness, gasping and lost for words every time a new human being enters the world. There are 250 children born on planet Earth each minute, compared to 500 volcanoes erupting every century, and yet this marvel still refuses to bow its head to the yoke of the commonplace.

I don't believe in God, I believe in the power of nature. It was she that I looked to when I gave birth to my children, I pitted her laws against the tumult and pain of my contractions. She is what my mind focused on while my body was torn apart, calculating resistance and viscosity, the way the earth's crust rises above a magma chamber, how the land slides apart and the shaking increases until the quakes make it known that the time has come and the eruption starts, the magma forces its way through the layers of earth in the eruption channel and up to the surface. I kept a death grip on my husband's hand, squeezed my eyes shut, and focused on the forces beneath me, under the mattress and the bed and the floor, I charted my course down through the basement and the foundation, through the soft, thick soil, the coarse gravel, and then the sheet of rock under the hospital, dearly beloved Reykjavík dolerite. My mind caressed the names of different kinds of rocks and minerals—olivine, andesite and gabbro, plagioclase, pyroxene and magnetite—names like magic spells, palliative prayers of redemption from out of the gray mists of antiquity, Anna peperit Mariam, Maria Christum, the forgotten names of all mankind's foremothers who conducted this ancient force through themselves before me. And beneath it all, the mantle plume arose in front of me, fiery and taut, the earth's charged, white-hot core, molten, swollen ore beneath all our feet, the head of the needle that we all dance upon, every last one of us.

It's okay to show some emotion, dear, said the midwife, but that wasn't what I needed down there where I was encased by the hot, healing earth. I writhed with each contraction, and then they slid out of me, soft and strong and alive, smelling of freshly baked bread, and I cried when I took them in my arms.

I'm going to take care of you, I whispered, and laid him on my breast.

I stroked her cheek: I'll never leave you, dear heart, I will protect you, till my dying breath.

$C_8H_{11}NO_3$

This isn't complicated, I say. You're out of your mind, says Tómas.

We're sitting across from one another at a little coffeehouse near the harbor in Grindavík, each with a cup of coffee and open-faced sandwich, his with smoked salmon and chives, mine with egg and shrimp. I thought we wouldn't know anyone here, but the waiter greeted me warmly by name, I've started talking to you about volcanoes and earthquakes on the TV screen, it's good to know there's such a competent person on the job. You'll take good care of us.

I smile stiffly and thank him for his trust, pay for the coffees and carry them over to the table where my lover's sitting, my hands shaking so much that the coffee splashes into the saucers. He's wearing a leather jacket, his helmet and gloves on the seat next to him, I'm in my Gore-Tex jacket and hiking pants, told my husband that I was going to Krýsuvík for a site visit.

Lucky you, getting to work outside in such nice weather, said my husband, kissing me on the cheek, drive carefully, I bought some stuff to throw on the grill tonight. I mumbled something into the collar of my fleece, ashamed to be telling yet another lie, there are so many now that they've become a part of me, a long row of abscesses under my skin. And here I was thinking I couldn't tell untruths.

But this time will be different.

At any rate, he's right, the weather is gorgeous today, it's one of the few sunny days we've had this strange gray summer; the boats bob merrily in the harbor, and most of the coffeehouse customers are sitting outside with pints of beer, inside, we're left alone in the shade. There's a folder with photos of the eruption on the table between us, like props, evidence to prove this is a work trip, not yet another of my attempts to end my relationship with Tómas Adler.

He's staring at me like he doesn't know if he should be mad or laugh at me.

Do you mean to say you've invited me here to tell me you've found the chemical formula for love? Are you feeling okay?

Love is a relatively simple biological process, I say. I've been reading up on it, everything I can get my hands on. It's simply a question of hormones, neurotransmitters, and time, how long it will take our bodies to process it, how long it will take for us to get over it.

I smile but keep my hands under the table so he won't see how they're shaking. I want to touch him, I haven't seen him in a week, a whole ice age of longing, wakefulness, poor appetite. But today I'm determined and hopeful, I've researched this condition, this strange illness we're grappling with; I know that we can best it, armed with information and sound arguments, if only we're dogged and patient enough.

I crack some pepper over my eggs and place the grinder on the table between us: Look, I say. We love one another, desire one another, but what we're calling desire is, in reality, a flash in the pan, love of the flesh. Lust. A primitive neurological phenomenon, much like hunger and fear, an instinct that all mammals possess and that compels them to reproduce. The brain pours a cocktail of sex hormones and adrenaline out into the bloodstream and creates a desire to mate. It's just animalistic instinct.

I reach for the sugar caddy on the next table and place it beside the pepper grinder.

It's this same instinct that's causing us to be so intensely attracted to one another. The thought of you engenders physical symptoms in me—dizziness, trembling, a sense of well-being—I lose my judgment, I can't eat, I don't sleep. These are sure signs that I'm in love with you.

He smiles tenderly and reaches his hand toward mine, but I yank it back; no, listen to me. This isn't a declaration of love, but a fact. Our brains are saturated with dopamine and noradrenaline, neurotransmitters that control well-being and excitement, while serotonin, the brain's other brake lever, which heightens our instincts and a lack of behavioral control, drops. We are, in other words, entirely in the power of primitive urges, like cats in heat.

How can you talk about love like this? About the way we feel?

Wait, let me finish.

I pick up the saltshaker.

Now things get complicated. I've made a number of momentous and poor decisions in recent weeks. My first mistake was that I didn't stop seeing you when I felt attracted to you. Then I realized this attraction was reciprocated, and I still didn't cut off the relationship. I lost control and I touched you, that was my third mistake, and then I went all the way, I went to your place and . . . we made love. I betrayed my husband, my family, and myself, and I still am, betraying them, as long as I keep seeing you.

I put the salt next to the sugar and the pepper.

My feelings for my husband fall under the third group of neurotransmitters, which control friendship, affection, and lasting bonds. This kind of love is controlled by oxytocin rather than that dangerous blend of dopamine and noradrenaline that draws me to you.

Look, I say. I write on a napkin:

$$C_8 H_{11} NO_3$$

and then hand it to him.

This, I say, this is what's wrong with us.

Anna, he says, but I don't let him interrupt me.

Look, it's not our fault. Yes, we've made poor decisions, but they've just been perfectly natural responses to primitive neurological processes.

Now we have to make a decision. Are we going to put all our faith in these animalistic instincts, hormones, and neurotransmitters? Should I divorce my husband, dissolve my home, and endanger my children's happiness, or should I wait for these neurotransmitter fluctuations to stop, go back to my secure and happy life, and put my faith in oxytocin?

I point at him: And you? Are you going to risk cursing me, bitter and unsatisfied, if this so-called love of ours turns out to just be a temporary metabolic fluctuation? Would you be able to bear the accusations, the guilt, if it came to light that you didn't really love me? We were doing fine before we met, we were happy, we can choose to go back to that, or we can bet on an uncertain future together, based on disturbances in our brains' neurotransmitters.

Anna, you don't understand anything.

Tómas looks at the napkin and shakes his head.

You're so dense. Such an idiot. You, with all your intelligence and talent and university degrees. The smartest person I've ever met. And you need me, a silly artist who never even finished upper secondary, to tell you that love isn't a formula, that our feelings aren't neurotransmitters. I'm not in love with you because of some dopamine fluctuation. I'm in love with you because you're you, because you have a dimple on your left cheek and always tuck your hair behind your ear when you're anxious, just like that. Because of the curve of your back, the little heart-shaped birthmark on your butt. I love your voice, how enthusiastic you are when we make love, the laughter that sometimes shines in your eyes when you're trying to be serious. I even love this absurd literal belief of yours in rationality, the way you try to apply scientific arguments to things that cannot be reasoned with, that won't bow to any learning or intellect. Things that just are, and always have been, and are older than we can imagine, and I could give a damn about all your formulas and logic. I love you with my whole, tormented heart and my life means nothing without you.

My love sits there across from me with the sun in his green eyes and his wild locks falling across his forehead, and I love him, too, with every fiber of my whole, ruined, wretched being.

Your heart, I say in a broken voice, is just a muscle that pumps blood through your body.

You're right, he says, tugging the collar of his shirt down, taking my hand and placing it on his chest.

Here, he says, do you feel it beating? It pumps every last drop of that blood for you, just for you.

I close my eyes, and then we both go out to my car, drive to an out-of-the-way spot near Mt. Þorbjörn and make love in the heather, mounds of lava at our backs and the sun in our eyes, fine ash swirling up and falling over us, I look up into the bright blue sky and sob with hopelessness; my heart is falling to pieces with love.

LOVE IS WORSE THAN DEATH

It's late August when I tell my husband that I'm in love with another man.

We go on a walk through the wood next to our house, it's raining, and the heather and twigs snap under the heavy wet leaves. He knows something terrible is coming when I ask him to come with me; gives me a questioning look, knows me well enough to hear the quaver in my voice. We're done with dinner and cleaning up, rinsing the plates and putting them in the dishwasher while our everyday conversation flows without effort, comfortable chatter about phone calls and the projects of the day, insignificant work incidents, commentaries, trifles, peanuts, and the whole time, this merciless knowledge is drumming in the back of my head: The time has come, it can't be avoided, you have to tell him.

I wish I could say that it was my conscience and guilt that overpowered me and forced me to admit everything, put an end to the lies and my double life, but that isn't the case. The two women I've become comfortably cohabitate in my body; one of them keeps living my old life as if nothing is wrong, reads to my daughter, cooks, makes sandwiches and fluffs the pillows on the couch, kisses my husband on the cheek, laughs with him and buys him a new sweater; the other fabricates reasons to leave work early, drives with a pounding heart and tears in her eyes to her lover and throws herself into his arms, barely makes it out of her coat before she's fallen onto that awful stained futon. She runs her fingers through his hair and touches his eyelids, his cheekbones, lips; he bites her jaw and throat, she twines her legs around him and cries when she comes, cries with joy, sadness, anguish, every single time is the end of the world, the destruction of everything that's dearest to her, and yet, she can't stop. She hides the bite marks on her neck with silk scarves, fixes her hair, puts on lipstick and sits outside in the car as though nothing's happened, and the first woman takes back over. Buys food for dinner on the way home, flips between radio stations, parks in front of the garage, and no one suspects a thing.

Or at least, that's what I steadfastly believe until Elísabet comes into my office, closes the door behind her, and sits in the chair across from my desk.

Something up? I ask, but she doesn't answer. Just looks at me with those clever gray eyes through her smudged glasses.

What? I ask, looking back at her.

She sighs.

This is obviously none of my business, she says then. And I wouldn't say anything if we hadn't worked together for twenty years, if you weren't my closest colleague. But people are starting to talk.

I open my mouth to say something, but nothing comes out. My lips and tongue have turned to stone, my whole face is numb, my hands ice-cold.

You've been seen together. Walking hand in hand at Krýsuvík, kissing in the car. And people have heard you—you know how thin the walls are here, you can hear everything that goes on from room to room. And Anna, dear, the break room is just on the other side, whatever possessed you to bring him here? You, always so sensible? We got out of there, no one wants to be an accidental fly on the wall.

I say nothing, Elísabet bows her head.

It's your life, you make your own decisions, we're not judging. We're your friends, we wish you well. But we're all under a lot of pressure right now, we've got a lot of balls to keep in the air, and there are people who envy your position, who think they belong on the Scientific Council, want to be our spokesperson. And it's such an easy weakness to exploit, they'll say you aren't focused, that you're shirking your obligations, that you aren't reliable anymore.

I take a breath, but she lifts a hand and stops me: I don't agree with them, I trust you implicitly, you know that. I'm just worried about you, can see the weight you're carrying, and you're wearing yourself out. You're under more than enough professional stress, the situation as it's been, without adding this on top of it.

She gives me a pleading look: And I'm fond of your husband, Anna, he's my friend too. You have to talk to him.

I open my mouth again, and this time, I can speak, it's like a dam has burst and the words and tears come flooding out: I love Tómas Adler, I'm in love, for the first time in my life, and love is the most terrible thing that has ever happened to me. Love is worse than death, worse than the end of the world. I have no control over anything, I can't be trusted with anything. I neglect my work, betray my family, lie right to my husband's face. He doesn't deserve to be treated like this, my dear, sweet, good husband, my best friend, no one has treated me better than him. But he isn't enough, my family isn't enough for me, my happiness isn't enough, I'm sacrificing everything for this terrible sickness in my heart, this unquenchable addiction, this god-awful love that's sunk its claws into me and refuses to let go.

I weep, and she stands up, comes over to me and gives me a hug, holds me tight. Oh, sweetheart, she whispers, my poor, dear heart.

And I sob, gasping with relief, because this is the last thing I expected when this big ugly secret of mine was uncovered. I expected contempt and shaming, not compassion and tenderness, not to be held in Elísabet's soft, understanding embrace, to get to cry into her old pink wool sweater.

You know what you have to do, she says then. You know it can't go on like this. You have to talk to your husband, tell him everything. You owe him that.

I snuffle and nod, I know, I've always known. And then I go home and ask my husband to come on a walk with me after dinner.

He looks at me in confusion and then concern, nods, sure, of course, and we go out. We're dressed in fleeces and Arc'teryx jackets, triple-layer Gore-Tex, his turkish blue, mine orange, my hands are shaking when I zip it up, lace up my hiking boots. We're going out for a short walk, he shouts. Can I come? yells Salka from the piano, no, we both answer in chorus, keep practicing, we won't be a minute.

I'm so scared I feel sick, but I also feel an underlying relief, like I've been hanging from the edge of a cliff and am finally permitting myself to let go, make my peace with the unavoidable and plummet into the abyss to meet my fate.

IT RAINS, AND MY HUSBAND'S
HEART BREAKS

Volcanic eruptions are so disparate. Not one resembles another, some are felsic, viscous, and hateful, they belch out fiery, tempestuous clouds and spare no one; others are subdued mafic effusive eruptions during which lava flows serenely across the landscape. It all depends on the chemical composition of the magma, how much of it there is, its journey up through the earth's crust and the conditions that await it on the surface. Whether it comes up through a focused stratovolcano or a hiccuping fissure swarm, in the uninhabited wilderness or a bustling, built-up area, whether it's had to break its way through many miles of glacial ice or encountered the ocean itself, so massively heavy and murky that the largest volcanoes on earth have come into being on the seafloor without revealing any sign of themselves on the surface.

What should I expect from my husband when he realizes our marriage is over? Will he be furious and throw me out or turn silent, a cold wall? Will he lose control, cry, resort to violence? There's no one in the world I know better, we've shared a life, a bed, and conversation for over two decades, and still, I don't have the faintest idea how he'll react to my betrayal. Elísabet is worried, offers me her sofa if he throws me out.

I'll just wait out in the car, be within earshot when you tell him.

I shake my head.

Just to be on the safe side, she implores.

He's not a violent man. He's a good man who's going to get bad news, he can take it.

And yet, I'm in no way prepared for his reaction when the moment comes, for how hard he takes the blow, it's like I've lunged at him instead of saying simply:

I'm in love with another man. I don't know if I can be your wife any longer.

He stops, doesn't look at me, not right away, stands completely still in the same spot and looks at the ground under our feet, then sinks slowly down onto his heels, puts his arms around his legs, hides his face between his knees, folds his long, thin body together into a ball, as if to protect himself from blows. His breathing is shallow and spasmodic, and when he looks up, his face is a grimace of pain. He doesn't say anything, just looks at me and draws breath in ragged gasps, his eyes dry and imploring.

I feel terrible, I say, and I can hear that I'm crying. The twilight around us is unusually silent, the mist thickens and becomes rain, the sodden deep blue sky empties itself upon us, everything is still and silent. The heather holds its breath, the entire world is in suspense, and then the loon emits its plaintive cry, which echoes across the lake: Where are you, my love?

My husband doesn't say a word, and I try to go on, to organize my erratic thoughts into comprehensible sentences: I can't even ask you to forgive me. My behavior's been unforgivable. You don't deserve any of this, you've been a good husband.

Anna, he says quietly. Anna, sweetheart.

That's it, nothing more. He rises slowly to his feet, straightens his knees and back, and walks along the path away from the house and into the rain-drenched wood, slowly and stiffly, as if he's learning to walk all over again. I follow him, unsteady on my feet.

Kristinn, I call through my tears. Don't go. What should I do?

He shakes his head, doesn't turn around, doesn't answer.

Will you talk to me? Do you want to know who he is?

Tómas Adler, he says quietly. I know who he is.

You know? Have you known this whole time and not said anything?

He turns around, his delicate eyebrows furrowed, rain streaming down his pale face.

I think I've always known what was happening, from the first time I saw the two of you together. And when you danced with him. I'd never seen you like that before, you were an entirely different woman.

His head tilts, as if his neck has no choice in the matter, his eyes dim with sadness.

Have you slept together?

Yes.

How many times?

I don't know.

What's your guess?

Ten times, maybe. Twelve.

When did your relationship start?

At the end of June. Before the Krýsuvík eruption began.

And where do you meet?

At his studio. And my office.

Your office? Do all of your coworkers know about it?

I don't know. Or yes, some of them.

Who?

Elísabet. Jóhannes Rúriksson. I'm not sure.

Why are you telling me now?

Elísabet told me to. Before you found out from someone else.

The answers flow out of me even as I feel a weight on my chest, almost too heavy to draw breath. We're facing one another and looking each other in the eye, he interrogates me and I answer, prosecutor and defendant, victim and aggressor. Each one of his questions is a blow, each answer of mine inflicts a lethal wound.

Is he a better lover than me?

Kristinn, dear heart, don't do this.

He looks away and down at the toes of his hiking boots, his arms hanging at his sides. Suddenly so gray and stooped, like the last few moments have been a decade in passing, like my answers to his questions have shortened his life span by half. The rain falls around us in gray sheets, disappears into the dark woodland floor and the withered grass on the edge of the path, puddles in the creases of our jackets, in the dirt at our feet.

I've known about it for a long time, he says. I don't know how to describe it. It was like the scent of you changed, the sound of your voice. You were happier, and yet it was like you were never entirely present. As if the heat and weight of you was gone and some fancy Sunday Best version of you had been left behind. A simulation. And I've probably been shutting it out, been in denial. Hoping deep down that if I acted like nothing was wrong, that it would just end. That you'd come back to me and everything would be the way it was before.

He raises his voice.

And all that time, while I've waited and hoped, you've gone behind my back, you've fucked like animals and laughed at me. Laughed and made a mockery of my innocent, trusting love. You've lied to me, you've betrayed me, made a fool of me. And you're my wife. My best friend, my life partner, the truest and best thing in my life. You've destroyed everything, ruined everything, trampled it under your dirty shoes. What am I supposed to say, Anna? What am I supposed to do now?

He cries and I cry, too, and say, I'm sorry, I'm so sorry, I didn't mean to hurt you like this. I wish that none of it had happened, but I can't take it back.

What are you going to do? What happens now?

I don't know, I'll leave if you want.

No. Don't leave. Please.

He's holding his face, thinking, thinking, then takes a deep breath and looks up, looks at me in distress, but decisive.

We need time. We need to be rational and to think this over, decide what we're going to do next. We can't rush into anything, can't make irrational decisions. There's too much at stake, our marriage, our children, our family. We have to think about this.

He walks over to me and puts his hands on my shoulders, looks deep into my eyes.

We've had a good, beautiful marriage for twenty years. I'm not going to let it be destroyed in an instant, in such a vile way. We have to at least discuss what our choices are, whether there's any chance we can save our relationship. You've made a terrible mistake, done a great deal of damage, but maybe we can still put things right. Maybe we can fix this.

Do you think so?

I don't know. But it would be irrational for us not to try. Don't you agree?

And, of course, I should say no, dear Kristinn, I think that ship has sailed, I don't love you, I am so endlessly fond of you, so truly sorry to have hurt you so, to leave you in this way, but it's the only right thing to do, I just know it, every cell, every nerve ending in my body is shouting it. But I don't say this, I'm too relieved to be in this warm, familiar embrace, to imagine to myself that I have the chance to go back, that maybe everything can be almost like it was before, so reliable and comfortable and predictable, that I could stop loving Tómas Adler and go back to being the old Anna, wife of Kristinn Fjalar Örvarsson. Maybe it's just cowardice that makes me say: Yes, I agree. It would be irrational not to try.

He looks at me, downcast and angry and relieved all at the same time. He is, in spite of everything, stepping back into his old role: comforting me, saving me from myself, tidying up after me.

EXPLANATORY NOTE IX

SWANS EN ROUTE TO SUMMERLAND

A typical volcano in Iceland is a long, volcanic fissure that generally does not erupt again and again, but rather opens far and wide over a large but circumscribed area. This must be accounted for when analyzing the impact of volcanic activity here in the country.

Páll Imsland. 2013. "Risk of Volcanic Eruptions." In *Natural Hazards in Iceland: Volcanoes and Earthquakes,* ed. Júlíus Sólnes. Reykjavík: University of Iceland Press.

I didn't understand the term *fissure swarm*. "Swarm" didn't describe fixed, stationary things like earth and stones, but rather large writhing groups of living, flying creatures—bees or sparrows. I found it strange to use that term for a cluster of eruptive fissures in a volcanic system, confusing, irrational. Fissures can't swarm like birds or insects, I said to my father.

He was sitting at the kitchen table with his coffee cup and a copy of the Social Democrats' paper, the radio warbling something about drizzle and light wind; I was sitting across from him with my buttermilk and cornflakes, reading *Fire in the North*, a collection of papers published in honor of legendary geologist Sigurður Þórarinsson's seventieth birthday; fifteen years old and burning with newfound rebelliousness and critical thinking, brand-new, sharply honed tools with which to examine the world. Dad suddenly seemed painfully conservative and complacent in his science, I took every opportunity to strike at him, demand answers to my questions. He received all of them affectionately and never lost his patience, outside of the one time when I aired Thomas Kuhn's postmodern idea that the natural sciences were based on subjective values; that got him so worked up that he dropped a pot of potatoes on the floor, spun around, and narrowed his eyes at me: There is nothing subjective about scientific facts, Anna Arnardóttir!

But he was happy to talk about fissure swarms.

Alright, look at this, Stubby, he said, and got to his feet, went into the living room, and pulled a big yellowed file folder from the bookshelf. He pushed our coffee cups to one side, placed it on the kitchen table, and opened it carefully, tenderly drew a finger across a black and white map of northeast Iceland. There were nine maps of different parts of the country, each crisscrossed by dense parallel lines. They ran in different directions: horizontal in the central highlands and vertical out east, diagonal on the Reykjanes Peninsula, northeast to southeast, with lines that wound around them and seemed to symbolize some kind of undulation.

What're these? I asked.

These, Stubby, are Þorbjörn's magnetic maps.

Dad's expression became solemn, Þorbjörn was his friend and mentor—they'd both come to geoscience from unusual directions, Dad from astronomy and Þorbjörn from nuclear physics. Þorbjörn was an inventor at his core and boyishly daring out in the field. One of his fertile, enterprising mind's primary areas of interest had been the earth's magnetic field, so he had invented a device to measure the magnetic field of rocks from the air, learned to fly, and bought a plane off which he could hang his invention.

And then he simply flew over the country, back and forth along those lines, and measured deviations in the magnetic field, said Dad. There are corrugations in the lines. And we got to float along with him, two by two, his puppies, as he called us young men, and try to locate the plane on the map. This was before we had the LORAN navigation system, so Þorbjörn had scrounged up a telescope that a Russian lady scientist had left behind in the country. One of us students would stare through it into the starry sky and the other down at the ground through a hole to look for landmarks—rivers and mountains, crossroads and easily recognizable buildings—in order to figure out where in the world we were. Þorbjörn bounced around the plane like a pinball, so worked up about the measurements that he could hardly sit still to steer it, so the flights were rather herky-jerky. And we got so airsick, my God, how we puked, liver and lungs every single trip, and all of it went onto the flight recordings: the coordinates, the landmarks, the puking, and all Þorbjörn's yapping.

But it worked, Dad shook with laughter—Þorbjörn pulled off what he'd hoped to do, he mapped out the magnetic field of Iceland. He played a big part in validating Wegener's plate tectonics theory and showing how oceanic plates have formed the Mid-Atlantic Ridge—and how Iceland came into being on a plate boundary.

What does this have to do with fissure swarms? I asked. Dad pointed at the map of the Reykjanes Peninsula.

You see the corrugations? How they get bigger along the transcurrent fault, and see here, how they follow the plate boundaries through the land? They're like birds flying in V formation. Our island is always moving, the plates are pulling it apart, the mantle plume rises up under it, and the motion moves through it from the southwest to the northeast, like a flock of migratory birds, swans en route to summerland in the spring. The movement just happens so slowly that we don't perceive it.

My father looked at the magnetic map, then he looked at me and his eyes were shining: Our world is so beautiful, Stubby. It's governed by simple and perfect laws, and it's the role of science to learn them and understand their effects on the physical world. It's the most amazing project a person can undertake. Without science, we're just animals at the mercy of nature's forces.

I rolled my eyes: Okay, Dad, it sounds like you hit your head or something. Talking like a poet about animals and swans flying to summerland or whatever. I still think it's weird to talk about fissure *swarms*. I'm going to use another term instead, maybe, like, *fissure rows*.

That doesn't describe the phenomenon at all, said Dad. You think that the fissures are fixed and stationary, but they're not. They're moving at quite a clip, like a murmuration of starlings, while you're moving at a different speed and can't perceive it. It's you who's the problem, not the fissures.

The first time I properly saw what he meant was during the Holuhraun eruption in 2014. The eruption was actually in another place entirely—the magma came out of the chamber under Bárðarbunga, the great volcano under the Vatnajökull glacier, and then worked its way through the fissure swarm until it surfaced at Holuhraun Lava Field, some twenty-five miles from its source.

A fissure swarm isn't a place but a mode of transportation.

If I'd only remembered this conversation, this simple truth that my father tried to instill in me about these natural laws and movements, about the journey of the swans to summerland. That a fissure swarm isn't stationary, fixed, and unchanging but rather the magma's pathway up to the surface. And its intentions are veiled from us because the earth moves at a different pace from people, it has other concerns and entirely different plans from those of us scrabbling about on her surface for the briefest of moments. For her, *one day is like a thousand years, a thousand years a day*, as the old hymn goes.

So while we're revolving around that pretty little tourist eruption at Krýsuvík, considering the course of the lava flow and sulfur pollution, advising on closures and stricter gas measurements, while we're granting permission for a viewing platform and helicopter flights for visitors, while we're weighing what all of this will cost against potential revenue, the deep-down burning heart is plotting another journey—one far more frightful.

A square mile of lava probably doesn't sound like a very big deal—you can see a full mile, a decent jogger can cover that distance in eight minutes. But as soon as a mile becomes a *square* mile, mi^2, now that becomes a decent-sized swath, and, if you throw in a third dimension, mi^3, some five thousand feet up into the air—now we're talking about a whole mountain. And it's this mountain, and more, that is biding its time deep within the earth more than nine miles straight down under our feet, 2,192 degrees Fahrenheit of constructive destruction, or *de*structive construction, depending on how you look at it. It's groping its way up to the earth's crust, seeking out fissures, weak points it can exploit and force its way through before rising higher and higher, up the eruption channel that it opens in the bedrock until it finds a comfortable mode of transportation, an express train, a fissure swarm. This conveyance can carry it dozens of miles horizontally across the land until it decides the joke's gone far enough, that this irresponsible subterranean joyride has to come to an end, that it has work to do on the surface: land to build, ravines to tear open, white-hot lava to pour over houses and streets and gardens.

And that's where I foundered—me, who's been called the nation's leading expert in the behavior of fissure eruptions, that's where I failed the test I've studied and prepared for with unflagging diligence for over four decades, ever since I was a small child clutching a rough chunk of lava in my fist, look, Stubby, our earth, fresh from the oven. I fixate on meter readings, put my faith in the models and the scientific method, carefully compartmentalize the chilling scenario playing out in my head, shut out the memories and the quiet thrum of warning bells clanging in the depths of my subconscious.

I lose sight of the big picture.

FAULT PLANE SOLUTIONS

The main fault plane solutions on the Mid-Atlantic Ridge
show normal faulting, which indicates a divergence at the
ridge axis.

Páll Einarsson. 1986. "Seismicity along the Eastern Margin
of the North American Plate." In *The Western North Atlantic
Region,* eds. Peter R. Vogt and Brian E. Tucholke. Boulder:
Geological Society of America.

The city is shaking like a beast in its death throes, I start from dark,
difficult dreams to find our bed rippling like a flooded moor.

That was a big one, I mutter, but there've been so many since the
spring, I rest my head back on the pillow and wait for my heartbeat to
calm. The shaking has also woken my husband, he starts talking before
he opens his eyes.

You've broken the law, you know. At the very beginning of Article 2
of the Law in Respect of Marriage from 1993, it says that spouses shall
be faithful to each other, support each other, and together guard the
interests of their home and family. You've broken that clause.

I lie still and unmoving beside him, my eyes closed, try to breathe
naturally, maybe he'll think I've gone back to sleep, maybe he'll stop
talking.

Today, I could demand a legal separation on the grounds of marital infidelity, he continues. In the eighteenth century, you'd have probably been drowned.

That's where I draw the line, I spring out of bed, stand in the middle of the room shaking with anger.

Charge me, then, divorce me! I have no claim to you, you can throw me out if you want. We decided to try and work through this, come to a logical conclusion. That doesn't give you the right to subject me to this abuse. It means that you have to be a man of your word and try to find a solution.

But there's no solution, is there? It's hopeless, he says. I've never been so entirely alone in my whole life.

He lies still, and I can now see that he's crying. The tears run down his temples and dampen the pillow, his body is racked with sobs under the duvet. I throw up my hands, sink to the bedroom floor next to him, take his hand, kiss it, and press it to my cheek, you're not alone, dear heart, I'm here. We'll find some way through this.

Some way, sure.

We just have to be rational.

We just have to keep talking to each other.

There's a knock on the door: Mom, you left your phone in the kitchen, some guy's calling from the Met Office and asking about the eruption.

We're coming, we yell, and hurry to dry our tears, look one another in the eyes. We've got to pull ourselves together, quit acting like scared, sad children, straighten our backs and fix on deliberate, stern expressions, put on the air of the almighty parents.

I love you, he says.

I look away, I know.

Five missed calls, what am I thinking, how can I forget my phone somewhere all night, battery almost dead, as lava streams out of the fissure near Seltún and the levels on the gas meters rise. There's been unusual seismic activity along the Krýsuvík system, says Júlíus, come as soon as you can.

Salka's sitting on the toilet, looks at me wide-eyed with her feet dangling: Mom, can we go see the eruption today?

I sigh, my child has this eruption on the brain. She's come with me several times, stood hypnotized on the edge of the lava, staring into it as if her eyes could bore their way through the black crust and into the red magma beneath; followed my colleagues in the field like an inquisitive little shadow under an all-too-big helmet.

We'll have to see, Stubby. There's a bit much happening at the site right now, a lot of earthquakes, so we might need to find another day when there's not so much going on.

But, Mom, you promised!

I know, but we have to be sure it's not dangerous. It might be better to find another day.

Then you can't go either. Not if it's dangerous.

I stroke her head: This is my job, Stubby. You don't have to worry about me, I'll be careful. But it won't be fun to come with me if everyone has too much to do to pay attention to you.

But when, then?

We'll see, maybe you can come with me later. Right now, I have to run to a meeting downtown with Civil Protection first and talk to them, then we'll see if you can come too. And then I'll either pick you up from school or we'll find another day.

It's 7:02 a.m., today is Tuesday, September 4, and I have my eruption gear on, hiking pants and a fleece, I'm just going to have one cup of coffee before I go. I put a pod in the machine, Fortissio Lungo, and while the black liquid drips down into the cup, it suddenly occurs to me that I've always hated this machine, this repellant hunk of plastic and its unnatural quick-service coffee in expensive packaging. I'm gripped by an irrational disappointment; I want real coffee, roasted and freshly ground, brewed on a Primus stove, midgale, up on a mountainside, bleeding its aromatic oils.

I inhale deeply and try to get a grip, sip my coffee and make another cup for my husband.

He's come upstairs, is sitting at the kitchen table in his striped pajamas and robe and staring at the table. He's changed, looks emaciated and gray, his outline's darker and sharper, like an old knife. He looks up when I put the cup of coffee in front of him.

I've learned something, he says. You don't have anyone. Not your spouse, not your children. You've got no one but yourself.

Kristinn, sweetheart. I have to go to work.

He looks down into his coffee.

You go when you want. I've never had you, although I've wished that I did. I really believe that. But I think I've always known you had something like this in you. This selfishness. That you could just up and decide to change your mind, out of the blue, to throw everything away. Somewhere inside me, I've always expected it. That's why I'm so calm.

You're not calm, I say.

What do you expect? he asks. I've been happily married for twenty years, a dependable and loving husband, I thought I was one of the lucky ones who find their soul mates, their best friends, their life partners, who live happily until the end of their days, and then one fine day, I get hit in the face: My wife loves another man. Our future is being swept aside for this great love of hers. She's going to trample everything that's been holy to me, our marriage, our children, everything I've worked for.

Don't talk so loud. Salka will hear you.

And what difference does that make? It doesn't seem that your children have mattered all that much to you of late. All you've done is think about yourself. You've made fools of us all.

I cover my face, he lowers his voice.

I'm sorry, I didn't mean to fly off the handle.

I have to go, I say. There's something happening at Krýsuvík. You'll take Salka to school, right?

But I can't just walk away from him, so downcast and desolate, hunched over his cup of coffee. I sit on my heels in front of him and hug his knees, rest my head in his lap. He strokes my hair.

I love you, he says. I can't help it, no matter what you've done to me. I can't stop loving you. But I'm not sure I can forgive you.

I deserve that, I say and cry into his pajama pants. I can't forgive myself for how I've treated you.

You don't have to forgive yourself, he says. You're not like that. You can keep going without ever thinking about the past.

Do you think I'm a sociopath?

No, you're not a sociopath. I know you know the difference between right and wrong, you've always judged people rather harshly. Judged yourself hardest of all. And then comes the day when you seem to simply be able to bypass it all, leave everything behind and keep going like nothing's happened. After all these years, it comes to light that you're exactly like your mother.

Don't say that. Kristinn, sweetheart, don't compare me to her, I snuffle and cover my face.

She at least had an excuse, though, she was mentally ill. She didn't string someone along for twenty years, playing the part of the perfect wife and mother.

Now I flee, I stumble into my shoes and jacket and run out to the car. Tears are blinding me, but I see him in the rearview mirror as I drive away, barefoot in his robe in the driveway, he shouts my name, he's crying too.

And I will admit that when I walk into the coordination center of the National Police's Civil Protection Department that Tuesday morning, I'm not entirely present. I call Tómas on the way there, he doesn't answer the first two times, when I finally manage to get through on the third try, I nearly drive off the road: Oh, ástin mín, God, it's good to hear your voice.

What's wrong? he asks, fuzzy with sleep. Are you crying? Is he driving you crazy?

No, but it's so hard. He talks constantly. And he's so hurt, I feel so horrible for him, I care about him so much.

Tómas doesn't say anything, and I hasten to add: I don't love him like I love you, but I still do love him, in my way. He's always been good to me. And then I treat him like this.

You can still go back to him. If he's so good to you, if you love him, in spite of it all.

Tómas, ástin mín, don't say that. How could I go back? I love you.

You love me, but it still sounds like you regret everything, he says morosely, I hear a toilet flush, but the sound is muffled, like it's coming from the other room.

Is there someone else there?

Who would be here? I just got up, I was up late. I woke up when you called.

I'm sorry, I didn't mean to wake you, go back to sleep.

He hangs up, I've stopped crying, I stare at the road in front of me. A wet, cramped sadness has given way to something cold and hard in my breast, the fear is like a stranglehold. He sounds so distant and disinterested, why did he get up so late? Who flushed the toilet?

I park the car outside of the coordination center, sit there for a moment and focus on regaining control of my breathing. It's shallow and jerky, I'm holding on to the steering wheel so tightly my knuckles are white, and I gasp as horror, sadness, and anger run vicious rings around my head; he doesn't love me anymore, he's turned his back on me, he's going to abandon me now, when I need him most.

I open the car door and throw up in the parking lot, some of the spray getting in the car, the coffee-colored bile almost pretty against the creamy leather interior. Everything's falling apart, my life separating like a split sauce. I sniffle and spit and get a paper napkin from the glove compartment, dry my face and wipe up the sick, collect my shredded judgment and head into the coordination center to make decisions about the welfare and safety of the nation.

BATTLE FATIGUE,
I THINK IT'S CALLED

And what do you suggest? shouts the national commissioner. That we put the whole of southwest Iceland on Emergency Phase? Have you lost your minds? Are you trying to frighten the living daylights out of the entire nation?

Júlíus projects a map of Reykjanes onto the screen as I walk into the conference room, it spans from Eldey Island off the southernmost tip of the peninsula and longways east toward Þingvellir; it's covered in green stars, all the spots where there've been earthquakes with a magnitude of 3.0 or higher, there were two thousand quakes last night, he's saying, fifteen of which were over 4.0. I think we can all agree that this is anomalous behavior.

Stefán, the Ministry of Justice rep, nods, adding: There's been damage to homes on the outskirts of the city, and the Road Administration has notified us of large cracks in the underlying structure of Rte. 1 where it crosses the Elliðaá River—it's like the city's ripping apart.

But what precisely are you warning people about? asks Sigríður María, chewing on her thumbnail, scraping its pink polish off with her teeth. I mean, there's an eruption in full swing just around the corner—is it so strange that we'd be having some earthquakes too?

Milan looks at me with a frown: Anna, are you okay?

Yeah, I'm fine, I say, trying to ignore the pounding in my head and the nausea, to shake the fog from my mind.

What's your assessment of the situation, based on these latest earthquakes? Do they indicate that the Krýsuvík eruption is changing?

It's unusual, I say. Typically, earthquakes stop when an eruption begins. But although they abated when the Krýsuvík eruption started, they're picking back up again. This could indicate a new magma intrusion, that the magma's moving. The problem is simply that we don't know where it's moving to. The quakes are traveling along the peninsula from one end to the other, they aren't bound to a specific area or volcanic system. It's very unusual and hard to say what it means.

Which is why I'm recommending that we announce an Emergency Phase for the entire Reykjanes Peninsula, says Júlíus. Both due to risk of an eruption and of major earthquakes.

We're already at Alert Phase, says Stefán. For a six-mile radius around Krýsuvík. We can't frighten people unnecessarily. Two-thirds of the nation lives in this part of the country.

If we announce an Emergency Phase, we could end up with pandemonium, adds the commissioner, stuffing a cream cookie into his mouth. A crush on the roadways—burglaries and looting. And as it stands, there doesn't seem to be an obvious reason for us to level up. We'll look like fools if we do so for no reason.

I look at him, aghast: Burglaries and looting? Are you for real? Do we have any examples of either happening in emergency situations, outside of American disaster movies? It's been my general observation that people receive Civil Protection's recommendations calmly and with composure.

But we've also never announced an Emergency Phase due to volcanic activity in such a densely populated area, says the commissioner.

The greatest risk doesn't just stem from an eruption, says Júlíus, but also tremors. We could have major earthquakes here, well over 6.0, chasms could open up, homes and buildings could collapse.

There are twenty-three thousand tourists in the southwest as we speak, says Sigríður María. The Krýsuvík eruption is drawing them like bees to honey. An Emergency Phase might scare them off, they'll be afraid of getting stranded here. It could irreparably damage the country's reputation, destroy all the infrastructural work we did this summer.

Milan looks back to me: Anna, I'm relying on your assessment of the situation. Your professional judgment.

I try yet again to cut through the fog in my head, stare at the projection on the wall, refer back to the spreadsheets and maps on the table in front of me, systematically review the GPS readings, the age of the lava, the position of the fissures. Look at Júlíus: Will you pull up the frequency distribution curves, just to be sure?

He nods darkly, reaches over to the keyboard and signs into the Met's geomonitoring system. A series of neon-colored, continuously refreshing images appears on the screen, all of which are being uploaded by their dense network of seismographs in real time. Everything looks normal, green and yellow, while the stations closest to the eruption are coming up orange. The volcanic unrest is bound to Krýsuvík; there, it appears as bright red pulsations.

This is what's causing us concern, says Júlíus, pointing to the lines showing the most recent earthquakes on the peninsula. They haven't consolidated much, and only a few have exceeded a 4.0, but they've increased. They also seem to be happening at shallower depths, which could indicate that the magma's getting closer to the surface.

But are these concerns enough to merit throwing society into disarray? asks Stefán. There's a volcanic eruption happening twelve miles from here, we've announced an Emergency Phase because of that. The ministry's position is that it would be irresponsible to engender social and economic upheaval unless there's ample reason to do so.

We sit around the oval conference table, six people drinking weak coffee in chipped mugs and charged with a surreal responsibility: deciding what's best for the public at large. Two police officers, one representative from the government and another from a special interest group, two geoscientists; we sit in front of open laptops, looking over maps and graphs, making tenuous attempts to be of some use, each from our own perspective. Later today, I'll replay this chain of events countless times in my head, wonder what I could've done differently, what other conclusions my calculations could've led to. Ask myself why I didn't listen to that vague premonition I had—given that a shot for a change. Why I didn't consider that feeling alongside the model. And the answer to these obsessive questions is always the same: I can't absolve myself of responsibility for what's about to happen.

But here, in this moment in Civil Protection's conference room, I believe I know exactly what I'm doing.

Earthquakes connected to volcanic activity are usually rather mild, I say. The likeliness of there being a major earthquake is pretty low. And regarding an eruption, one of the characteristics of the fissure swarms on Reykjanes is that most of the volcanic activity is concentrated in the middle; there's less of it the farther you get from the plate boundaries. Búrfell is the northernmost volcano in the Krýsuvík system; we've never had an eruption farther north than that. And in that case, the only neighborhood in the capital area that would be directly threatened would be Vallahverfi in Hafnarfjörður—it's built on lava that extends from Undirhlíðar Pillow Lava Ridge, but we'd always have many days' advance warning to evacuate the residents before the lava flow reached them.

I look at Milan and deliver my assessment: We should wait and see. We're in a position to respond if anything changes. We should issue a press release saying that the Krýsuvík system is still being closely monitored and that there's risk of earthquakes on Reykjanes but that currently, we don't see any reason to increase our preparedness level to Emergency Phase.

Milan nods at me: Good. But we've got to be ready for anything. You'll all be called out if there's the slightest change in conditions.

We stand up from the table, black dots dance in front of my eyes when I get to my feet, I have to grip the edge of the table to keep my balance. Milan asks to have a word once the others have left.

Are you okay? he asks again.

Yes, of course, I say.

He looks at me inquiringly.

Anna, we've all been under a lot of stress in recent months, he says. You've started to remind me of some of my colleagues in the army police before I left. Not the new recruits, but the hardened, experienced officers. They could work without ceasing, fight like lions for months at a time, but then, all of a sudden, something would change. They'd get confused, lose sight of the big picture without realizing it, start committing pointless acts of violence. Battle fatigue, I think it's called.

Now wait just a minute, Milan Petrovic. Battle fatigue? Are you serious? If you don't think you can trust my judgment anymore, just say so and find someone else.

Don't get angry, I trust you absolutely, says Milan. I'm just worried about you. You're my friend.

I have a PhD in volcanology and geophysics, have led research on every single volcanic eruption that's happened here in the past fifteen years. I'll allow myself to say that there's not a single geoscientist in the country who has as much experience, education, and/or sense of the bigger picture as I do, no one who's as good at making rational decisions about how we should respond to these eruptions.

Milan runs a hand over his buzz cut, his eyes are sad and gray and bloodshot from lack of sleep, just like mine.

You know, Anna, you're the most intelligent person I know, but intelligence can be stupid and prideful too. It can give a person a false sense of security. Sometimes, it makes you think you have control of things that it simply isn't possible to control. Sometimes, rationality is just an illusion—sometimes, you need to take other things into account: intuition, feelings.

I'll let you know when natural disasters start hinging on people's feelings, I say. Should be about the time that hell freezes over. No: these events hinge on simple laws, physics, and calculations. And knowledge and logic are the tools we have to make sense of them. Don't worry about me and my stress levels. I've never heard anything so ridiculous in my life. Now, if you'll excuse me, I'm going to go out to Krýsuvík now to familiarize myself with the conditions there, we can reassess later today.

Then I storm out, piqued and dead sure of myself, sure in the arrogance of my arrogant rationality, as if I have everything entirely under control, as if I know everything, can rely on my infallible judgment and knowledge, never mind the storm raging inside my head.

And everything certainly looks as it should, the models are all finely calibrated, the potential scenarios all precise. The formulas add up, every constant and variable is in its right place, but somewhere in the depths of my consciousness, deep in the past, my dad is tapping out his pipe and narrowing his eyes:

Look, Stubby. A fissure swarm isn't a place, it's a mode of transportation. Like the swans, remember, on the way to summerland.

But I don't hear him, I don't let him in.

NUÉE ARDENTE

Nuée ardente, which translates into English as "burning cloud," is a hot, almost incandescent cloud of volcanic gas and ash that spews out of a volcano and down its sides at incredible speed (up to 500 km/hr).

Sigurður Steinþórsson. 2019. "What Is *nuée ardente*?" The Icelandic Web of Science.

I make a lot of mistakes this morning. Or actually a series of forgotten decisions, memories, and promises, and one of the things I forget is my earlier conversation with Salka, when I half promised to pick her up from school and take her with me to see the volcano. The question flits through my head at the meeting—is it advisable, as things stand, to take an eight-year-old child to the edge of the lava field? But the question flew in one ear and out the other without waiting for an answer, the thought vanished, the promise forgotten.

Later, I'll try later to work out this equation in my mind, figure out where we would have been at 10:34 a.m. if I'd picked her up. Would we have been out at the eruption site with Jóhannes and Halldóra and my other colleagues, would they have given her a friendly pat on the shoulders and extolled her: this girl's a real chip off the family block. Or would we have gotten held up at school, had to go home to get better shoes and a warmer sweater, been snug in the car? A thousand chances and choices could have changed the course of the events—a flat tire, a traffic collision, an urgent phone call, a run of red lights—but the dire, unalterable fact remains:

I forget Salka.

I don't drive straight out to Krýsuvík like I told Milan I was doing. If I had, I'd have remembered my promise, detoured back to our neighborhood, and picked her up. Instead, I'm driving out there, my champagne-colored jeep zipping along its intended route when suddenly, it somehow ends up in the wrong lane, and before I know it, I've taken the exit that runs through the industrial neighborhood where Tómas Adler's studio's located. I hesitate for a moment as I park in front of his door. What do I mean by showing up at his place uninvited, jealous and looking for a fight? What am I seeking—to confirm his love or to unearth some horrible, unknown betrayal? I pause, but then walk through the unlocked door without ringing first, open the inner door to his workshop and call:

Halló? Anyone home?

I stop to listen for gasps, commotion, the futon screeching, but the only thing I can make out is "Wild Horses" and the faint scent of pot. He's at his computer going over images, poring over details in black and white, looks over his shoulder in surprise when he hears me come in, a smile appearing on his face: Hey, wasn't expecting you! How nice, to what do I owe the pleasure?

I'm dizzy with relief, ashamed of my insecurity.

I just had to see you. I missed you, it was a difficult morning.

Ástin mín, he says, standing up. I missed you too. I'm so glad you're here. Sorry I was short when you called, I can be a real grump in the morning.

He puts his arms around me, hugs me close, and I tremble in his arms, relieved and happy he's still glad to see me. I don't really care about any of the rest of it, about the disarray in the workroom and my head; how conscious I am of how homely and middle-aged I look in this fleece, my hair scraped into a scraggly ponytail.

Why didn't you tell me you were coming? he asks, giving me a kiss. I would have cleaned up a little, made you some coffee.

There's an edge to his voice, something new, and I look into his eyes. Suddenly, I think I see something flicker there and look around; the futon's unmade, there's an ashtray on the coffee table with the butt of a hand-rolled cigarette, there are two red wine glasses in amongst the dirty dishes next to the little galley sink, and if my eyes don't deceive me, one of them has the outline of lipstick on the rim.

Was someone here yesterday? I ask neutrally, as though I'm just inquiring about the weather.

Why do you ask? he replies, which makes me suspicious: Am I not allowed to?

An old acquaintance stopped by, wants to work with me on a series about the Krýsuvík eruption for *Iceland Review* or some publication like that. It could potentially turn into a book.

Why didn't you tell me?

It just didn't come up, you didn't ask before now. I meet with a lot of people.

Are you "meeting" anyone besides me?

The question flies out of my mouth before I can stop it, reveals my pitiful fear. He jerks back, looks at me wide-eyed, wounded: Anna! Ástin mín, how can you ask that? Don't you know me better than that?

Clearly, I don't know you as well as I thought I did. I didn't know, for instance, that you do drugs.

He rolls his eyes: Kristín had one joint, it doesn't bother me.

Oh, so this acquaintance has a name all of a sudden? Kristín?

Kristín, my friend. She's a journalist, a freelancer, we work together sometimes. And I rarely touch the stuff myself.

He takes my face in his hands, unshaven and unkempt in his old metal-band T-shirt and sweatpants, his breath a little sour: My dear, beautiful beloved, I know you're tired, I know you're carrying the world on your shoulders and that things are hard at home, but you have to trust me. I love you and you love me, and nothing else matters. You are the light of my world, my life is in your hands.

He speaks so prettily, my lover, he's so boyishly handsome and relaxed in his soft shabby clothes. He talks like he moves, soft and strong and lithe, he walks like a dancer, speaks like a poet, it's so easy for him to pacify me, to make me laugh and stop me asking difficult questions. I don't know him very well, I know so little about him other than what he wants me to know, don't know anything about the women he's loved, who've loved him, and now, out of nowhere appears this woman friend who smokes pot and drinks red wine and is planning future projects with him. Jealousy wells up inside me in hot red jets, but the words that come out of me are ice-cold: Sometimes, I don't understand you, Tómas Adler. Sometimes, I think everything that comes out of your mouth is just a pretty fiction, yarns you spin to appease me. It's like there's nothing behind any of it.

He laughs at me: My dear, Dr. Scientist, you want hard facts, concrete confirmation that I love you? You want me to feed our love into an algebraic equation and solve for x? It doesn't work like that, you have to trust me. Trust love.

You tell me to trust you and trust love, and then you laugh at me? Do you find me laughable, sensitive and vulnerable like this? I've thrown away everything for love and for you, Tómas Adler. My marriage, the happiness of my children, the respect of my colleagues. What has Tómas Adler sacrificed for me?

He's angry now, his eyes glitter: I've never forced you to do anything. It was you who took the first step. It was also your decision to tell Kristinn about our affair, that you loved me. You've had some agency in all of this, you have to take responsibility for yourself.

I can hardly believe my ears: Affair? Now we're calling this an affair? You, who've always talked about our grand love, the greatest adventure of your life, you, who've begged me, tears in your eyes, to leave him and be with you, now you're calling this an affair? And I'm the one who needs to take responsibility?

My blood screams furiously in my ears, I kick the coffee table and send the ashtray flying to the floor: You don't get to treat me this way, you hear me? You rip my life to shreds and then tell me to pick up the scraps. You tell me to take responsibility. You should talk.

Anna, he shouts at me. What in God's name has gotten into you, woman? What did I do?

You did nothing, that's the whole problem! You just talk and talk about love and beauty, and then there's nothing behind it. Absolutely nothing. I'm leaving.

I storm out and hear him calling after me as I slam the door. Get in the car and peel out, eyes brimming with tears, speed away from the second man on the same godforsaken morning. I drive as fast as my car will carry me onto Rte. 41 and from there, turn off toward the pretty little eruption purring there in the best possible location and showing its best possible side to two busloads of tourists and thirteen geoscientists poking around the edge of the lava with their meters and picks and shovels, with their thermographs, sample vials, and tape measures—the absurdly didactic, useless weapons that science wields against the forces of nature.

I dry my tears on the arm of my sweater, I'm so angry my mind swims, my stomach churns, I have my hands full trying to keep the car on the road. I roll down the window to get some fresh air, realize too late that the churning isn't just inside me. Don't realize this until the wood on one side of the road suddenly disappears, is plucked away as if by magic, the road left behind in the void, a strip of pavement leading into nothingness—it's like an isthmus, the surrounding land is gone. The car glides through the air, a champagne-colored arrow cleaving through a cloud of dust, there's no sound but the screams of the deep as the earth shudders and then breaks apart.

And then that falls silent, too, and everything goes black.

BLACK

DEFINITION:
EXTREME RISK—NATIONAL
STATE OF EMERGENCY

Events that fall into this category demand immediate action. Namely, these are events wherein the number of potential casualties is significant, as are the projected economic losses with their extensive, attendant societal repercussions, and/or those in which the environment is subject to irreparable, irrevocable damage. The severity of events in this category is such that their management must be of the first and highest priority. It is essential to have in place a contingency plan that alleviates the danger by means of mitigating actions.

"Civil Protection Risk Assessment: Executive Summary." 2011. Ed. Guðrún Jóhannesdóttir. Collaborative report between the national commissioner of the Icelandic Police and the Department of Civil Protection and Emergency Management.

CHINESE LULLABIES

This is how it ends. I'm dead, have been absorbed into the soil.

I wake encased by the earth. She has me in her power, holds me tight like an insect in her dark velvety palm.

I try to move my head, but it doesn't budge. I open my eyes and close them, full of darkness, once again. Best to keep them closed, to concentrate on just doing that.

Don't think.

Don't let my mind wander to the thought that I'm dead, that this is what it's like to be dead.

This wouldn't actually be a bad way to go. To fold my wings and be absorbed into the soil like a honeybee in autumn. That's where we all end up in the end, down in the soft, tightly packed darkness, decomposing and returning from whence we came, bees and scientists, just and unjust, the earth makes no distinction between us. For her, we're all just lumps of sentimental carbon.

I almost want to laugh, but if I did that, my mouth would fill with soil, and I'd suffocate. And I can't suffocate. Not yet, at least. I can't even think about suffocating, about the fact that there isn't any oxygen down here. That I probably have only a few seconds to get moving before the darkness blackens and I die for real, become yet one more organic splodge the earth secretes away in her dark recesses. Try instead to create a little more space around me, to claw at the soil and gravel with battered fingers, clench my toes in my shoes and then point them, try to use my hands and feet to push off

—and out.

My left arm's out, all the way up to my elbow.

I lie still for a moment, racking my brain over what to do in this unimaginable situation, but then my body's had enough. It takes control, my will to live takes over and writhes and kicks and thrashes with all its primal strength, a cold blast of air blows in through the paper-thin margin between myself and the earth, is sucked in between my cracked lips and clenched teeth, down into my screaming lungs, that heavenly blend of oxygen and nitrogen in precise proportions, 22 percent oxygen, 78 percent nitrogen, what splendor, what a miracle that this exact chemical compound exists in the world and makes our terrestrial existence possible. I direct all my energy into breathing, then I hear a shout and calls, someone grabs my hand and yanks, there's scraping and digging above me, under me, next to me, and all of a sudden, I'm out, hands grip under my arms, pull me up, and I gasp for breath, gulp the wonderful air down into my throbbing lungs. My eyes are expecting painful brightness, but I can't see anything, I put my hands in front of my face—have I gone blind?

No, there are my hands, both of them, ten sad, dirt-encrusted, but unbroken fingers. In the hulking darkness, I can't make out the faces of my saviors. Dark eyes over gray masks, someone hands me a bottle of water and says something I don't understand, I drink the water greedily, my eyes slowly acclimatizing to the darkness. We're at the bottom of a ravine, a brand-new landslide. The tail end of a small bus sticks out over the verge, the passengers have crawled out through the back and then dug me out of the scree with their bare hands. The earth has literally swallowed us.

Hvar erum við? Hvað gerðist?

Where are we? What happened?

The people shake their heads, they don't understand me. Foreigners, maybe tourists from China. They speak to one another in soft, musical voices, a short gray-haired woman in a red jacket sits down next to me and takes hold of my shoulders, brushes the dirt from my face, speaks to me in a soothing voice. She hums softly, *yao yao yao*, something that could be a lullaby. That's when I first notice I'm crying. Shaking like a leaf, sopping wet, and muddy from the landslide, my phone is gone, my jacket's lost. We're enclosed in freezing coarse-grained darkness, black sand rains from the heavens, and I realize that the thunderous rumbling in my ears isn't because of the unbearable pain in my forehead but is rather the instantly recognizable roar of a phreatic eruption in close proximity.

This kick-starts something in my befuddled mind, which tries to organize my thoughts into something resembling a logical plan. One by one, the lights in my head switch on, like the control panel of an old machine coming back to life after a short circuit. I'm sore and wet and cold and completely exhausted, but I know one thing for sure: the base of a landslide near a volcanic eruption is the worst place you could be. We've got to get out of this pit before the poisonous gases come crawling, slip their devious fingers over our mouths and knock us out.

Follow me! I shout to the poor tourists in English and then attempt to climb up the scree, but my feet won't support me. Searing pain has wrapped itself around my left ankle, I can't stand up. Two men hold under my arms and help me up to the edge; one is slim and wide-eyed with fear, barely older than twenty, the other could be his father, a composed, balding man with a focused expression. They go back down and fetch their suitcases from the bus, the rest of the passengers struggle single file up the hillside with their own luggage. I wait up top like a petrified stone, gaze out over what remains of the world as I knew it.

Walls of flame are slicing the land apart as far as the eye can see, glowing jets of lava spurt from the scorched landscape like sharp red teeth. The earth is showing her true face, the enchantress has cast off her beguiling mask and is ripping volcanic fissures into the peninsula, from one end to the other; the black shadow of a formidable volcanic plume casts its night over the landscape, we're standing amidst a blizzard of ash. I'm completely disoriented, try to locate myself in place and time, but the world is unfamiliar, black and buckled, my feet ache and my head pounds, and the sun has vanished in the blackness. A shrill, high-pitched keening cuts through the heavy rumbling of the volcano, like the shriek of a smoke alarm, I can't tell where it's coming from.

The Chinese tourists have opened their luggage and are helping me into a neon jacket over my muddy clothes, I wince when they shift my injured leg to get me into waterproof pants. They talk to me in soft, melodious voices, put a dust mask over my mouth and nose and an absurd hat with an embroidered puffin and a pom-pom on my head, then carefully lift me to my feet.

We appear to have come up on a road, spider-cracked and crumbling, all around us is old lava, crisscrossed by new crevices and landslides, soil and stones still tumbling from the edges. The land's been torn apart by terrible quakes, but I can't remember where I was or what I was doing before the earth swallowed me.

The high-pitched sound gets louder, a painful, shrill sound of alarm; I look sluggishly down at my feet and can make out a movement in the black ash, the shrieking is coming from a field mouse running in circles, keening in terror, mourning its burrow, its home and the world as it was, frenzied and anguished in this dim, unfamiliar milieu.

Poor little thing, I think, but then the earth shakes again, there's a sharp jerk, and my benefactors cry out and start running, in what direction I don't know, just out into nothingness, away from the screaming flames, dragging six Chinese suitcases and one Icelandic geoscientist along with them. The father and son half carry me, I'm holding on to their shoulders for dear life, running on my hobbled foot and crying silently because I've finally figured out where and when we are, understand what's happened. We're running away from what was once the viewing platform over the pretty little Krýsuvík eruption, but Krýsuvík is gone, my colleagues lost in the murk. The only place this coal-gray plume could be rising from is tranquil Elliðavatn, the lake that once lapped amiably at the shores right by my house on the outskirts of the city.

The migration of the fissure swarm, remember, Daddy? The swans en route to summerland.

The fiery haze and ashfall rob people of their will to live. I've seen plucky geoscience students slump over in apathy and pessimism after a few hours in such murk, lie down and pull their sleeping bags over their heads. It's a primitive response, and the reason is simple: We're children of the light and lose our sense of direction in the palpable darkness as it streams up out of the earth. The cindery torpor has no less an effect on me than my saviors, but I'm trained and prepared and driven onward by a wholly different anxiety. It didn't take long for them to stop running, not least because it's no easy thing to drive yourself onward along a splintered road in the dark when you can barely see one step ahead.

Keep moving! I yell. Our lives depend on it! But they don't understand English or simply can't push themselves any harder, their progress is slowing by the minute. Their suitcases are strewn behind them like twigs on the roadway, they weave onward, bent over and dragging their feet through the lapilli, the gray-haired woman whimpers softly with each step. Finally, she sits down, a man and woman who could be her son and daughter-in-law pull her to her feet and pull her along, but after a few minutes, she gives up once more and sinks to the ground. They try to drag her to her feet, but she shakes her head, refuses to get up. They stand over her for a moment before the daughter-in-law continues along the road, the son stays behind. The gaps between us get wider, I lose sight of those who fall behind. The father and son seem to be supporting me more out of sheer force of will than real strength, and then the son looks at me apologetically, lets go, stops, and is swallowed by the darkness of the ashstorm.

Please don't give up, we have to keep moving, I shout at the father, he doesn't seem to hear me, doesn't understand, bends his hat-clad head forward and keeps moving as though it's all he can do, like an ox that has dragged the same plow for its whole life. In the end, he gives up, too, and lets go of me, his arms hanging at his sides. I take his hand and try to lead him onward, please, I say, but he just casts a sad look at me, his eyes bloodshot over his grimy dust mask, then sits down in the ash that's collecting in drifts along the road.

I keep going, stumble for a few yards on shaky feet, then give up and fall to my knees, crawl on all fours, crawl and cry and swear. After a time, the chaos in my mind slows down, my thoughts become muted, my conscious existence left behind on the road. Everything's sucked into the blackness, my work and reputation, my pride and my dreams, my ambition, my vanity, my parents and home, my husband, my lover, my children. In the end, there's nothing but darkness and love, a longing for everything that lives in the light, and the snippet of a verse that echoes in my head after everything else has gone black:

> The dandelion is sleeping
> in a meadow fair
> a mouse under moss

and then that goes silent too.

EXPLANATORY NOTE X

GRÓTTA

. . . none of this has anything to do with anything, not really, I don't know why this is what comes to me in the darkness. This scrap of land at the end of Seltjarnarnes Peninsula, just west of Reykjavík; it's actually below sea level, but its shores are surrounded by stone walls to block out the waves that attack it from all sides. Once, it was a broad meadow covered in flowers, but over time, the sea carved more and more of it away, the land has eroded and sunk and left behind a tear-shaped bowl in the sea. You can't even call it a real island, due to the narrow strip of land that connects it to the shore like an umbilical cord; it's an outpost, a negative space fighting not to sink into the sea.

I've lived less than two miles away, on the west side of Reykjavík, in Vesturbær, for my whole life, all twelve years, but I've still never been to Grótta and the lighthouse there. Not until Guðrún Olga drives me in her little wine-red and black car, past all the big single-family homes, and parks in front of the car repair shop near the end of the peninsula. She takes a giant backpack and picnic basket out of the car and hands it to me, the pack's so heavy she can barely get it on her back. Then she sets off and I follow, burning with fear and curiosity.

I don't dare ask what we're doing here. Most of the time, Mom hardly notices me, but now, all of a sudden, we're taking a trip together.

I didn't even know she had a car. But she's waiting for me when I get to her house that morning, excited and happy with a strange light in her eyes, says: Tonight is Midsummer Eve. A night for adventures.

Does Dad know about this? I ask uncertainly.

Yes, she says, he wanted to surprise you. That's why he didn't say anything.

I know this isn't true, of course, Dad has never tried to surprise me, not once. If he knew I was going on a field trip like this, he'd have given me a lecture on the geology of the area, lent me his rock hammer and made me at least three sandwiches with liver spread and cucumbers. But I don't say anything, I'm too surprised and happy she wants me to go with her.

We have a long way to walk, I get tired and trade off carrying the basket on my left and right arm. We turn onto a gravel road that runs along the sea toward the lighthouse. Then, when that road ends, we wade through meadow grass and buttercups, then lyme grass and kelp, before finally, we reach the sea. It's started to lick the rocks that make a narrow path out to the little island.

Come now, hurry up, says Guðrún Olga, we need to get across before the tide comes in.

But, I stammer, won't we get stuck out there?

Just for a little while. It's okay. This is an adventure.

She almost slips when she steps on the first rock, manages to get her balance, and then picks across the stones with the giant pack on her back. I stop and think before following. She's not a lot bigger than me, thin as a blade of bluegrass, her lace-up leather boots are slippery on the wet stones, she's wearing a red dress under her black coat. The wind blows her long dark hair in all directions, I'm afraid that she'll get blown off the stones, fall into the sea and not come back up again. It's hard to jump from rock to rock with this heavy picnic basket, I feel a prick of fear in my stomach, but it's alright, I think. There's nothing weird about going on a trip to the seashore with your mom, moms are probably doing stuff like this with their kids all the time. I don't have to worry so much.

The sun is shining, but the wind is cold. There's nothing on the island but the lighthouse, three old outbuildings with boarded-up windows, some stressed-out oystercatchers, and about ten thousand vicious Arctic terns who nest there. They dive-bomb us over and over, plunge out of the blue sky, shrieking loudly. I feel a wing brush my hair and just manage to put on a hat before one of them takes a peck at me.

They're going crazy! I shout to Guðrún Olga, who's standing in the middle of the tern tornado, but it's like she doesn't notice me or the birds. She walks toward the lighthouse and leans the pack up against the wall.

We'll camp here, she says, opening the bag.

Is that allowed? I ask, looking around; the ground is covered in bird poop and little wriggling heaps—newly hatched tern chicks. They huddle together and try to make themselves invisible while their parents prepare for their next attack from above.

She looks up, an angry expression on her face: You're too obedient, Little Anna. You need to break the rules sometimes, do things you're not allowed to do. Girls need to learn to be disobedient.

Okay, I say tiredly.

Stop that, she says, still angry. You don't have to say okay. You don't have to obey and excuse yourself and shape yourself to other people's demands. You have to talk back and ask why, demand things of the world around you.

Why?

Because the world is going to try and keep you down so it can use you. It wants to use you to clean and cook and birth children and wipe their butts and do the laundry and work an unbearably boring job in the service of others. You've got to break free of the demands of your environment, Little Anna, you have to learn to serve your own interests, not other people's. You need to be disobedient, or else you'll be squashed like a bug.

But, I say, but she's stopped listening. Digs through the backpack and pulls out a colorful tent, a couple dusty wool blankets, and a stack of books. I try to help her pitch the tent with three rusty tent pegs; in the end, we use a big rock to hold down one corner.

There, she says, satisfied as she brushes the dirt from her hands. It smells bad in the tent, like when Dad forgets to take the laundry out of the washing machine, but it will air out soon, she says, lighting a cigarette and exhaling the smoke into the tent.

She sits on the ledge that encircles the lighthouse, takes off her shoes and socks and stretches out her skinny legs. I try not to look at her feet, but I can't help it, her toenails are long and yellow and thick as the claws of a falcon. I'm suddenly frightened, nothing is as it should be.

We're surrounded by the sea, but otherwise, everything is oddly familiar. I walk around the little island, from one side to the other; there's Mts. Esja and Akrafjall to the north, to the south are my and Dad's mountains—Trölladyngja, Keilir, and Fagradalsfjall, I tear up when I look out at them. He's going to be so worried if I don't come home for dinner. I'm not used to spending more than three hours twice a month with Guðrún Olga. I don't think it was her who asked for the visits. Think it was probably Dad who decided I should see her sometimes.

I look at the mainland, the city. The sea has risen over the strip of land, I'm stranded here, stuck in Mom's adventure.

She's sitting with her eyes closed when I come back. Come here, she says, sit with me, and then lets me rest my head in her lap. She gently strokes my hair and starts singing, quietly and a little off-key, a strange verse:

> The dandelion is sleeping
> in a meadow fair
> a mouse under moss,

gull on the waves,
bloom on a bough,
star in the sky,
hart on the heath,
and fish in the sea.
May you now sleep soundly
and victorious.
Sleep, my dearest love.

Then she's quiet for a long time, just stroking my hair. I lie there with my eyes closed, don't dare move.

Are you hungry? she finally asks. I sit up and nod. She reaches for the picnic basket and takes out a white tablecloth and two plates with faded gold borders, a bag of dried fish, a can of sardines, and a packet of butter crackers. She wrapped a tea towel around two wineglasses and now opens a bottle of red wine and pours some out. I peek in the basket looking for water, don't dare ask if she brought anything for me to drink. She hands me one of the wine glasses and lifts her own: *Na zdorovie*. That means *skál* in Russian.

Do I drink this? I ask, and she shrugs, if you want. I sniff the wine and take a sip, it's sour and smells terrible, like spoiled apple juice, but I'm so thirsty I just swallow it down, finish the glass in one gulp. She doesn't say anything, just pours me another, then opens the bag of dried fish and hands it to me. I don't like *harðfiskur*, but I take a piece anyway, eat a few butter crackers, and then I'm thirsty again. I'm stuck between a rock and a hard place—I'm so hungry, but if I eat anything, I'll only get thirstier. The wine's made me dizzy, there's a burning in my stomach, and I want more than anything to burst into tears, but I don't. Guðrún Olga looks at me, examines me closely as if she's seeing me for the first time.

Have you gotten your period? she asks out of nowhere. I shake my head and feel my face getting hot. Don't tell her that I haven't even started getting breasts, I'm by far the smallest of all the girls in my class and am actually relieved to be a late bloomer. I don't want to stop being a kid.

You have to be careful once you get your period, she says. After that, you can get pregnant. And if you get pregnant, you'll be faced with a choice. You'll have to decide.

I look down at the tablecloth, blushing, I don't understand why she's talking like this. I don't want to talk about this, not now, not ever.

You must always be deciding who you want to be, she says. Whether you're going to be who you're told to be, or whether you're going to be yourself. Whether you're going to be obedient and good, or whether you're going to be strong and independent. And if you have a child, that complicates matters. You can't be yourself if you have a child. Then you have to be a mother. You have to give so much of yourself that there's nothing left. You stop existing as a person.

She looks down, her hair falling across her pale cheeks.

I wasn't going to hurt you, she whispers. No matter what they say. I was just so confused, and you were crying all the time. Wouldn't sleep, wouldn't let me touch you. There was fire in your eyes. We were dying. I was trying to save us.

She looks up, her eyes glinting like black stars.

They wanted to take you away from me. I shouldn't have trusted the geoscientist. He was in league with them the whole time. Was just using me, always meant to take you away from me. Which is why I took the stroller down to the sea, to get you away. I'd never have hurt you, no matter what they say.

Where were you taking me? I ask, confused. Why did you take me down to the sea?

She shakes her head impatiently: I don't remember, I was so confused. And you were always crying. There was fire in your eyes, I thought I needed to put it out, to save us.

She reaches out her hand, touches my cheek with her fingertips.

Love, she whispers. Love is the most dangerous thing that can happen to you. It ties you down and changes you, it erases you. You have to decide, Little Anna. You have to decide whether you're going to choose love or yourself.

I look at her and don't understand anything, don't understand what she's trying to tell me. I'm so tired and hungry and very thirsty, scared to death and a little drunk, and when the police come in the ICE-SAR boat to pick us up later that evening, I feel like they're saving my life, I'm so relieved to be in Dad's arms that I burst into tears. He stands on the shore with his hands in the pockets of his coat, his face all scrunched up with worry, he holds me tight in the police car on the way home, there now, Stubby, it's gonna be okay. He heats up some lamb soup for me and then carries me to bed when I fall asleep at the table, sits at the foot of my bed for a long time and holds my hand until I drift into a fitful sleep.

After this, I don't see her for a long time, not until I'm no longer a child. Grótta becomes an unclear, uncomfortable memory, a little scar in my past; I bury it deep in the dim recesses of my mind. Don't allow myself to recall and investigate it with my full-grown, full-fledged consciousness, to see that this Midsummer Eve adventure was my mother's ineffectual and broken attempt to give me an explanation, to ask for forgiveness, to tell me she loved me.

I buried it all, deep down in the crushing black darkness.

SEARCH AND RESCUE

. . . it's nothing but dumb luck that we saw you. We'd have driven right over you if you weren't wearing such a conspicuous jacket, with the visibility now. And then, of course, I recognized your face from TV— they can't say the word "eruption" without you popping up to explain.

Little by little, the foggy outline in front of me solidifies and becomes a sturdy woman sitting behind the steering wheel, her voice strong enough to be heard over the perpetual din and calls on the TETRA. The ICE-SAR jeep rattles down the road, full of grim-faced people wearing red and blue jackets and white helmets. The darkness is an almost tangible thing outside, the windshield wipers are pushing the gray sludge back and forth on the windshield. The man next to me hands me a Styrofoam cup with some dregs of coffee in it, here you go, try to drink this. You look like death warmed over.

I open my mouth to say something, but nothing comes out, it's like the ash has ossified my face. My eyes are burning, my eyelids scraping them like sandpaper every time I blink, it's best to just keep them closed. I swallow, clear my throat, try to loosen whatever has lodged there, but it doesn't work until I throw up on the floor of the jeep, a puddle of black slime.

Goddamn it, says the man next to me. Okay, lady, take it easy. It's gonna be okay.

The people, I manage to stammer, up on the road to Krýsuvík. You've got to go get them.

Search and rescue teams are on the way, says the woman. There are people all over the lava field who need to be picked up. It's going to take as long as it takes, what with the visibility as it is now.

They're dying, I sob. They saved my life.

She shakes her head: Sorry, lady, we can't fit any more people. And we have orders to get you to the coordination center in one piece.

The coordination center?

Of course that's where we're going, but I bristle, first I have to find Salka and Örn, I need to call Kristinn. And Tómas, anxiety goes through me in waves, where are my loved ones? Can I borrow someone's phone?

The ICE-SAR guy in the seat across from me carefully lifts my feet onto his knees, takes off my hiking boots, and palpates my swollen ankle, asks me to try and move my toes and foot. His hands are warm and careful, but I wince when he touches me.

I don't think it's broken, but it's badly bruised. They can take a better look at it at the coordination center, give you something for the pain, wrap your ankle. And the phones are down, there's no point in calling.

Can you use the TETRA to find out what happened to the people in Vatnsendahverfi, the residential neighborhood up by Elliðavatn Lake? Would you do that for me?

The driver shakes her head: Don't you see the ash plume? That neighborhood's gone. The residents only had a few minutes to get out before everything went to hell. She gives me a sidelong glance in the rearview mirror, raises her voice: People were stupid enough to trust you all, you scientists, no one suspected a thing. Then everything blew up in their faces.

That's enough, Nína, says the man next to her, turning to me. We don't really know anything yet, friend. We're the Sigurvon search and rescue team, we answered the call and came up from Sandgerði in the south. The capital's in total chaos, it's been about an hour and a half since this started. All transmitters are dead, the only things working are the TETRA system and long-wave radio, which no one uses anymore. People have been trying to flee but are stuck in their cars in total deadlock, and we don't know how long the police can keep the situation under control. It's not good.

The ICE-SAR jeep crawls along the road, and we shake inside it, seven downcast heads in white helmets, the eighth swiveling uselessly on her shoulders, muddy, bruised, covered in scratches and filled with terror, darkness, and regret. I stare through the little window from which the wipers are struggling to scrape the raining gray mire and am completely overwhelmed; the driver is right, the responsibility is mine. People were stupid enough to trust me. Why didn't I foresee this? The morass that my life has become appears before me; I've destroyed everything, betrayed my husband and pushed away my lover, everyone I love is in danger, and it's all my fault. I trusted prediction models and called them scientific fact, allowed pride to impede my vision, was blinded by foolish, excessive faith in my own wisdom. Didn't listen to the voices of those who tried to warn me—at meetings, in my head, from the past—the responsibility was mine, and I failed, I failed, I failed; I put my hands over my face and weep quietly in despair.

There, now, the ICE-SAR guy next to me pats my shoulder. It'll be okay, try to rest now.

He's just a young bright-eyed boy, and yet there's something deep and tender and fatherly about him, and I decide to let him reassure me, feel myself relax, feel the waves of despair ebb and become a soft buzzing in my head. I lay my head on his shoulder, close my smarting eyes, and let the shivers and exhaustion overcome me, the TETRA receiver crackles and hisses on the dashboard, the broken voices of Civil Protection management echo through the car:

Coordination center calling, Emergency Phase, Black. Emergency Phase, Black.

This is an all-hands call. All ICE-SAR teams report to Civil Protection operations control. Black.

I repeat: Black. Emergency Phase, Black.

I wake up outside the coordination center, I've no idea how long it took us to make our way through the ashen darkness and the honking, wheel-spinning traffic jams; the angry, terrified faces of the people in the surrounding cars breaking through my drowsiness. Police waving us through roadblocks and closures, the look in their eyes both stern and anxious. Headlights sending pale cones out into the darkness, the city is without electricity.

The ICE-SAR people help me into the center and leave me in the hands of an energetic nurse who gives me a shot in the ankle and wraps it, cleans and sanitizes the scratches on my face and hands, gives me a can of a cloyingly sweet energy drink and commands me to finish the whole thing.

It'll revive you, she says. If anyone needs to be able to think clearly right now, it's you.

The operations room is a study in focused chaos, a wriggling mass of people who walk quickly and talk quietly, hunch over computer screens and telecom equipment, try to get the upper hand on a situation that nothing in human power can control, are fighting tooth and nail to preserve life, to save what can be saved. The only information being transmitted to Civil Protection via the radio system is from the police, ICE-SAR, and the firefighters attempting to push through the terrified multitudes fleeing the city's upper neighborhoods, away from Elliðavatn Lake, which has been transformed into a boiling, shrieking volcanic crater.

Anna! Thank the Lord!

No one pays attention to my arrival except for Ebba, who leaps up as I hobble into the room, runs over to me, and hugs me with all her might, and as I stand there, shaking in her arms, I realize that this gaunt, undemonstrative woman in her snagged wool sweater is probably the only lifelong friend I have.

Her eyes are filled with tears when she releases me.

Good Lord, I'm so glad to see you, she says. So many are gone, I thought we'd lost you too. Jóhannes, Eiríkur, Halldóra, Jean and Mogens, a number of techs from GeoSurvey and the Met, God only knows how many others. The tourists. All those poor people in the residential areas up there. It's an absolute nightmare.

Ebba, I've got to get home.

No one's going up to the lake now, no one except the fire department and the ICE-SAR teams. The best thing is for you to stay here at the coordination center, you'll get all the information it's possible to get. And Milan's waiting for you.

He's standing in the eye of the storm, at the Civil Protection control panel with a headset mic on, buzzcutted, methodical, and serious. He allows himself a moment to look up and shoot me a small smile, reaches out his hand and takes mine, as if to confirm that it's really and truly me.

Good to have you here, he says, just give me a sec. Then he keeps talking into the mic: We need you to keep evacuating the neighborhoods west of Vesturlandsvegur and south of Reykjanesbraut, go house to house, check basements and garages. Search well, be careful, don't take any unnecessary risks.

Milan, my family is up there. I have to get out there.

He looks at me with his sad gray eyes, I can't lose you, so many scientists are gone. We're in a national state of emergency. We all have families that need us. We can't allow ourselves to give anyone priority.

He points over to one corner: The Red Cross is compiling a list of those who've been rescued, reported themselves safe, been taken to the hospital, or . . . you can talk to them. But then, you need to help us.

The Red Cross should, yes, be maintaining a list of the missing, comparing that with the list of names of people who've been reported safe, reuniting families and getting them to shelter. But the representative at the table is at a total loss, the computer system isn't up and running, the internet isn't working, they haven't started the registry yet. I drop into a chair and rest my quivering leg, Ebba hands me a sandwich and a cup of thin, scalding coffee, holds my arm as if she's afraid of losing me.

How many dead?

We don't know, she says, wiping her nose. No one knows anything. No one has the full picture, but she lays out what fragments they do have. She tells me about the series of earthquakes that began around Eldey Island last night and then, while I was arguing with Tómas, jostled eastward along the peninsula and reached their apex at Undirhlíðar Pillow Lava Ridge with one major quake of a magnitude of 7.0 right before 10:00 a.m. These quakes carved the land apart, opened crevices, tore up the roadways and destroyed houses and man-made structures in the capital area until the earth gave way under the road to Krýsuvík and swallowed my car and a small bus filled with Chinese tourists. Shortly after, new volcanic fissures opened, a phreatic eruption began at Kleifarvatn Lake and another out at sea, just beyond Kerlingarbás Cove, where the first eruption took place in the spring; and then, finally, a new, far more powerful lava flow forced its way through the fissure swarm and surfaced at the southern end of Elliðavatn Lake on the outskirts of Reykjavík.

We got a call from the group that was on-site at Krýsuvík just after the first quake. They were trapped, boxed in by the new eruption fissures. We—we were sure that you were there. Everyone thought you'd died with the others. You can't imagine how relieved we were to hear that the team from Sandgerði found you on the road. One bright spot in the darkness.

Was there really nothing that could be done? Why weren't they picked up? What about the helicopters?

Anna, dear, it all happened so fast. The ashfall was so heavy, coming from all directions, there was no way to get through it. It was so awful—there was nothing we could do. Just had to listen until the connection broke.

Ebba holds me while I cry for them, try not to picture them out there—Halldóra's clever face, Eiríkur's myopic eyes filled with terror, and Jóhannes, my friendly foe, that warm, rough-edged volcano cowboy with his beloved Hekla erupting on his forearm—try not to envision them standing face to face with the glowing lava, huddled in a knot, holding one another and awaiting the horrifying death that was crawling toward them, slowly but certainly. I hope with my whole soul that the gas got them first.

Forgive me, whispers Ebba. I should have listened to you, taken you seriously. Encouraged you to pursue the idea about a big magma chamber. It just flies in the face of all the data, all the research, all the models. This shouldn't have been able to happen. There's never been an eruption so far north in the Krýsuvík system.

I failed them, I say, drying my tears on my sleeve. I've failed you all. We should have announced an Emergency Phase, closed the entire area.

How exactly were you supposed to foresee this? Nothing indicated that this eruption would be dangerous. And the unrest from the eruption at Krýsuvík was enough to overshadow all signs that another one was beginning to the north.

Do you remember Holuhraun? I ask through clenched teeth. Do you remember Krafla? A fissure swarm is a mode of transportation, not a fixed place. We should have been better prepared. I should have known better.

The last message from Jóhannes, over the TETRA: May God have mercy on our souls. Iceland's burning heart beats within her.

I know Milan needs me, but I have to try and find my family. And Tómas Adler.

Dear heart, I don't know about your family, says Ebba. But Tómas is here.

My love, my lover—the world is on fire, my colleagues are dead and my family's missing, but still, I rejoice with my whole sick, selfish heart to see him. He's with a group of reporters up on the second floor, in amongst the chaos of computers, tripods, and cameras, is sitting there with his back to me, I'd know that unkempt nape anywhere. I say his name, and he leaps to his feet, his face lights up this whole horrible void, I reach my arm out to him like a drowning woman.

We embrace, hold each other tight, earthquakes shake the city, radios crackle and sirens wail, the control panel glows, and none of it matters. For one single moment, it's just the two of us in this world, he and I, the fact that he's been spared and that the fates have brought us together, here and now.

The embrace doesn't last long, we release each other gently, my God, ástin mín, to see you, he says, stroking my bruised, swollen cheeks. I'm so happy to see you, to get you back from the jaws of death. They thought you'd been trapped with Jóhannes and the others, had fallen to the lava. But I couldn't believe that, you couldn't go like that. And then suddenly, we got word that you were on the way here, safe and sound. I've never gotten better news in my life, ástin mín.

I just cry and smile like a fool, like all the sorrow and worries of the world have been lifted off me. Like something's been solved, just by finding Tómas here, scruffy and green-eyed, beautiful, unharmed, and I love him uncontrollably. He speaks softly to me, as he might to a frightened animal, strokes my dirty hair. Tells me about the quakes that rattled his studio, the earsplitting din of a thousand cars slamming on their brakes at the same time, of concrete cracking in houses across the city. And then there was a deadly silence, as if the world was holding its breath, and you know what, Anna? I knew something bigger was coming. I could just feel it—that something had broken, deep in the bowels of the earth. Felt it coming before I heard it, the scream from Elliðavatn Lake. And when it came, you were the first thing I thought of, where you were, whether you were okay.

He'd sped to the coordination center, gotten through all the traffic jams on the road on his motorcycle and used his Civil Protection ID to get in, hoping against hope to find me here.

And this is where I found out, he said. That Krýsuvík had suddenly changed, that the eruption had transformed. It tore open new fissures that circled the first one and then continued on toward the city and into it, much farther than anyone predicted. And to make bad worse, an eruption also started out at sea, just beyond Kerlingarbás. It's raging out of control, no one has a good grasp on the situation, not even Milan.

We go down to the control room; a map of the Reykjanes Peninsula has been projected on the wall over the control panel. It's covered with big red circles for the earthquakes, black stars symbolizing submarine eruptions out beyond the tip of Reykjanes. The on-land eruption fissures have been drawn in with black streaks, they're organized into two separate branches that start at Mt. Trölladyngja and Krýsuvík respectively, run into Kleifarvatn Lake, come together at Undirhlíðar Ridge, and then vanish in front of Mt. Búrfell before appearing again in the neighborhood where I live, Vatnsendahlíð, and running out into Elliðavatn Lake, flaming arrows traveling northeast, into the capital. Like swans flying in V formation on their way to summerland.

The fissure swarm, I say bitterly. There was a magma chamber under us this whole time. Krýsuvík is a full-fledged central volcano after all. And the systems are connected.

It overwhelms me, I need to sit down, this is my fault. I knew it. But I refused to believe myself, just shut it out. Didn't even run the simulation model, never included it in the possible scenarios.

Anna, are you okay? asks Milan. Are you in a condition to help us?

I'm not sure that I'll have anything useful to offer, I say. All the advice I've given up until now has done us nothing but harm. We should have closed the area a long time ago. Expected that this could get worse. We should have warned the residents of the upper neighborhoods. That was our job—my job—to make Civil Protection aware of the risks. To force you all to take it seriously.

Milan shakes his head, it does no good to get into this now. We don't have time for critiques or accusations. Those will come later. Right now, we need to try and get the big picture, to save what can be saved.

No one could've seen this coming, says Ebba. Do you think Halldóra and Jóhannes and all those veteran scientists would have been out at the volcano if they'd thought there was any chance this would happen? This is mischance, an unforeseeable disaster. Things like this happen, that's all there is to it. We can try, but we can never be completely sure we've got control over the situation. You've always known that.

I nod, my father packs his pipe and leans back in his chair, brushes some loose tobacco off his old argyle sweater: We've got to remember that the eruption belts in this country can erupt anywhere, at any time, in any way.

But that's such a simplification, I argue. There can't be an eruption just anywhere.

He lights a match, sucks the flame deeper into the tobacco, its warm aroma hangs over the room.

Alright, Stubby, look: it's more likely in some places than in others. Science helps us run simulation models. But they're no guarantee of anything—we can never be sure of any of it.

And yet I was so goddamn sure of myself.

Milan seems to still have faith in me, and I still have a debt to discharge with the nation's Civil Protection department. We need to form a picture of the disaster and save what can be saved while we wait for help to arrive from abroad. The Nordic militaries are on the way, but the planes will have to land in Akureyri, and the first ships won't be here for another day. That's a long time under these conditions. I speak with the Met Office and try to puzzle together a fractured picture of the volcanic activity as it stands, we calculate and trace out possible routes that the lava, volcanic gas, and ash might take; I draw lines on the map for Milan, he compares them with the information coming from the field and tries to plot out routes for the first responders. Slowly but surely, the map fills in and the picture becomes clearer: black eruption fissures stretch into the lake, destruction crawls into residential areas in a red wave, scorching houses and covering the streets with lapilli; the ICE-SAR teams are flickering blue dots that sporadically inch forward against the red line, searching houses and then falling back, retreating from the glowing tephra, heat, and lava that has begun its slow merciless campaign down the slope in the direction of the sea.

I give it my all, but I have to force myself to stay focused on the work at hand. To sit amongst all these blinking lights, these crackling transceivers and chirping alarms, and try to shut out thoughts of my family, to work against the clock, short of breath and trembling. The haughty scientist is gone, replaced by an exhausted, terrified wreck of a person with a pounding headache and sand showering from her hair and onto the control panel. Maybe I'm dead, maybe I died, am buried there in the earth, maybe it was some other woman the tourists dug out and the Sigurvon search and rescue team fished off of the roadway. The fact that I've survived is illogical, I don't deserve it. My colleagues perished in the eruption, my saviors languished in the conflagration, and my family is missing, my children perhaps in grave danger, and here I sit at the control panel in the Civil Protection coordination center, acting like I know anything about anything, shaky-handed, ineffectual as a ghost.

Milan, I say, after saving the last lava flow model. I have to go find my family now.

I know, he nods, I understand. Go, we're in a good place. Ebba will take over for you, we're in contact with Júlíus and his people from the Met. Shelters are up and running, the Red Cross should have started publishing its list of names, you can talk to them and ask them to help you look.

I stand up, supporting myself on the table, put as little weight as possible on my weak foot.

Milan, I'm so sorry, I say. I'm sorry that I miscalculated so badly, that we didn't manage to warn people.

He looks at me and smiles sadly: Anna, dear, you don't have to apologize for anything. You did your best. You didn't foresee this, but you're not omnipotent. That's an unfair demand to put on yourself. You worked with integrity, dedicated yourself entirely to the service of science and the safety of this nation. And then you came here and worked alongside us, tried to be of some use. That's no small thing. Not everyone would have done that.

He gives me his hand and squeezes mine tightly, good luck, he says simply, then turns back around to the control panel and continues answering emergency calls, urging first responders onto new streets and into half-collapsed houses in search of survivors.

I totter toward the Red Cross table, the representative is running around in circles and doesn't seem to have the slightest idea about what she's doing at the coordination center. Volunteers have begun recording the names of people who've come to the shelters, but the list of the lost is getting long fast.

This is total madness, says the woman despairingly. All the buses in the city were deployed up there, they were supposed to evacuate the schools and nursing homes, but people don't listen. They raced out in their cars to pick up their kids and old folks, their dogs, all kinds of junk, clogged the roads trying to rush home to save their computers, paintings, flat-screens, and travel trailers. The police have no control over anything, the buses can't get through, drivers are giving up and abandoning buses on the roadways. It's hopeless.

Though not entirely. I badger her, beg until she gives in and uses her TETRA even though it's not allowed, jams up an important transmission channel for two minutes in order to inquire about my family.

Good news, a voice crackles on the transceiver. We've got two registered here under the name Kristinn Fjalar Örvarsson.

I'm so relieved my legs nearly go out from under me, I have to hold on to the table so I don't fall to my knees. Kristinn and Örn have both reported themselves safe at the shelter at Smáralind Mall, Salka must be with them.

One adult family member is registered as missing, says the voice on the transceiver. Anna Arnardóttir.

That's me, I whisper so quietly she doesn't hear me, take a deep sigh of relief, thank providence, God, whoever is out there for sparing my family.

And one child.

What did you say?

One child, Salka Snæfríður Kristinsdóttir, age eight. She's also on the list of the missing.

EXPLANATORY NOTE XI

KATLA 1311

The jökulhlaup started the Sunday after Christmas and continued through Candlemas with much water and glacial flooding. It wiped out all the settlements that remained on the Mýrdalssandur outwash plain.

Markús Loftsson. 1930. *Essays on Volcanic Eruptions in Iceland*. Reykjavík: Ísafoldarprentsmiðja.

. . . and I can picture him when the flood wave comes barreling along the plain, headed straight for the farm, a coal-gray scythe come to cut down the settlement and everything that draws breath, his first and only thought in that moment is to run in and grab the child from the crib beside the bed. Commend yourselves to the Lord's mercy, he shouts before running back out, leaving his wife and entire household behind to perish in the floodwaters, and jumping, babe in arms, up onto a wall and, from there, onto a large ice floe that the glacial flood carries past the farm and all the way out to sea.

What goes through his head all those days he's stranded on the floe, shivering and powerless in the dark of dead winter, ash raining unremittently from the heavens? Does he regret having saved himself instead of meeting death with his loved ones, does he consider standing up and stepping off the ice floe into the sea? He's felt his child growing ever more still as hunger and exposure sap her of strength, he's seen her eyes drooping. He tucked her under his tunic and next to his skin to keep her warm; prayed that God would protect them both, show mercy on their souls; he's berated himself for trying to outmaneuver Katla and survive. Takes his knife out of its sheath, his fingers bent and blue from the cold, thinking, in his despair, that it would be best to cut the child's throat, put her down gently like a suffering lamb, but his little girl has awoken and is pitching her face at his chest, searching for his breast with her mouth, taking hold of his dry nipple and sucking zealously before releasing it and wailing piteously.

He cries, too, a full-grown man, tears stream down his bearded, weather-bitten cheeks. He moves the knife down, takes hold of his nipple and closes his eyes, clenches his teeth, and cuts it off. Then he places the child to his breast. She drinks, recoils from the unfamiliar salty flavor, lets go and howls in protest, but her hunger wins over her anger, and she suckles greedily. Now and again, she lifts her face from his breast and screams, her mouth smeared with blood, and her father lifts his face to the heavens and screams, too, screams with all his might; they have nothing, nothing but each other, the blood and thirst for life that they share under soot-black skies, the storm is blowing from the west and the ash from Katla follows them eastward along the shoreline like a curse.

They were saved, I say, the little girl and her daddy, but my father shakes his head: Don't waste your time on such nonsense, Stubby, it's just a folktale. Poppycock.

I don't say anything, close the book and put it back on the shelf, but I don't forget the story, rather store it away in my mind. I think it's true, the story of the man with his baby girl at his breast, I can picture him cuddling her to him under his black coat, far out at sea, screaming into the darkness: You're not going to get her, do you hear? I'm going to save her, at all costs.

His name was Sturla Arngrímsson. More than seven hundred years have passed since that disaster, which was named after him—Sturluhlaup, the Sturla Outburst Flood.

SHE'S IN THE SYSTEM

Smáralind: High-capacity shopping mall in Kópavogur. Possible to make use of this facility when large numbers of people must be sheltered but extensive services aren't required.

Evacuation Plan for the Capital Area

I hold on to Tómas for dear life, bury my face in his leather jacket. He drives through the crush like a maniac, along traffic islands and sidewalks, the motorcycle zigzagging between stationary cars. People have given up and abandoned them, are weaving along the sidewalks in the dark, dragging their children behind them, cloths over mouths and noses and eyes frozen in fear. The occasional driver honks, opens their car door and screams at us, but I couldn't care less. I hold on to Tómas like a drowning woman, press myself closer to him and feel the terror building in the pit of my stomach, hardening into a painful tumor. His body leans left and right, I feel his shoulders, stomach, back, how every single muscle is focused on this drive, on getting us to the mall as quickly as the bike will carry us. I try to follow his movements, put my thumb on the scale to speed our progress, hope that the tears and snot flowing out of my eyes and nose won't ruin my mask. It and the gas meter were the last things I got from Milan, after he tried to talk me out of going in search of my daughter.

There's no point, he said. The best thing by far would be to leave it to ICE-SAR and the police. The Red Cross will reunite families, it's just going to take some time.

I'm going to find her. If it's the last thing I do.

You're just going to get stuck on the roads, he replies, looking concerned. That doesn't serve anyone—not us and not your daughter. You'll be in a much better position to search for her here than out there amongst the masses. Be rational, please.

He gives up in the end, seeing that he couldn't even appeal to my professional conscience. I've become an ungovernable machine with a single goal: to find Salka. I won't be any good for anyone or anything until she's safe and sound.

The schools in the upper neighborhoods were evacuated quickly and to a person, says the woman from the Red Cross, the children should all be at Smáralind. They probably just haven't reunited Salka and her father yet, I'm sure they asked him to put her name on the list of the missing until the computer system could bring them together. Or maybe they have been, and the system simply hasn't updated yet. It's just a function of the registration process—red tape, nothing more.

I'll come back as soon as I've found them, I promise Milan. Ebba will take over in the meantime, she knows a lot more than I do anyway.

Maybe about Katla of yore, she says as she hugs me goodbye, but not this monster. Don't worry about us. Good luck. If I were lost, you're the person I'd want coming to find me.

My arms and knees squeeze Tómas tightly, it's like we're one body hunching over the handlebars, jostling as the bike goes over curbs and traffic islands, slips in ash when we take turns, the engine whining with stress. It should be broad daylight, but darkness is being drawn across the sky in thick veils; the people of Skaftafell have a name for the dark pillars of ash emitted in the volcanic eruptions that regularly ignite in the north: *morbálkar*, cinderwalls. They blot out the landscape, cast it into shadow; occasional flashes of lightning illuminate the smoke, thunderclaps drown out the constant rumbling of the volcano. My lover drives along narrow and barely visible verges, his sole purpose to get me to my husband—this may well be a high-water mark for the mess my life's become, but that doesn't matter now. All that matters is finding Salka, finishing this never-ending journey to that ugly mall, which finally appears before us like the promised land, its flickering lights powered by a weak reserve power generator, but at least they're on, sending their dim rays out through the thick clouds of smoke. I get off the bike and hobble through the door, into the throngs of dirty, terrified people, shouts and calls, children crying.

Tómas takes my hand, I hold it tight as we elbow our way through the twilit mall. I ask where the Red Cross has their help center, and people point me deeper in, by the escalator, someone says, but then I suddenly see a dark head atop blue and orange work coveralls, I'd know it anywhere, I let out a cry, shove my way through the crowd, throw myself in the arms of my beloved son.

He's been burnt. My eyes well up looking at the blisters on the backs of his hands and forearms, but they aren't serious, not enough for him to be given priority at any of the nursing stations that've been set up on the mall's third floor.

It's okay, Mama. It isn't serious.

Örn tries to calm me, and I hug him as tightly as I can, so blissfully happy to see my sweet boy, to feel him, alive in my arms.

He'd just come home from the night shift at the smelter and gone to bed when the big quake passed through, he says, then the fissures appeared, and everything went black. The glass in the living room windows shattered, and when I looked outside, I thought the lake was on fire. But Dad knew exactly what to do. Threw me into my work coveralls, got our ski helmets, wrapped a fire blanket around his shoulders. We took the car, but the traffic was at a standstill, we couldn't get through. We left the car behind and ran down to the school to get Salka, but by then, the kids were gone. So we just kept running. Away from the eruption. It was like being in a nightmare, Mom, like burning snow. Things started going up in flames around us, houses, too, and then we couldn't see anything for all the ash, couldn't hear anything for the noise from the eruption. We ran and ran, and people were screaming all around us. So many injured and burnt, it's so horrible.

He looks at me with his big brown eyes, so like my own, so like his grandfather's. Sad and frightened, agitated like when he was a little boy, my dear sweet love, I hug him tight, filled with gratitude to find him in one piece.

We haven't found Salka, Mama. They've been telling us not to worry, that all the children were evacuated, but her school's here, and the teachers say they don't know if she got here. It's a total mess. Dad's going insane. He's been hulking over the Red Cross people at the table over there and reading them the riot act.

I've got to help him.

We shove our way through to the Red Cross table, force our way through masses of frightened and angry people, crying children. The mall's full of shivering people with aluminum blankets around their shoulders, they're sitting on the floor, up against the walls, some have sought out shelter in the stores, where employees are either trying to make them comfortable or are acting like nothing's wrong, like this is just any other normal Tuesday in September, and try to ignore the filthy phantoms passing by. The sporting-goods stores have been given over to nursing home residents, the old folks have been outfitted in colorful jackets and sweaters to keep them warm, the floors are covered in multicolored tussocks.

My husband looms over the Red Cross service desk with his arms crossed, staring down at a young man in a red fleece who's staring miserably at his computer. He doesn't say anything to me when he sees me, just sends me an anguished look and holds out his hand, I run into his arms, bury my face in his sweater, and sob. My dear husband holds me in a death grip, as though I'm the solution to all the world's problems.

She's missing, he says, and his voice breaks. They can't find her. But my God, I'm so happy to see you. We thought . . . but we hoped . . . I'm just so glad to see you. Safe and sound.

I'm happy to see him, too, inhale his familiar scent, sandalwood and Cedrus under all the sweat, the smell of burning; it's like a warm blanket, like everything's going to be okay, just the way it was. It doesn't last long, he stiffens, releases me.

What's he doing here?

I look up, Tómas Adler is standing to one side and watching us, his eyes resting on me.

He drove me here on his motorcycle. Kristinn, dear, I take his hands, his large, warm, capable hands that have stroked my child's head, that can mend almost anything, hands that I wasn't able to love: We have to solve this together, find Salka. Nothing else matters. We have to put everything else aside.

Kristinn nods, slowly and reluctantly, breathes deeply, angrily, at the end of his tether, but always, beyond anything else, rational.

Go, then, talk to the school. They're up on the third floor, at the movie theater. Take them with you, I'll be here, waiting for any news.

Again, we push through the hordes, between our neighbors, coworkers, people we've sat in traffic with, met at the grocery store, while out walking the dog or at a soccer game cheering on our kids; here, everyone looks the same, unrecognizable with ash in their hair, shaking under the aluminum blankets that the Red Cross handed out to keep people warm. Dusk descends on us, black drifts cover the glass ceiling of the mall and the lights flicker. The heavy rumbling of the volcano can be heard in the distance, but the thunderclaps are closer, the city shakes as they move overhead.

They're showing an animated movie in the theater to amuse the exhausted, frightened children, the teachers are standing outside the auditorium and trying to direct traffic to the bathroom, make sure that the candy counter isn't emptied out. I catch sight of Salka's principal, who helps me find her teacher, who shakes his head unhappily, he just doesn't understand how this could happen. He confirms that he saw Salka on the bus, he took roll, was 100 percent sure that no one was left behind. I'm so, so sorry, he says, but I don't have time to listen to apologies.

Where's Máni? I ask, and the teacher leads me into the dark auditorium where stupid yellow critters are dancing their frenzied dance on the screen and asks my daughter's best friend to come talk to us.

I don't know, he says, looking at me stubbornly through his thick glasses. I don't know where she is.

I did already ask him, says the teacher in a resigned voice, but I go down on my knees and talk as clearly and gently as I can: You're her best friend, no one knows her as well as you do. You're so good at remembering things, do you remember anything she said?

He's silent, shakes his head again, lips pursed.

Máni, sweetheart, please try. None of this is your fault, I won't be mad, I promise, no one is going to be upset with you. She might be in trouble, I have to find her and try to help her.

He looks down at his toes, I don't know. Maybe she went home. Maybe she was going to find her dad, get Almond and Raisin.

The rats!

Of course. Wasn't it me who was always hammering home that she couldn't forget them, that she should look after her dad and brother, take care of them, be responsible? Be a good girl and use her blasted common sense like her mom?

I scramble to my feet and start running, don't say goodbye to Máni or the teacher, see Örn and Tómas at the theater entrance.

Home, I say, my voice catching. She's at home.

We shove our way back through the mall, find Kristinn in the same place we left him, by the Red Cross table. His severe expression turns to abject horror.

Do you hear that? he hisses at the young man from the Red Cross, she went home, Elliðahvammsvegur 8. Tell operation control: they have to go find her.

The boy types something into the computer system, then looks at us in confusion and shakes his head. They've already searched all the houses in that neighborhood. The firefighters and ICE-SAR teams have been instructed to fall back, the area's too dangerous.

She's only eight years old, I say, fighting to control my voice. They have to look for her.

He shrugs, I'm sorry. She's in the system, at the highest priority. It's all I can do. They'll search if they can. I have to ask you to take a seat and be patient. There are other people who need assistance.

We stand there as though frozen, our helplessness breaking over us like waves. My face is numb with fear, I look in turn at each of the three men I love. My son has his hand over his mouth, is close to tears, his father is grinding his teeth in a helpless rage and looks like he wants to flip over the service desk; Tómas has crossed his arms, is looking at me with concern, waiting for me to make the next move. I try and catch my breath, I have to take control of the situation, consider the options.

We really only have three. We can stay here, wait for news, put our faith in ICE-SAR teams that have already stopped searching the neighborhood. This option doesn't merit consideration. I can go back to the coordination center and try to convince Milan to send in a team to find my daughter, but I know there's little hope of that. It won't make any difference if the request comes from an exhausted man at the Red Cross or me—Milan would never give me preferential treatment at the expense of someone else. The third option is the only viable one.

I'll go myself, I say. I'll go back up there and find her.

I'm coming with you, says Örn immediately, but I shake my head. Nope, buddy, there's no way I'm letting you come along. You and your dad will stay here. Tómas and I will go on the motorcycle. It's the only way.

Kristinn looks at me as though he doesn't believe his own ears: You mean to take him with you to look for Salka?

It's his motorcycle. It's the only way to get there.

She's my daughter.

I know that, I say, taking his hands and looking into his eyes, dim and anxious. Kristinn, sweetheart, one of us has to stay here to meet her in case she's found. In case ICE-SAR gets to her before me.

Then I'll go with him. You can wait here.

No, I'm going. Tómas and I have IDs that will get us through the road closures. The police have to let us through. And I know volcanoes. I know these conditions. If someone's going to make it all the way, it's going to be me.

He is going to fail you. Kristinn's voice is shaky. He's not the man to go the distance with you.

I stand between them and hold both of their hands. Tómas looks down at the floor, as if he's ashamed of himself, Kristinn glares at him, enraged and sorrowful in equal measure, looking for all the world like he wants to murder him. I squeeze their hands, look at them in turn.

We need to take a cold, clear view of this. Put everything else aside. We need to do what we have to do to find Salka. This is the only way.

Kristinn falls silent and closes his eyes, breathes heavily and swallows. He looks at Örn: Get undressed.

What?

Take off your coveralls and give them to your mother. They're fireproof.

We say goodbye, I hug my big sweet boy, he's shivering in his boxers and T-shirt. Hug his father, too, he vibrates with suppressed anger but holds me tight.

You be careful, woman, he says. May God and all gracious beings protect you, find my child, bring her back to me safe and sound. You come back to me, the two of you, you hear?

IT'S RAINING FIRE

How far are you prepared to go for love? What would you part with? Your home, your work, your reputation, your financial security? Are you ready to go all the way, to sacrifice your life and peace of mind, venture gladly into hell, trudge through fire and brimstone for your love? Or are these just things we say, is this too much to ask?

And how does one prepare for a journey to hell, what does one take? Tómas and I opt for water, plenty of water, a little chocolate, CO_2 meters, masks, and fire blankets, then head out into the darkness. There's a bit of a break in the clouds, the light is hazy and gray, but we can only see a few steps in front of us. I try to see Tómas's face through the visor of his helmet, can only make out the shape of his eyes.

Thank you, ástin mín, I say, hugging him, thank you for coming with me, for helping me find my little girl. Thank you for standing with me through this trial, for not failing me.

He doesn't answer, just rests his helmet against mine so that our foreheads bump lightly. We get on the bike, him clad in leather, me in Örn's far-too-large coveralls, the crotch hanging almost all the way down to my knees. Tómas revs the engine, the bike rumbles underneath us, ash and tephra spit up from under the tires. We head north, into the blackness, barrel between parked cars, along traffic islands and sidewalks.

We don't stop until we hit the first roadblock and a slim police officer wearing a helmet and a gas mask holds up her hand. I pull out my Civil Protection ID, it gives me unrestricted access to disaster zones, she looks at it front and back and then looks at me in consternation.

You want to go up to the lake now? Don't you know what conditions are like up there? It's raining fire. There's no one there.

I look up, up the hillsides where I once had a home, realizing that I've avoided doing so until now, have unconsciously looked away and refused to face the horrors awaiting us at the lake. Ash falls in black sheets, but up in the darkness there's a fire burning, I can just make out glimpses of it through the smoke, the houses on the hill protrude from the glow like teeth in a monstrous red jaw. Bolts of lightning flash within the ash plume, thunder booms like two mountains crashing together; only an insane person would demand entry to this inferno.

I'm on the Scientific Council, we're here on behalf of Civil Protection, I say as commandingly as I can, looking at her like I'm the one who holds the power, hoping beyond hope that she doesn't whip out her TETRA to ask the coordination center about our expedition.

She takes another good look at my ID, shrugs, hands it back to me and holds out her hand to Tómas. He sticks his hand into his pockets, unzips his jacket, and gropes in his breast pocket, then looks from her to me.

Damn, he says. I must have lost it on the way. I don't have it.

A bolt of ice shoots through me.

Check again, I say. Turn all your pockets inside out, check inside your shirt. Then I look to the police officer, these are unusual circumstances, we have to get up there. Can't you make an exception and let us through?

She shakes her head, you can go if you want, but I can't let him through if he doesn't have a valid ID.

I look around in desperation, there are only two police cars and one motorcycle, the roadblock is nothing more than a few orange cones. It wouldn't be hard to get through, I whisper to Tómas, we have to try.

And drive up there with police cars chasing us, lights flashing? Forget it, he says. They'll catch us for sure—there are more roadblocks farther up, we won't make it through all of them.

We've got to try, I say, but he shakes his head, takes my arm and looks into my eyes.

We should go back, he says. Ástin mín. It's the only sane thing to do. Let's go down to the coordination center and talk to Milan, get him to send ICE-SAR in after her.

No!

Anna, we tried. We did everything we could.

This floors me, my desolation throbs hot and black in my chest, but I refuse to give up. Stalk over to the bike and start rooting through the bags and panniers, gnashing my teeth in frustration, he grabs my arm and tries to stop me, Anna, don't do this, but I manage to open a little compartment under the handlebars and wouldn't you know it: there's his Civil Protection ID.

I whoop for joy, hand it to him triumphantly, euphorically—problem solved!

He looks away.

I'm not going. I can't do it.

You can't, or you won't?

I look at him stupidly, don't understand. We're here, on the bike, have permission to go through: what's the problem?

Anna, this is absolute madness. The whole area is on fire, do you not see the flames? We're walking into certain death.

We have to try, Tómas. She's at home, I have to save her. She's my daughter.

But she isn't mine.

He stands before me and all of a sudden, I see him for what he is. Not a bad guy, not a villain, just a scared, weak man who loves himself more than anyone else in the world. More than me. I can't blame him, stooped and bowed and yet unforgivably resolved, I can't hate him for not following me to death's door, all the way down to hell. After all his beautiful words, all his promises and passionate declarations, his love doesn't go any deeper than that. There's nothing he can do about it.

I look away, he holds out his hand and looks at me imploringly, c'mon, Anna, we should turn back.

No, I say, getting on the bike. I'm not turning back.

And then I go.

TRIUMPH BONNEVILLE

I've never driven a motorcycle in my life, but I've seen Tómas do it. The bike rockets forward, so fast that for one terrifying moment, I think it's going to kick back and throw me, but I manage to get control and hiccup ahead, past the roadblock and through the flakes of falling ash.

Tómas shouts something and runs after me, my silver-tongued, long-limbed love with the laughing eyes, and then I lose sight of him in the smoke, I have nothing left for him but disappointment and these blasted tears that are filling my helmet visor and drenching my gas mask, as if it makes any difference now whether my heart is broken, whether the love that took over my life, changed me and opened all these new rooms within me, has turned out to be nothing but a veneer, has gone up in smoke and fizzled out the moment it was put to the test. I've got more important things to worry about.

I rev the engine, urge the bike onward and weep, drive this familiar route I've taken a hundred thousand times before, past the quiet apartment complexes, single-family homes, shops, churches, schools, and parking lots—everything is hollow and vacant, abandoned, a pointless stage set: life's gone out of the world. There's nothing left but the ferocity of the earth and my small deranged journey into the eye of the storm, into the hazy, terrifying glimmer of the fires to the west.

The road conditions get worse the farther I go, ash flakes get thicker, the tephra coarser, it sticks to the tires and gets under the fenders, the engine has to work harder and harder. Please keep going, I moan through clenched teeth, please, just a bit farther, up to the next crossing, but it isn't to be. The engine's making sounds that remind me of Salka's asthmatic gasps; it finally gives in, the rumbling fades and dies.

Damn, I shove the bike away, start groping my way along the street, against the falling ash. Despair squeezes my heart, it's going to take me such a long time to get there, to trudge through these black drifts, how I will I ever make it home in time? The coveralls get tangled around my feet, I slog forward like a distraught emperor penguin in an Antarctic blizzard, try to focus on putting one foot in front of the other, fight my way forward against the onslaught of the ash. It's gotten grittier, the clacking on my helmet is getting heavier, slowing my progress and depleting me.

Getting struck by a two-inch piece of pumice isn't life threatening, reels off a voice in my head, but repeated blows could be harmful. A blow from a two-inch stone shard at a hundred miles an hour could be lethal. The only death during the Hekla eruption in 1510 was caused by a blow from falling tephra . . .

The monotone lecture drones on in my head, the smoke is getting thicker, the roar of the eruption more deafening by the minute. I'm numb and confused, have to really focus to not lose direction, it feels like the noise is coming from all sides, from above, from the left, from the right, from behind. It sounds like an engine.

Anna!

I turn around slowly, as slowly as a plant turns to face the light, I can't believe my ears, but Tómas is here, for a moment, I'm sure I'm hallucinating, that the glow has blossomed and swallowed me, but it's him, it's really and truly him, riding an enormous police motorcycle. He takes off his helmet and grins boyishly, he's delighted to see me, pleased that he's taken me by surprise.

I long to run to him and embrace him, to kiss him a thousand times and thank him, tell him that the world can fall to pieces if he's with me, if I don't have to be alone when it happens, that I can face anything and everything with him by my side. But I don't say any of this, just stand there as if nailed to the ground and look at him.

Tómas gets off the bike, puts a hand over his eyes to shelter them from the ash, tries to see my face, becomes unsure of himself.

Forgive me, he says. Forgive me for losing my nerve. I failed you. Everything seemed so hopeless. Then I watched you drive off and knew I couldn't let you go by yourself, I had to try and help you. I could never have lived with myself if you'd gone alone, knowing that I'd failed you. I think the policewoman understood that. She ended up loaning me her motorcycle, said it was breaking all the rules, but it wouldn't be responsible to let you go alone. And . . . yeah, well, here I am. I'm coming with you.

He grins, he's putting on a brave face, but he's scared, scared to death. Tephra's falling in his hair, his beautiful dark hair, the light from the volcano illuminates the western sky and is reflected in his eyes and I make a decision. I march over to him, take five decisive steps and shove him so hard he falls back into the ash.

Anna, I made a horrible mistake, he says, sitting on the ground. But can't you forgive me?

Go! I scream. Get the fuck out of here! Just leave.

I said I was sorry! Ástin mín, I regret what I said about Salka—that she wasn't my child. It was an ugly, stupid thing to say, unforgivable, I know. But I'm here to help you, for God's sake. I love you!

Go, I say again. I don't want you here. I'm doing this alone. I don't love you.

He recoils, as though I've kicked him.

Don't love me? Liar. At least take off your helmet, let me see your face!

But I don't, just grab the handlebars of the police bike, lift my feet with some difficulty and sit down. He scrambles to his feet and takes my arm: Please, Anna, don't leave me here. What am I supposed to do?

Go, I say. Turn back. I don't want you coming with me.

My voice is firm, he can't see my face through the visor. I start the bike and speed off, up the hill and into the black. My lover, my beautiful love vanishes in the smoke, I tremble with sorrow, tears running down my cheeks, but this is how it has to be.

He's strong, he'll make it back.

He will survive. Him and Örn and Kristinn. I comfort myself with that.

The bike struggles up the hill, I look out over the wasteland that was once my neighborhood. The lake has almost vanished, it's evaporating, incandescent craters have started sprouting up around it, black and glowing red. The magma jets up in sharp yellow tongues, a hundred yards into the air, thick ash plumes tumbling out of them. The fissures extend into the burning wood and out into the dead, scorched lake bed that runs along the residential streets. The houses closest to the lake are getting buried in ash, many are already in flames amidst the glowing lapilli spitting from those red jaws.

The gas meter in my breast pocket emits a long drawn-out wail, like the loon that once lived on this lake. I turn it off, take out my fire blanket and wrap it around my head to protect the helmet, rev the engine and head toward the lake, toward the black mass that is my home. All that remains is darkness and fire and terror, but I don't give in, I drive into the blackness, toward the burning heart that beats and burns and wreaks destruction upon the world.

Now it's just me and you, I think.

I'm coming.

PAVANE

She's hidden herself in the back of my closet. Is curled up amongst my old heels, resting her head on an old sweater. It's soft, maybe it smells like me. Maybe it's made her feel like I'm with her, like she isn't alone.

She's holding on to her little pets, the degus, hugging them to her chest. They're stiff, but her body's still soft and light, her head lolls back when I pick her up, as if she's sleeping. I lay her on the floor, take off my mask and try to breathe life back into her, tilt her head back, open her mouth, and blow, once, twice, three times, four, but my breath becomes a moan, she's cold, so cold, the ash falls on her open eyes, her pupils dilated and frozen, seeing nothing. Carbon dioxide is a covert killer, it slinks through cracks and crevices, pushes the oxygen from its victims' lungs and gently smothers them.

My tears dampen her soft dark hair, I rock her like I did when she was little, mourn my sweet baby, my little girl. My tears become a lullaby, I nuzzle my face into her hair and breathe her in, the lyrics are long forgotten but the song used to relax her, soothe her asthma, quiet her tears.

And although there's no longer any life in the little body I hold in my arms, although my heart is breaking and light has gone out of the world, there suddenly awakens within me a wonderous peace. I look at her delicate face and kiss her bright forehead, I cry in grief, but also in gratitude, because I had the chance to love her. Her and her brother, their father and Tómas, my father and my poor suffering mother. I have loved, I have been loved, I had this life that I lived, and this is how it ends.

I lay her gently on the bed, take off my shoes and put them away, tidy at the end of the bed with the laces tucked inside, and then lie down behind her, spreading a blanket over us. Encircle her like a fox curling around its cub, hold her slender body and sing quietly in her ear, the words coming back to me little by little before they're drowned out by the thundering volcano.

> The dandelion is sleeping
> in a meadow fair
> a mouse under moss,
> gull on the waves,
> bloom on a bough,
> star in the sky,
> hart on the heath,
> and fish in the sea.
> Sleep, my dearest love.

Ash rains in through the shattered window and covers us in a soft black mound.

SKAÐI

N 64°05′08″ W 21°45′34″

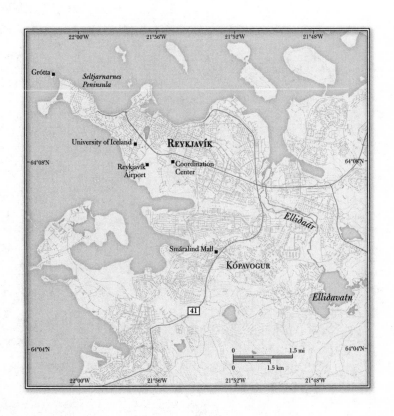

Skaði, meaning "damage" or "loss" in English, is an 850-foot volcano on the border of Reykjavík and Kópavogur where Elliðavatn, a shallow lake on the outskirts of Heiðmörk forest, used to be (See also: Skógarhraun, or Forest Lava Field). Skaði was formed in the first years of the Krýsuvík Fires, which destroyed a large part of the uppermost suburbs (See also: Borgarbruni, City Lava Field). Eighty-seven people died and nearly three hundred were injured when volcanic fissures opened at the Krýsuvík geothermal area, as well as at Kleifarvatn and Elliðavatn Lakes. Most deaths were a result of CO_2 poisoning.

ABOUT THE AUTHOR

Photo © 2019 Benedikt & Sigurjón Ragnar

Icelandic author Sigríður Hagalín Björnsdóttir studied history in Reykjavík and Salamanca and journalism at Columbia University in New York and previously worked in Copenhagen before moving back to Reykjavík, where she lives with her husband, children, and stepchildren. Her bestselling debut, *Island* (2016), was nominated for the Icelandic Women's Literature Prize in 2017. When she isn't writing, Sigríður works as a journalist and television news anchor at the Icelandic National Broadcasting Service. Her highly anticipated third novel, *The Fires*, is a bestseller and viral hit in Iceland.

ABOUT THE TRANSLATOR

Larissa Kyzer is a writer and translator of Icelandic literature. She holds an MA in literary translation from the University of Iceland as well as an MS in library and information science and a BA in comparative literature. Her published translations include novels, short stories, children's literature, nonfiction, and poetry. Her translation of Kristín Eiríksdóttir's *A Fist or a Heart* (Amazon Crossing) was awarded the American-Scandinavian Foundation's 2019 translation prize. The same year, she was one of Princeton University's translators in residence. Larissa served as cochair of PEN America's Translation Committee from 2019 to 2021 and runs Jill!, a virtual Women+ in Translation reading series. Find her online at www.larissakyzer.com.